Coming to Light

BY THE SAME AUTHOR

Short stories
The Spark
The High Tide Talker
The Night of the Funny Hats
A Traveller's Room

Novels
Providings
Creating a Scene
Climbers on a Stair

Coming to Light

by

Elspeth Davie

HAMISH HAMILTON · LONDON

HAMISH HAMILTON LTD

Published by the Penguin Group
27 Wrights Lane, London w8 5TZ, England
Viking Penguin Inc, 40 West 23rd Street, New York, New York 10010, U.S.A.
Penguin Books Australia Ltd, Ringwood, Victoria, Australia
Penguin Books Canada Ltd, 2801 John Street, Markham, Ontario, Canada L3R 1B4
Penguin Books (N.Z.) Ltd, 182–190 Wairau Road, Auckland 10, New Zealand

Penguin Books Ltd, Registered Offices: Harmondsworth, Middlesex, England

First published in Great Britain 1989 by
Hamish Hamilton Ltd

British Library Cataloguing in Publication Data
CIP data for this book is available from the British Library

ISBN 0-241-12861-7 HBK
ISBN 0-241-12860-9 PBK

Printed in Great Britain by
Richard Clay Ltd, Bungay, Suffolk

ACKNOWLEDGEMENTS

The author gratefully acknowledges help from
the following books:

The Story of Astronomy in Edinburgh
by Hermann A. Brück
The Royal Botanic Gardens, Edinburgh
(1670-1970)
by Harold R. Fletcher and William H. Brown
Royal Scottish Museum: The Early Years
by Jenni Calder

PROLOGUE

An annual Garden Party? But this place was never a garden. It is a huge park overlooked by an ancient volcano and backed by what had once been described as 'an imposing and picturesque crescent of beetling cliffs'. On one side is the old Palace, often open to the public but seldom used officially except for rare royal entrances and exits. Nevertheless, Royal Garden Parties are treated as most important occasions. Absolute exclusiveness is the crux of the matter. Gathered together on this summer afternoon are all the high dignitaries and big brass of the place – The Lord High Commissioner, The Lord Provost, The Moderator of The General Assembly, the judges and magistrates of the city, with leaders in Law, Medicine, Education, Church, Army, Navy and Airforce. The top sporting personalities, and heroes and heroines of brave deeds are honoured with the rest. Now, if ever, medals, ribbons, crosses and chains come out of their quilted boxes. Wives are dressed up to the nines, but even the stoutest have the frail aspect of those who dread the usual gales and downpours. Naturally 'garden' is too domestic and flowery a word for this place. The flowers are to be found mainly in the hats, in the patterns of dresses, or occasionally in the buttonhole of a dark suit. And anyone who has the divine right to wear a kilt wears it on this day.

There is some grace in the proceedings particularly as Royalty is never protected by the vulgar gun or even by the sword, but by the Old Company of Archers in their green. In fact, the head of this Company, with his bow at the ready, never leaves their side. Thus he is able to hear every word that passes between them and their subjects. The words of these subjects are unlikely to be threatening, but they will be very well rehearsed, well enunciated and probably unlike any other conversations in the land. At all such gatherings here very well-defined circles are immediately formed. It is a matter of tradition. First there is the close, inner circle of chosen people who can both see and hear, who will, in time, be able to report back the smallest details of what is happening. Further out – at a deep, respectful distance – stand the second circle of spectators watching the inner crowd jealously. But at a still greater distance is the huge circle of the also-rans, a seething, craning crowd on tiptoe with binoculars, trying to see between top-hats and plumes, but in fact seeing little and hearing nothing. Here there is always great frustration. Perversely, this circle is trying to guess impossible things. What is the colour of those jewels round Her neck? What is the design of His tie? After a time an even greater frustration comes with the certainty that there is no use even attempting to reach the sumptuous, white tea-tent, splendid as a sailing ship on its clipped green waves. In the far distance people can be seen emerging from this tent carrying plates piled with exquisitely cut sandwiches. They are eating them hungrily and even going back for second helpings. 'Oh, the dreadful heat there'll be inside that tent!' exclaim those who have absolutely no hope of reaching it. 'Just wait. One or two in there will be carried off in ambulances before the afternoon's through!'

But there is another circle of persons even further out. They are the true outsiders, the would-be gate-crashers if there were gates to crash. This is the unruly, ungovernable crowd beyond the confines of the park. There are real obstacles here to seeing anything at all. Large cars and police on duty are crammed together and few persons are allowed through. Nevertheless, even here people can get an occasional glimpse of the strange scene inside. The whole hill above the old Palace becomes more crowded as the day goes on. People are picnicking or standing staring at the spectacle below. The Scots have never been averse to praise. A journalist writing on the first Royal visit to Edinburgh by George IV reported it thus: 'The steep of the Hill was so thickly crowded with well-dressed persons that it seemed as though the population of a hundred cities had been piled up with only the heads visible for the very purpose of giving effect and grandeur to the scene. As His Majesty advanced the hill of heads was perceived to move. The heads were uncovered, the visages were seen, and the nearer they were approached the more strongly did the bold fronts indicate the possession of an active and discriminating intelligence.' As his carriage took him towards Calton Hill, packed with this fashionable crowd, the King was moved to exclaim: 'Good God! What a spectacle! But where are the working people? This seems a Nation of Gentlemen!'

Today, as then, the working people are, of course, at work. But in this far-out circle there are others in various trades and professions who have come up in a free moment to take a look at what exactly is going on inside the park. A dentist, for instance, glances across the wall for a second and wonders what gives the Royals such a dazzling and even-toothed smile. He has seen nothing like it in twenty years of work, except when he himself has fashioned this white smile, tooth by tooth. But quickly he puts aside all suspicion from his mind. It is simply the result of the old brush-and-toothpaste routine familiar to all his sensible patients.

There are other unlikely persons up here. Early in the afternoon, long before the crowd gathers, a garage-man has come up in his lunchtime, hoping to try out an old car on the rough road circling Arthur's Seat. The strong arm of the law immediately prevents him and the first vehicles on the scene block his path. Nevertheless, he stays on to see the cars gathering. Cars are his livelihood, but few like these will ever stop at his workplace. They are almost as sumptuous as the padded carriages that had once taken the crowds up. Most are black as polished ebony. But there are coloured ones too – regal purples, deep blues and greens, with the occasional cheeky, scarlet sportscar. The garage-man pointed out to the man beside him that so rich and gleaming were these cars that they might have been newly bought for the occasion.

'I've no doubt,' the other replied, 'but in my trade I go in for colours you can actually live with.' He said he was a house-painter and added, staring at the Palace, 'I wonder what it's like in there, for instance. It's rooms that interest me. I was once asked to paint a room dark crimson from floor to ceiling. What do you think of that?'

'Terrible,' says the dentist who happens to be near and is thinking

of white-walled surgeries. 'But remember in the old days they sometimes hung the walls with dark red velvet.' The three stand together
for a moment until the jostling crowd elbows them apart.

A foreign tailor is up here seeing it all for the first time. He has a
feeling for drama of every kind, and indeed he himself makes costumes
for the theatre. Today he would like to have seen even more
pageantry. For him there is never enough. He would like to have
seen crowns, jewels, coronets, courtiers and velvet trains. He has
always been an unashamed romantic both in this country and in the
country of his birth.

So dense is the hillside now it is difficult to make out anything
between the close-packed groups. Yet those staring intently up are
aware of the thin figure of a boy weaving downhill from side to side,
knocking into people, tripping over their belongings, being yelled at
and yelling back himself.

'Look at that!' say one or two who've caught sight of it. 'The
rudeness of them these days!' They don't know where they're going
and don't give a damn who they knock around! He'll learn one of
these days when he gets knocked about himself!'

But every teacher, staring at the hill, knows that some time or
other she'll have just such a boy in her class. He will be neither loved
nor hated by her. He will simply be a familiar figure who will appear
again and again in different guise as time goes on. For two or three
years they will form a close relationship of strife and compact,
defiance and agreement, of peace and anarchy in turn, all continually
appearing and fading out again like sunlight and shadow across a
rocky hill.

CHAPTER

1

During the whole of one year Martin MacNab, a dentist, had been worrying a great deal about his back. To make matters worse he lived in a city of steep hills, precipitous flights of steps, and walled, narrow lanes, glaciated for a good part of the winter. His street was named after a King and his flat looked down upon this Majestic figure on a high pedestal, a figure blissfully oblivious of the cars and buses swirling and honking around him day and night. The King was straight-backed because he was a King. Martin was straight-backed because it was all he could do to prevent the crick in his spine from becoming permanent after bending from morning till night above his patients' flat-out chair. Martin laughed at the interesting exchanges and discussions other men put forward as the reward of their professions. As for him, sounds were limited, after his probings, only to his patients' sighs of relief that they were not to see him again for another six months, and then only if pain forced them. For the most part there was silence in his room. Down below, the King was himself always silent, regally stout, and staring fixedly to the south, possibly wishing himself home in London. It had rained very hard during much of George IV's visit. Nowadays, though high and dry, he took everything that was flung at him, including advice that he should get back to England. Others had endured this too. But they were not kings.

Martin occasionally had people who wanted to talk. Usually they were persons who seemed to see him as a doctor, who asked his advice and took him into their confidence. This happened one afternoon when a middle-aged woman – the last of his patients – was leaving. She paused at the door. 'May I ask if you have children?' she said.

'Oh, I have two – a boy and a girl.'

'I was wanting to ask you about our youngest son, Niall.' The dentist stood waiting, polite but impatient, holding the door. In the hall he saw his receptionist closing the heavy appointments book and sticking a pen back into a mug of coloured Biros.

'You see,' said the woman, 'his mind is on nothing but horrors, terror, ghastly sights of every kind. He talks, reads and thinks about it from morning till night. Maybe he dreams about it too. I've no idea.' She looked both angry and anxious as she spoke.

'A common enough stage,' Martin replied. 'I was exactly the same myself. 'They also discovered I had what was politely referred to as "a vivid imagination".'

The woman ignored this, staring at his white coat. 'They say you're good with children,' she said. 'Perhaps you could help him, though he's hardly a child now, of course. He's nearly fifteen.'

'If you're worried, why don't you see a doctor?' said the dentist, putting a slight emphasis on the last word and opening the door wider into the hall where the receptionist was now unhooking her coat and looking back impatiently over her shoulder. 'Of course he should come along if he has any trouble with his teeth,' he added. 'Then he can look at all my instruments of torture if he's interested.' He said goodbye with a smile and watched her walk slowly away down the street.

That evening he took off his white coat with relief. Bloody or clean, it had got him into trouble before this. He wondered what white coats stood for in people's minds. Secret sadism or total dedication to humanity? What labels to live with! On the whole he was sorry for the various laundered coats. Such saintly, single-minded whiteness was a target both for adoration and mud-slinging.

'Nobody should wear white as a uniform,' he said to his wife later that evening. 'Except perhaps the Pope,' he added in a heathenish attempt to redeem himself.

'Him least of all,' she replied. 'That laundry! Hand-done, as likely as not, and every last fold to the greater glory of God. Women will never learn.'

Martin seldom had time or energy for things apart from work.

One day, however, he picked up a list of Evening Classes and studied it for the first time. As he went through it he saw, in a flash, that he was getting tired of teeth. 'Tired to death,' he murmured. He was tired of the look of them, the feel of them, tired of descriptions of pain — stabbing, gnawing, bearable, unbearable, agonising — tired even of his patients' weird passivity as they lay, prone and helpless, in the metal chair under a blinding light. He realised they resented this position. It was undemocratic, undignified, no doubt. Even his expensive modern equipment and the huge goldfish tank in the hall, bought to amuse and calm children, had not paid off as far as he was concerned. Most of all he'd begun to abhor the thick, opaque window of his surgery. For almost the entire day he was shut off from the outside world behind grey, bubbled glass, on which, one after the other, the moving, faceless shadows slid past like fish, without a sideways glance. He seldom mentioned the strange draw-backs of his trade, seeing everyone believed, not without reason, that he was making money hand over fist. What else was he supposed to want from life? In fact he wanted a great deal more. He went back to the list of classes. His choice, in the violence of the moment, wavered between a course in Non-Aggression and one on Active Volcanoes of the Earth. On second, calmer thoughts his choice became Astron-omy. His main interest had always been in the sciences and dated back to childhood when, searching in an attic cupboard for football boots, he'd found an old pile of popular science magazines with his mother's name faintly pencilled inside. She'd not much time in her life for reading, she'd maintained, little use for novels and none at all for romance of any sort. Yet she'd subscribed regularly to a magazine, and was a secret reader — or rather, the magazines had been made difficult to find. Martin had found a second lot of copies crushed into a shelf at the top of a wardrobe behind hats, gloves and piles of old handbags. The crushing and creasing of the magazine pages and their torn corners, he remembered, had made them seem to date so far back in time they appeared almost like ancient lore. Their hiddenness made them at once essential reading. Here petty guesswork about strange phenomena was mixed with spectacular and learned dis-coveries. Under the word Science was revealed the appalling distance of the stars alongside the difficulties of rearing pet tortoises and the phenomenon of sex-change in human beings. Fascinating photographs accompanied the articles — exotic flowers and fruits, the unknown life under the sea and the stones deep inside the earth. Poisons, remedies and drugs were here. Two-headed animals stared from the page, the fattest people in the world, the hairiest, the tallest and smallest, the most beautiful and the most grotesque. Terrifying illnesses were described and wild guesses about life in distant parts of the universe. The conception and birth of all creatures — human, animal and insect — were laid bare in graphic detail. He was fascinated to know how he'd been conceived and stared at his grave father and mother with a certain grudging admiration mixed with generous and total astonishment. He wore strong-lensed glasses at this time, and whether he was reading of the singular revolution of nebulae, great clerics of the world, peculiar penises, dangerous poppies and their uses, or the thunderous mating of dinosaurs, his appearance was always studious and cautious. He had known that here before him, albeit madly jumbled and tangled, lay the choice of what he would eventually take up.

There had been other magazines in the house, of course, but they were there, as it were, by accident and scarcely opened — virgin-smooth cookery books, unspotted by gravy or butter, gardening manuals, unearthy as the day they were bought, unthumbed church magazines, pristine clean from the hands of unwelcomed elders, needlework patterns lent by neighbours and never opened. Early in life Martin felt himself on the road towards medicine and surgery. In time his ideas became more matter-of-fact than romantic. He became a dentist and a very good one, partly because his maternal grandfather had been a dentist and a very bad one. As a child he'd been taken to visit his grandfather's surgery in a decaying quarter of the city. The dentist, a miserly old scoundrel, hadn't bothered to keep up with anything, neither the first rules of hygiene nor the latest findings in his profession. On their few visits Martin and his mother had crunched over bits of old teeth as they made their way to the window to be shown a view of the Castle between rows of black chimneys. The old man had made a good deal of money out of suffering persons, unwilling to walk further, and only too thankful to land up quickly on his grubby doorstep. 'He's a good extractor' was the recommendation given by the companions of these aching and speechless ones, just as in former times they might have said 'a good executioner'. His grandson hadn't seen an executioner, but this old man with his thin, white face, his sharp-nailed fingers and the gold ring he removed when on the job, might well have passed for one skilled in the art of torture. At the end of the room his grandfather had a shelf of yellowing books on dentistry. Martin's mother vowed that behind these were other books – 'dubious' books – she called them. 'Dubious' was the word for anything she thought indecent. Amongst these, picture books were for her the worst, because 'picture books' held the idea of innocent childrens' stuff as well as the pornographic. Martin, because of his wild readings as a child in his mother's fascinating hoard, was never sure of the word 'innocent'. What was it? Were people born with it, or did they gradually become innocent and lose it again? Or were they born without it, gained it over the years, and died innocent people? And innocent about what?

On brief visits by himself to his grandfather, Martin gathered he had a mistress or sweetheart – names good for any woman, young or old, at the time. Yet neither of these seemed to fit the strangely regal woman whose long, navy-blue skirts brushed past as – giving him an absentminded smile – she stepped from the hall into the street. Had they been lying on the tooth-gritty floor, he wondered? What other place? A highly acrobatic act achieved on the swivel chair seemed out of the question. In bed at night Martin would think it out to the last detail. So his grandfather with his sharp fingers had assisted this dignified and absentminded woman to lift her skirts. He couldn't tell what he thought of this idea. After a time the painful drill, red blood and water swirling in a bowl, combined uneasily in his head, passed quickly from head to body and were mixed, not unhappily, in a frantic dream.

The possibility of high salaries had begun when Martin was in the early years of his profession. He could afford attractive rooms and all the things that went with success. His wife was an intelligent and charming woman who kept a family life and social life running smoothly together. The dentist had the staying power and dexterity needed in his work. His eyesight was keen. He was also fairly perceptive about people. He noticed that when he was introduced outside as a dentist, people automatically dropped their glance from his eyes to his smiling mouth. The thing was wildly unreasonable. Firstly, they were expecting him to have perfect teeth, and secondly, if they hoped to become patients, they were expecting him to give *them* perfect teeth. Boiled sweet and biscuit crunchers, life-long smokers, and paid-up members of the anti-toothbrush league, all hoped for a gleaming, royal grimace when he'd done with them. Certain people sat down almost with relief in his chair. There was a large school in a street not far from his surgery. Exacting as his days were, he'd often reason to be thankful they were relatively quiet. He'd met most of the teachers and some came in as patients after school – tired people, only too thankful to put their feet up, even to lie flat out in his reclining chair, drill hovering overhead.

'I'm sorry it's not a proper couch,' he remarked one afternoon to an exhausted Maths teacher.

'Don't worry, it soon will be. Some comfortable psychiatrist's couch up there in the mental hospital will do for me, if this goes on. What do *you* do, by the way, to take your mind off your work? Or perhaps you don't need to.'

'I'm thinking of taking up stars,' said Martin. 'Not the filmstars. Evening Classes.'

'Time enough when I'm retired for that,' the other replied. 'The very thought of more classes! I correct a load of stuff in school. When I get home I take my shoes off, wash the chalk from my fingers, and that's the finish of it for the day, thank God.'

He spoke with bitterness of educational theorists who'd never set foot inside a classroom in their lives, who hadn't an inkling how to tackle thirty-five or more thirteen-year-olds. Let them do one week of that and keep their cool!

Occasionally Martin's teaching patients spoke of the history of their profession – one of the old Edinburgh schools, for instance, that had made a specialty of Writing. How wonderful if Writing could be their only worry!

Mr. Butterworth Moffat respectfully intimates that he has commenced his morning hours from seven to nine at 7, Infirmary Street where classes are open from nine to four. The hours from seven to eleven and twelve to two are especially adapted for Ladies as the very superior accommodation allows these classes to be quite *private*.

Improving a Bad Hand, with Private Lessons when Necessary.

Book Keeping.

Two hours, one for Ladies and the other for Gentlemen, are devoted to Penmaking on the first Saturday of every month.

Other private teachers made a specialty of writing in the eighteenth century, for example William Swanson. Of Swanson's School, Cockburn wrote satirically, 'Screech's shop was the natural resort of lawyers, authors, and all sorts of literary idlers who were always buzzing about the convenient hive. All who wished to see a poet or a stranger, or to hear the public news, the last joke, or yesterday's occurrence in the Parliament House, or to get the publications of the day, congregated there — lawyers, doctors, clergymen and authors. I attended the writing school of William Watson, the great handspoiler of the time, whose crowded classroom was on the south side of the High Street close by the cross and I always tried to get a seat next a window, that I might see the man I heard so much talked of moving in and out of this bower of the muses, or loitering about its entrance.'

Occasionally Martin would remind strangers of George Street. Perhaps they had noticed the statue of George IV as they came to his surgery? The most famous and long-lived member of his profession had practised in that same street and been given Dental Appointment to the Royal Household in Scotland, not only in George IV's reign but also in William's, and for a part of his old age, even at Queen Victoria's court. So that old dentist must have treated teeth ground down by the rich, gargantuan meals of that time. Chronically constipated the feasters would be, and with teeth rotted — every one of them — he'd no doubt. Things were a great deal better now. There were huge changes in his own profession. Future generations of dentists would have less work to do. There would be less rot and they would stop the rot wherever a speck of it occurred. Yet his tired teachers couldn't let him get away with such an ideal future. They themselves were in the endless struggle for their pupils' health, for the children of those pupils and their children's children. They weren't heroes. Did they have the time, the strength, the superhuman energy to combat the awful lure of sugar, the artificial colouring and the chewing gum? They reminded him of the hundreds of sweetshops cheek by jowl with schools, the stacks of Coca-Cola, the clouds of white fluff on sticks, the gluey, chewy bars, powerful enough to drag a tooth from its socket. They might combat the cakes, the chips, the pies, syrups and cigarettes. They couldn't take on the entire world single-handed, as well as climbing up the slow stages of History, uncovering the Basics of English Literature and helping the Faltering Steps in the awful struggle through Trigonometry.

Meantime Martin said nothing of his recent tiredness and discontent with his own work. Rather, he talked a bit about the origins of his profession. Before the twelfth-century healing of all kinds lay in the clergy's hands, but later they were prohibited from anything involving bloodshed. After that, all surgery was relegated to barbers and Guilds of Barber-Surgeons. As barbers were mostly in towns, country people had to rely on blacksmiths or charlatans, anyone, in fact, who could wield a tool – all of them itinerants walking from place to place or travelling in gaily-coloured coaches on market days. The tooth-pulling, in fact, became a spectacle like other outdoor performances. It was not merely a sideshow, however. The suffering patient mounted a platform to have his tooth pulled before expectant crowds, while a bugler stood by to drown his yells of pain. The fun caught on. In fifteenth-century Scotland not even a King was above trying his hand at tooth-pulling. More than that, King James IV paid his subjects for letting him do this. Some who heard of it asked themselves what strange desires this pointed to in the character of the King.

But soon jewellers, watchmakers and workers in wood and ivory adapted their skills to the making of dentures. The first successful denture-makers in Edinburgh originated with a Frenchman, Duchateau, an apothecary of Paris in the 1770s who wore false teeth himself. In

8

those days each denture was handcarved in one piece from hippopotamus ivory, and fitted a plaster cast of the mouth. But this ivory was very yellow in colour and also porous, giving teeth not only a bad shade but, worse still, a very bad smell. Soon hippo-ivory wearers were avoided by near acquaintances. Even close friends began to regret their closeness. The Sèvres factory, however, was not far away and soon porcelain was in fashion. The breakthrough was made by an Italian, using individual porcelain teeth with a hook attaching them to a gold and platinum plate. These teeth — fine though they were — were not a good shape. By the 1820s human teeth were still in great demand and were naturally called 'Waterloo teeth'. These, then, were the forerunners of John Lee, the Edinburgh dentist, who had a very great success making dentures in ivory. At eighteen he was adept at carving these teeth and was said to be one of the best workmen in Scotland at that time. Even more of a success, however, was another Scotsman, Robert Hogue, who, having trained in London, returned to Edinburgh where in 1883 he advertised that 'he was happy to state that after numberless experiments conducted and resumed at intervals during as many years as his professional duties would permit, he had at last succeeded in firing incorruptible teeth and gums, where requisite, of an entirely new and beautiful composite, surpassing the French Terra Metallic and other kinds of mineral teeth in toughness, lightness, perfectly natural in appearance, and not liable to break like these during mastication'. These teeth were indeed very strong, lifelike and durable. Their proud owners also had the bonus of carrying a precious metal inside their mouths. A good deal of gold had been used to position these teeth and to fill the cavities.

'So,' said Martin as he showed his last patient out, 'I'm afraid it was mostly a story of dentures. Today we dentists hope to be in the business of preserving teeth.'

'As far as I'm concerned it takes me all my time to preserve anything,' his patient replied, 'and there are a lot of things to think about. There's my heart, for instance. Is it going too fast or too slow? Naturally it begins to play up when it's thought about — either it gallops along like a racer or it slows down from beat to beat like an unwound clock. Then stops. Stops for *good*, I mean. What else would it stop for at my age? The lungs have their own tricks too, if you consider how they've had to keep going from that first gasp, often accompanied by a smack or two. Then there's my liver and kidneys. They're so smoothly tucked away I rarely think about them. I still have my brain to worry about, and most of all, my nerves. Can I stand the wear and tear of it all for another ten years or so? Of course if you read all the stuff that drops through the letterbox you can't miss being immortal. So if you actually die one day it simply means you've read neither the large print nor the small. Maybe you never even opened the envelope. You've just been bloody careless.'

The waiting-room was now blessedly empty. As soon as his patient was around the corner, the dentist got into his car and made for the nearest garage.

CHAPTER

2

The garage called The Duke was now owned by a Steve Kirkwood who'd been there since he was sixteen when he'd been taught everything he knew about cars by his uncle, the Duke – a name given by other members of the family who considered their brother to be a man with an enormous conceit of himself – a man who, whatever time he got home, dressed himself up to the nines and sauntered out for the evening, sometimes picking a flower from a neighbour's garden to stick in his buttonhole. If this happened to be their prize rose so much the better; if not, even a hedge flower would do. He carried an elegant stick with a curved white handle, smooth as alabaster. No one knew where he was going and no one ever asked. He'd been a first-rate mechanic and an excellent teacher of everything to do with cars. Yet – careless of the working of his own body – he died before he was fifty. At thirty, his nephew Steve took ownership of the garage. Now it was he who became the teacher, keeping a group of young ones under his eye, giving them everything he knew from tightening screws to performing the most intricate repair jobs. In between he initiated them into the art of placating suspicious customers who insisted on climbing out of their cars in order to scrutinise every move and finally to check over every penny of their change. Though Steve for the most part enjoyed the work, he was rather a severe man who'd had no time for his uncle's playacting, while secretly envying him his carefree outlook on the world. Yet, above all, he wanted news from this world. More often, however, it was machines, and more and more intricate ones, that he heard about. Computers were all the rage. Every man, woman and child, it was implied, ought to possess one if they were going to know anything at all about life. Sometimes he could hardly believe that grown men with good brains, hands and eyes could work themselves up into such a state of excitement about computers, even the smaller ones they could afford. True, the larger ones did some fantastic sums counting distant nebulae, particles, cells, and the living creatures inside dust specks. Their discoveries in medicine and science were fabulous. So naturally they were to become all but human in good time – speaking comfortably to the lonely, advising, scolding, teaching, healing, writing poetry, painting pictures, brewing beer, making tea, making love, brushing the floor of crumbs, scouring the universe for God, putting the baby to bed, quarrelling, arguing, standing up for women, standing up for men, as well as standing in for doctors, midwives, psychoanalysts and social workers. Then, of course, there was nothing messy about them. No oil, no dirt, no petrol, no smell, hopefully soon no sound and scarcely any movement. Before long, perhaps, they would mate by means of screws and pistons, and give birth painlessly to small, identical robots and computers. That would be the day. Some of the youths who worked for him already had a miniature computer at home and were saving up for larger ones. Before they'd learnt to polish a windscreen they knew what the earth would be like in a hundred or even a thousand years. Occasionally Steve would interrupt to point out that the earth might very well not be there at all in a hundred, let alone a thousand years. A huge nuclear reactor had already blown its top. The earth was dotted with others, all growing up, swiftly, silently, like innocent, white mushrooms in the night. At times they would listen to all this with genial patience. More often not. They were hurrying to be off for the night, and the future was aeons away. He would feel a terrified sympathy with them as he watched them donning their gear like soldiers, mounting the motorbikes and swerving off slowly at first, but only waiting for a clear, dark road to let rip beyond the speeding cars and far beyond the cautious bicyclists. For them there was nothing left in life but speed. Their helmets were not invulnerable. Long ago Steve had shared a side-ward in hospital with a young head-injury case. About this he still had nightmares.

Spending half his life in a garage didn't, as some assumed, give him a special feeling for cars and their drivers. He had more sympathy with the long-distance lorry drivers and their enormous grievances. The larger vehicles had their own stopping places. But he met men who'd once driven the great lorries and was curious to hear of the variety of stuff that was on the move. There were the problems of loading and unloading and the dangers of movement according to the kind of load. Huge cylinders of liquid, packing-cases, crates of animals or furniture, stacked blocks and boxes, bars and bags – all had to be clamped, roped, chained or manacled together. Some of the men had already driven in various parts of the world. They had taken their eightwheelers for hundreds of night-miles across Australia. Though they were driving small vans now, they looked back with pride to these night vehicles, lit up like long, moving houses from end to end. They spoke of the creatures that had raced away or raced towards these lights out of the black bush. They talked of the blinding red dust, the crossing of dried-up river-beds and the fear of flash floods. In scorching weather there was the danger of driving toward the near mirages on the road or the distant shimmer on the horizon. Steve had not travelled far himself. These accounts went down a great deal better with him than the car stories which consisted mostly of the difficulties of parking, the aggression or slowness of other drivers, the stupidity of certain women at the wheel. He hammered dents out of the cars, filled them up, washed them down, and listened to the story of their bashes, scratches and stupid women with a sceptical smile. A careful knowledge of the innards of cars had given him a fair working knowledge of most people who came here.

Sometimes he wondered if his bike-crazy youths were interested in cars at all. Long before they came to him they had the helmets, the goggles, the gear and the girls, and were ready to sell their machines for bigger and better ones before the month was up. Sometimes at night, under the yellow lights of the place, Steve would stand, rubbing an oily rag between his hands, watching these boys, wondering what would happen to them – this one so slow and secretive, another so slapdash and quick. They were already away when the dentist arrived at the place. People came from all the surrounding streets to this garage to discuss cars or listen to transistors. They had the whole countryside, their own homes and garages, and yet they came here. Technical colleges and university buildings were not far off, and once in a while people even arrived here with a load of books at the back of the car. Occasionally when the place was deserted, they sat on here, as if this dingy place with its hard yellow lights, filled with wrecks of cars, wheels, pumps and oil-containers, suited them better, in some grotesque way, than library or study. Steve had never thought of himself as particularly sociable and it was some time before he realised that, though they preferred to look too busy for conversation, they were often in dire need of talk and company. A great weight of print had taken the light from some of them. Others were learned but not bright – not as bright even as his group of youths who, at their best, could be as sharp and racy as any actor on the stage. Sometimes his customers read as they were being filled up, and Steve would think of them as pouring the stuff of print into their own heads. But, unlike the petrol, he could see that print didn't always make for speed. He wondered if it often made for despondency.

Steve saw his last customer come in and watched as Martin sat for some time in his car, frowning at a booklet in his hands and drawing a finger down its columns.

'You've got something interesting there, then?' he remarked as he came round from the petrol pump and glanced in at the open window of the car.

'I've just got the Evening Classes for the winter. Want to have a look yourself?'

'Wouldn't mind,' said the other, taking a corner of the booklet and studying its pages under the light. 'Better get a move on if you want to go,' said the man in the car. 'Some of them fill up quickly.' The garage-man looked through the list and gave a laugh. His only free night coincided with Dance through the Ages, and Geology. He pointed this out and together they studied the page again. Martin mentioned that only recently he'd gone off the idea of Non-Aggression and Live Volcanoes. He was now opting for Astronomy. He was anxious, he said, to get off the earth as quickly as he could, millions and millions of light years away, if possible. Just now the earth seemed foul indeed, seething with hideous bloodshed and war, murder, rape, famine, guns, bombs, drugs, disease and huge nuclear spills, plus the murderously honest faces of grinning world leaders. 'Pure escapism, of course,' said the dentist as he slid off into the dark. 'Maybe I'll see you around.' Steve wished him luck in his take-off from the earth. He brooded a long time in the empty garage, wondering if many of the cool-speaking types who came in here had this violent longing to escape. He wondered where his own escape might lie. It wasn't the outside but the inside of the earth that was in his bones. Rocks and ancient stones would suit him best.

Dancing! The garage-man smiled grimly at this idea. His uncle, the Duke, had most certainly danced, but his father and mother had never danced in their lives, nor had his grandfather who'd worked in his youth down the deepest mine in Scotland. Those had been the days when miners walked home in winter darkness off the night shift, lights on their caps, white teeth and eyes staring from black faces. On Sundays his grandfather had walked out, a pale whippet at his heel, to join the other racing men. No dancing man, he. Things improved a little in his father's time. 'As a treat' Steve had been taken down the mine one day as a child. For some long seconds he knew the sealed, black, stomach-wrenching drop of the cage, and came up later into daylight, shattered by such noise as he had never known before, and limp with the heat. Occasionally, his father told him, the ferocious vibration of the coal-cutter could dislodge a stone swift as a bullet and large enough to kill a man. Some miners, he said, had claimed a sixth sense for danger. They could sense, for instance, when part of the roof was unsafe by a faint creaking of the old wooden props before their replacement by steel. In one day the boy grew up. From then he saw his father differently as a physical being – a bending, stretching, struggling person with a stony backbone, living two totally different lives, below ground and above it. Though he and his brother worked hard – he in his garage and his brother with a large tool-making establishment – their work seemed nothing to his. In the proud boast of front parlours they had never 'needed to get their hands dirty' or not for long. Whereas their father might wash his hands forever; his clean hands would be rimmed with nails as black as soot. His grandfather, so scrubbed and spruce when he walked out on Sundays, had died of the coal dust in his chest.

Steve's feelings about the rest of his family changed too as time went on. His sisters seemed less well-known to him as they grew older. There had never been a deep affection between him and his mother. Yet he had sympathy for women in general and those in miners' families in particular. Soon women were making claims for themselves in different parts of the world, but in his experience there was as yet little of this in the small town where he lived. Women who were strong to take on everything during the day, were out of it when male talk got underway in the evening. After all, they were considered well able to look after themselves. Were they not the sex who, through the ages and in all places, had cast spells of one kind or another? These were seldom thought to be good spells. More often they were sinister, and men must be safeguarded. Taboos had hung round the necks of women. There were sacred places where they must never set foot, sacred talk they must not join in, tables they must never sit at and altars they were forbidden to stand behind. These bits of furniture might be desecrated, the shiny cloths tainted. This seemed to imply that the solid church furniture had been nailed together by God himself, the cloths stitched by angels rather than the Women's Guild. The old superstitions still held. Not only was it unlucky to have women amongst fishermen. To miners, setting out early, there was the mysterious danger of seeing a woman before going on the morning shift. Why, Steve wondered, was it women who carried these bad-luck burdens along with all their other loads? When and where was it ever very good luck to encounter a woman? He had not heard.

There was absolutely nothing bright about the house where his parents had lived, as if the slightest touch of colour around the place was a sort of insult to his grandfather's and his father's dark work. The front garden was a patch of green with iron railings, and the back was a slightly larger patch for drying clothes. There was no gaiety in his mother's life as far as he could see — very little smiling and no laughing, as if too much strength might be expended on this. It seemed to him, as a child, that all her energy had gone on washing and drying clothes. A warm, windy day that others might think of as a day for shopping, for chatting to neighbours in the next garden or even for sitting out, was for her 'a good day for drying'. She would pull out a heap of damp clothes from a basket, hang them up, and some hours later he'd watch her walking along the line, snatching off pegs, while she embraced the dry stuff, letting trousers, skirts, pyjamas, pants, overalls, sweaters and dungarees fall into her open arms. As a young man he'd thought very little about her life as wife or mother until one freezing, winter morning he'd watched her bringing in some of her own clothes that had been out all night. He remembered her standing, attempting to fold an uncharacteristically frilled and flimsy nightgown — a present from her sister. After the night's frost it cracked in her hands like a frail board. Thin ice splinters broke from its frills as it slowly thawed and dripped in pools on the kitchen floor. She bent and mopped them up. To him there was something poignant about the sight. He saw her for the first time as a woman stiffened and frozen by experiences he knew nothing about.

At that time they lived in a small, rather bitter community, cut off from most other workers by the hardships of a life with its own language, its own fears and illnesses, pleasures and sports, by a day-to-day existence relatively unknown and certainly totally unseen by most other persons. Their house had been in sight of the church and they would watch people walking past their windows on Sunday. Few of the miners at that time were church-goers. They opened the door cautiously and unwillingly to the minister, though they had nothing against the friendly man. Rather, it was a distrust of the whole language of light in church — the sunshiny hymn or flaring word. This divinely shining optimism seemed rashly overdone and faintly ridiculous to the men, thoughtful and critical as they could be of things underground as well as how the world above was managed, never mind heaven. As far back as he remembered Steve's house had been a centre for discussion one evening a week. It was an old house, partly modernised. When he was on nightshift Steve's grandfather had slept part of the next morning in an old box bed off the living-room, and such was the labour of the previous night, he could sleep soundly through all kinds of noise. Visitors were rare, but when they did come they were surprised that no one expected them to lower their voices.

Over the years Steve's father had got together a large collection of books. Volumes on History and Economics, political books and pamphlets had been his main interest as a young man. He had also old books about the district, books on Geology, a row of Encyclopaedias, a huge family Dictionary, and one or two works of fiction that interested him for various reasons. One of these was James Hogg's *The Private Memoirs and Confessions of a Justified Sinner*. His interest in this book, he claimed, lay partly in the fact that his grandfather, a man from the north-west, had been a strong-minded elder of the Free Church. Another reason, he would add, was that he could see the Crags of Arthur's Seat – the scene of episodes in the book – from his own back window.

Steve had married a woman who once seemed not unlike his mother. He didn't often look at her nowadays and seldom took the chance to talk to her alone. From the start romantic talk had not been welcome in the family. 'Falling in love' had been spoken of as men and women making fools of themselves over one another. Occasionally he might glance at his wife's, Ruth's, face and wonder momentarily if she was happy. But, reminding himself that millions of people in the world had neither time nor energy to ask themselves this question, he gave up thinking about it at all. She had once appeared a rather mild-mannered girl but, like his parents, had developed a sharp, sarcastic way of talking. She also laughed at his early ideas of travelling one day, of seeing new places and people, and remarked that, if he ever managed to do that, she would certainly not be going with him. It was in his mind now, however, that nobody could stop him in his travels underground amongst rocks and stones if he decided on it, just as nobody could stop the gloomy dentist from going to the moon, the planets and the furthest star if he'd made up his mind. He mentioned to his wife when he got home that he'd met a man who was planning his winter classes. 'What kind of classes?' she asked. 'Oh that sort!' She dropped the subject at once.

They now lived in a new part of town where rows of houses had grown up almost overnight. These were neat, bright, all similar in size and pattern as if squared and cut off to the last millimetre. Different colours of curtain, of car, of paint on the front door, of flowers in the garden, marked the contrasts here. People knew they were lucky to own one of them and worked hard to make these contrasts show. Shops followed quickly, swings and a concrete playground, often covered with splintered glass, a modern church with a green spire, and a new white school.

As to the landscape round Steve's old family home – that had all changed. Most of the mines below were long gone, but the signs of their disappearance showed in deep, unexpected faults, with humps and holes in roads and gardens. Movements from the caving-in of old, deep mines could sometimes be heard in the night like the rumbling of earthquakes. Afterwards, windows and doors wouldn't shut properly. Hinges hung minimally askew, and even the pictures on the walls were slightly crooked. To begin with, this displacement had a curious effect on certain people. It could seem like a slight change in the eye or even the judgement, an overturn of the laws of lines and angles. Right angles were now wrong. There was the usual uneasy question of what, then, was right or wrong in anything. Judging the moral law, the human rules, was bad enough. Now one was staring at a fractional change, perhaps an imaginary crookedness. It was a relief when the down-to-earth workmen arrived with tales of other buildings in the same plight. And sometimes the business of rescuing old houses had to be totally written off.

CHAPTER

3

A vacuum must be filled. It is a law of nature. And there was no doubt that this silent Festival city was grey and empty as a stranded shell compared to a few days ago. Things are said to rush into a vacuum – sometimes with a sound like a thunderclap. But in this place things move backwards or forwards circumspectly. Change can be stealthy. The last collections of pictures had been taken from galleries and strapped into boxes, along with thin, sculpted figures, now safely padded and quilted like Eskimos. The winding steps which housed hundreds of amateur paintings and dozens of interested buyers had resumed its darkness and urine dampness till the next summer. Halls were empty now and courtyards silent. Yet only days ago on a grey, Civic Building Japanese acrobats – seemingly within an inch of death – hung from their heels while bus after bus with screeching brakes and screeching people slowed down on the hill to stare. Not long before, the high balconies and turret windows had served as a stage where nervous Juliets and doomed queens had said their piece. The dusty room where three tramps had waited beside a tree had reverted to a storeroom where kitchenware was piling up along with linoleum rolls and jazzy samples of wallpaper. Soon the sinks, mirrors, basins and lavatory seats will come shunting back again like some flashy set for a bathroom drama. Meanwhile the true tramps of the city – the paper-pickers and metal collectors – begin to move in, this time finding an unnatural cleanness about the streets. But soon the lamppost baskets will fill up again while bulging rubbish sacks will be dragged down tenement stairs to tip over in gutters on windy nights. The strange silence may continue until the first autumn leaves scrape along narrow closes, gathering thickly in the vomit-sticky corners of pubs or plastering themselves against the stained-glass windows of old churches. The city will begin to withdraw into itself again. For only during Festivals does the place seem to forget, for three weeks, its rather chilling dignity and reserve.

'It certainly affords much matter of reasonable regret that in Scotland, a country distinguished for its learning and good taste in poetry and general Literature, music, in the liberal sense of the term, should be so little cultivated and so much less understood,' said G. F. Graham in 1815. For his 'reasonable regret' he might well have been booted out of Edinburgh, if not Scotland itself, except that he happened to be one of the Secretaries of its first Edinburgh Festival in the year of Waterloo. And there was nothing wrong with the list of 'Extraordinary Directors' either. It included Walter Scott, Esq., Principal Baird, Sir William Fettis and Lord Grey. Parliament House was chosen for the first performance. 'Early in the morning,' says a newspaper report, 'reconnoitring parties were seen in Parliament Square, some of which took post near the different entrances, while others returned home, terrified by the anticipation of demolished dresses and personal injuries. In consequence of the excellent arrangements and attention of the Directors on Duty the pressure and inconvenience to individuals upon the opening of the doors was inconsiderable. It was a fine day, the sun shining brightly and filling the room.' The article added that the Poet-Director who had published *Waverley* the previous year would be in his element.

Part I of the concert was all Handel. Part II was 'The Creation' by Haydn. The whole concert was a great success – evidently almost too great. The audience fairly let itself go in applause. Again Graham – that stern critic of human nature – wrote: 'So powerful was the general sentiment of pleasure that many were harried by their feelings, so far beyond the bounds of propriety and decorum, as to express their delight by plaudits, more becoming a theatrical performance, than a musical performance of the most grave and solemn kind. Fortunately a gentleman who had been to a similar occasion and knew how to behave, put them right.' After the description of 'a gigantic burst of harmony which thundered from the organ and all the other instruments . . . the idea of national importance adding to the whole', Graham feels forced to deliver another grave warning: 'Perhaps there is no country in the world where prejudice in favour of national music is carried to so great a height as in Scotland. The love of one's country is, within proper bounds, a most amiable passion but whenever it operates so strongly as to shut our eyes to what is admirable in a different country, it is no longer an amiable passion but a silly vanity.' Brave words indeed.

In an indirect and mysteriously moving way, even Beethoven – the great composer himself – had a connection with the first concert. It came about like this. There was a double-bass player who had performed in Parliament Hall at the first Edinburgh Festival of 1815. His name was Dragonetti and Beethoven had once met him somewhere and admired his playing. In fact, Beethoven presented him with a snuffbox, its lid decorated with a painting of eight men taking snuff. One might expect that most people would give their right arm to keep such a genius-given gift for themselves, but obviously Dragonetti needed his right arm for nothing but his own playing, and he presented this snuffbox to a Dr Mather at the first Festival. Evidently this Dr Mather didn't treasure it either, for the box soon fell into the hands of a Mr Boag who bought it in a job lot at a Glasgow saleroom. 'I bought it along with a couple of Bibles and some other things,' he says nonchalantly. Edinburgh was always packed with Bibles as everyone knew who had worked in the secondhand bookshops. What man or woman of Scottish descent had ever destroyed a Bible and remained free of guilt? Even wrapping it up in layers of fine, white paper and hiding it in a hedge or lowering it into clear, running water – these acts would be almost inconceivable to the Scottish temperament. Passing them on to a bookseller was the only decent thing to do with the huge legacy. After that nobody asked what happened to the piles and piles of old Bibles. A proper silence sealed the mouth.

When late visitors or even the inhabitants themselves begin to wonder what could possibly fill the after-Festival vacuum of the modern city they have, perhaps, forgotten that this was once and still is a place of learning – not necessarily a place of book-reading nowadays, but always one for storing knowledge cannily inside the skull. So, before many weeks have passed, before the scuttling leaves are frosted, there are occasionally new kinds of persons to be seen in the streets at night. Not the carefree world traveller who's seen it all before, nor even the citizen himself who's tried to feel at home in the midsummer jamboree, tried to get into the act of pantomine or high tragedy. No. There are different men and women to be seen around. They have got themselves a couple of brand-new notebooks, a bunch of pens and maybe a clipboard for extra notes. With these they are armed, and walk the dark streets with new confidence. The city belongs to them at last. Each person knows exactly where he's bound for. No one accompanies him. Evening Classes have begun.

The list has been out for some time. It reads like the history of life on earth, from Dinosaurs to Space Satellites, from Primitive Man to Robots. In between come Archaeology, Myths, Magic, and Religions of the World, Astronomy, Botany, Geology, Literature, Philosophy and Computer Studies, classes on how to conquer timidity, how to relate to others, to lose fat, reduce clumsiness and the fear of death. There are classes in Cookery, Painting, Engineering and Writing. There are classes to get the tongue-tied to speak. Indeed, eventually, and long before the winter's out, every single person there has slowly, perhaps, and tentatively, started to talk.

A generation or two of schoolgirls, schoolboys, students and their parents had sometime or other found themselves in an Extra-Mural Class. All ages had attended them. And they came from what was called 'all walks of life'. But nearer the present day the walks tended to merge gradually into the middle walk. It was not always so, nor meant to be. There were, for instance, the coffee-houses. As early as 1667, John Houghton, a Cambridge man and Fellow of the Royal Society, had compared the coffee-houses with universities: 'Coffee-houses made all sorts of people sociable; rich and poor meet together, the learned and unlearned. It improves arts, merchandise and all other knowledge; for here an inquisitive man, that aims at good learning, may get more in an evening than he shall by Books in a month . . . and he may in short space gain the pith and marrow of the others' reading and studies.'

Much the same feeling was expressed in a broadside of the same year:

There is the colledge and the Court,
The country, Camp and Navie,
So great a Universitie
I think there ne're was any,
In which you may a scholar be
For spending of a penny.

CHAPTER

4

The dentist who had wanted to get away millions of miles from the dirty earth was driving up the steep hill to the Observatory for the fourth night of the Astronomy class. Sometime soon during this course, a good viewing of the brilliant Venus had been promised. Halfway up he passed a group of girls, but circumspectly didn't stop to pick them up. In his headlights he saw flowery skirts and bright blouses under their heavy coats. To him they seemed like girls off to a party rather than to a study of the universe. He stopped, however, for an elderly man climbing laboriously on the last steep corner of the road before the brilliant dome of the place came in sight.

'Well, I suppose it's all worth it for Venus if we *are* going to see her,' the man remarked as he took his seat. '*Is* it though?' he asked, staring sideways at Martin. 'Is the world well lost for love? You should know at your age.'

'But you have the experience,' the younger man replied.

'You mean, because I'm nearly seventy you think I've had years and years of solid Venus?'

'Not all that solid, I hope,' said Martin, glancing at the unexpected mixture of white and black hair on the head beside him. 'You're a handsome man and you must have caught the eye of some good-looking women in your time.'

'In Italy and in Greece, yes. I'm Italian and a tailor. I've worked most of my life in those countries.'

'In this part of the world,' said Martin, 'the number of solid women is pretty high.'

'Not just in your country,' said the other. 'If she's anything to go by, the Venus de Milo would be a well-covered woman. A 40–42 bust, I suspect, and the hips to match. I've had to measure them and put the pins round many a one in my day. Greek and Roman matrons. Dignified and demanding. The trick is to let the cloth lie on them like a second skin, skimming the figure, as it were, so they move gracefully inside a sort of sheath. No buttons, no belt, and black wherever possible.' He looked sideways from the window. 'Those were very pretty girls you passed down there – all bright, belted, bundled-up – pulled and dragged in the wrong places. They *look* very bright, very flowery under those coats, you see, but not at all happy in their clothes.'

'You've dressed only the rich, I daresay,' said Martin. 'Whether they're happier I don't know, but they probably look more relaxed.'

The Observatory now shone directly above them, brilliantly lit against a dark stretch of hill – a lonely place where in midwinter the wind whistled through low trees and thorn bushes and where one forgot the frisky daytime dogs and their fearless owners. To get to the lecture room of the building the two men went through corridors and past small rooms where blue screens were flickering, where groups sat at revolving discs and large computers, making press-button calculations of the sky. Sunspots and flares and the intensity of starlight were recorded here. The lecture room was already full when they entered. A serious and enthusiastic crowd. Many were amateur astronomers who owned small telescopes and spent freezing nights outside. They knew their planets and their constellations. They were here to learn about things further out still – even the most distant objects of the visible universe. Some were ardent, silent followers of exploding stars, or fans of Quasars, Black Holes and Red Shifts. Down one side of the room were great windows overlooking the city far below which, as it grew later and darker, began to glitter with yellow, green and blue lights, cross-cut by moving streams of traffic in the main streets. Behind it all was a straight, black line of sea, pointed with occasional beams from ships, and beyond that the faintly twinkling coastline of Fife winding eastwards into darkness with the flash of a last lighthouse miles away. The room was warm. The girls in flowered skirts had removed their coats and were sitting in the front row. Martin had dropped his eyes to these skirts as he came in, as if to ask how flowers and stars could come together in this place, and got a defiant stare from some who guessed what was in his mind.

The young astronomer who took the class was a tall, thin man with long arms and large hands with which he made sweeping gestures of enthusiasm and astonishment. There was nothing smooth about him, neither his hair, his clothes nor his words. Often he would confess that he himself was as astounded at what he was showing them on the screen, at what he was telling them, as they were themselves. 'If your mind boggles at it, don't imagine ours doesn't too,' he would say as he showed them the close-up satellite pictures of the rings of Saturn, a distant galaxy tilted like a plate, or strands of blue nebulae veiling black space. The class warmed to this man. He was generous, respectful, even, of their meagre knowledge. They sensed a kind of patience in him that was not in their experience. No doubt it was not a better patience, but it was different − not the paltry patience they experienced in the endless setbacks of each day, the irritation of lost moments in queues and traffic jams. This man was used to waiting hours, days, months and often years, even a lifetime, for certain changes in the sky. On these huge explorations, huge disappointments were in store. Even tonight, as he looked out, he was preparing them for disappointment. Thicker and thicker clouds were floating in from the sea. 'No telescope, no Venus tonight, I'm afraid,' he said at last, 'but I've something interesting for you. Follow me to the library and I'll show you hundreds of plates of the sky we've been collecting.'

In the library the astronomer stood at the long cupboards, pulling out a series of sliding drawers. 'A map of part of the sky,' he explained as he put out dozens of slides on the tables. Everyone leant down to study them. At first they appeared to be photos of the dark sky speckled with stars. The astronomer, with something of the air of a magician now handed round small magnifying glasses and told them to look again. This closer look brought exclamations, cries almost of fear like those of persons presented suddenly with the mind-blowing after seeing only the unbelievable. Under their eyes each small star-speck had become a looped nebula, all grouped together with others in space. Back in the lecture room the astronomer spoke again about what they'd seen and talked of comets, reminding them that Halley's Comet was hurtling towards the sun, still many million miles away, but near enough for them to have their telescopes at the ready and their binoculars polished up. Lucky, he said, that few people nowadays were superstitious about the coming of plagues, earthquakes, floods, wars, famines and other catastrophes. At this point his audience were staring rather blankly before them. It seemed to them that already that year — comet or no comet — the earth had endured every one of these happenings, and that before this comet faded out there would no doubt be a great deal more. No, they didn't believe this object from space could be responsible. But there was a T V in every house and several daily papers. Who needed to be superstitious about the future? Disasters were happening every minute and every hour of every day.

A couple of weeks later, on one of the coldest nights of the winter, Martin met up again with the Italian tailor, Mario Viscosi, and went on to join the long queue waiting behind the Observatory. The big telescope, housed outside the main building, was open, pointing in the direction of two stars between which a faint blur was to be seen. This was Halley's Comet, only one of the many comets visible through the centuries — their course plotted by mathematicians and astronomers, their 'manes of hair', their 'tails' painted by artists, their meaning argued over by theologians and soothsayers. Of one comet, Rosa, it was written in the sixteenth century: 'It is so called for its pink colour; it is great and round after the manner of the sun and turns towards the yellow colour of gold and silver mingled. In days past it was seen red and inflamed, casting a light so great and bright that it vanquished the night: then later its greatness diminished little by little so that at last its brightness was altogether diminished and consumed. When this Comet appears it signifies the death of noble-men in the lands where it shows its face, and the things of the world shall be changed, and there shall be better things.' The Chal-deans said of this comet 'that when it appears it signifies the death of kings and of great and noble men, and the captives and prisoners shall be delivered and set free from their prisons'. This comet was seen by all Europe in the year 1460.

The two men had stood in many queues in the city, but this was unlike any they had seen before. Every head in the crowd was thrown back apprehensively for fear the precious patch of clear sky would cloud over before the telescope was reached. Only the tailor was not looking up, but showed himself more interested in the huge variety of winter clothing round him — the thick-eared helmet caps and double collars, the cloaks with hoods, the long, knitted scarfs covering up the cheekbones of some, and trailing around the short legs of others. There were shawls knotted across coats and wound around stomachs as well as outsize gauntlet gloves, arctic boots and climbers' knee-socks. These people were on an expedition to outer space, but they were fairly calm about it. In their bones they had always known how to dress for this. Bitter wind and ice were in their background. Nevertheless this place was black and steep. It was going to be a long wait. There was much comforting talk for the young ones of late suppers, of grandmothers waiting with piping-hot pies in the oven, of long drinks, and a warm bed at the end of it all. Signor Viscosi himself was fairly comfortable. He had clothes for every occasion, even the occasion of comet-watching. Tonight he wore a coat with a thick fur lining, and fine fur shields covered his ears under his cap.

It was an awkward pilgrimage all right, but there has been certain respites and encouragements along the way. A few small telescopes had been set up by the Observatory staff to give a preliminary view. For those with good eyesight a blur was pin-pointed, and some were satisfied with that. It was enough. Thankfully they started home. Others had set their hearts on climbing up inside the big telescope and were not to be tempted down by lesser apparatus nor by thoughts of food, drink and warmth. Hadn't the devil himself tried to draw all heaven-seekers down to comfort and acclaim by taking them up into high mountains in order that they should make the miraculous leap back into normal life — while at the same time warning them never to climb too high again or set themselves above the multitude?

Although he'd been looking into Astronomy during the week, Signor Viscosi told his friend, other things interested him more — sewing, embroidery and weaving for example, various types of needle through the ages, different dyes and colours and the thickness of threads, wools and silks. And of course, he explained, he had visited Bayeux in his travels. He had seen the splendid tapestry and studied every inch of it. And on the hottest day of the year, he added. Everything, in fact, had been the opposite of this present experience. The tapestry comet was a great yellow flaming thing like some huge, thick-petalled flower in the sky — not at all the faint, almost invisible blur to be seen above them at this moment. The tailor, because of his trade, was a champion of women, and proclaimed himself mystified to see only three women in the whole tapestry. Certainly there were none amongst onlookers at King Harold's coronation. Yet women liked wedding feasts and coronations, didn't they? At any rate they did all the work for them. So was the designer of the tapestry a mysogynist? he asked. That battle was a bloody business when you looked into it. Ecclesiastics weren't allowed to shed blood, of course. But then the Church had always managed to get around little drawbacks of that kind in wartime — always had and no doubt always would. After all, you could always brain a man with one mighty stroke of the club. Neater and probably cleaner. Droves of ecclesiastics and bishops with lethal clubs and maces rampaged across the Bayeux Tapestry from end to end.

They had almost reached the telescope, but not before a cutting wind had blown up from the east. Now everyone was loudly declaring the longing to get inside the comparative shelter of the building. Those almost at its door were still stamping, swinging their arms and occasionally cheering as, one by one, people emerged.

'Worth it? Worth it?' was heard all around when the incomers met those going out.

'Did you say "worth it"? What do you mean? Yes, of *course* worth it! What do you think we came for? We knew it would be worth it!'

It was curiously still inside. People were climbing the spiral stairs slowly, silently, as at the end of a long pilgrimage — stopping, starting again, and waiting patiently. There was something moving about the moment when they at last stood before the instrument. Each person, young or old, was requested to kneel for a few moments. Then they got up again. Often they gasped at what they saw — not so much at the dim comet, but rather at the way the black sky had come suddenly close, glittering with huge numbers of stars they had never seen a second before. Even the astronomer, directing operations, took on a certain radiance from these astonished faces.

'Did you see it?' he kept asking hopefully. Perhaps and perhaps not. But they had seen an awful thing, and it made them jubilant.

When Martin had stood at the Observatory window he'd looked down on a landscape of reflection and illusion. He'd seen distant water and the lights miles away flushing the sky, and the sky gleaming on sea. He'd seen stars overhead, and the blazing windows of an Observatory wing, adjacent to his, throwing panels of light onto the darkness outside.

All these were reflections, as it were, of certain articles on the History of Astronomy he'd seen years ago in his mother's old Science magazines. For the eighteenth-century Professor of Astronomy in Edinburgh, Robert Blair, had looked into all the phenomena that Martin had seen from the window. This astronomer had worked with the idea of optical illusion, with the properties of glass and mirrors. Above all, he worked on the use of fluid lenses in the study of the stars. Indeed there were many water images in Robert Blair's work. For this star-man was also a man of the sea. The early part of his life had been spent on board ship as a naval surgeon looking after the health of sailors — notably prisoners of the Napoleonic wars. One of his most important discoveries at this time was finding a method of preserving the lime juice which was used on long journeys to prevent the dreaded scurvy. Blair's post was more or less a sinecure — there being few astronomical instruments for the job at that time. But now a move was made to combine one principal observer in Astronomy with the Professor of Astronomy in the University of Edinburgh. The full title of this post was to be The Astronomer Royal for Scotland and Regius Professor of Astronomy in The University. It was a rather curious thing that in 1834 none other than Thomas Carlyle should have put in for this post — the reason being that twenty years before he had been a student of Mathematics at Edinburgh University.

31

'The case was this,' he says in his *Reminiscences*: 'We heard copiously in the Newspapers that the Edinburgh people, in a meritorious scientific spirit, were remodelling their old astronomical Observatory: and at length they had brought it to the proper pitch of real equipment, and that nothing now was wanting but a fit observer . . . . I had hardly ever looked through a telescope, but I had good strength in Mathematics, in Astronomy, and did not doubt but I could be at home in such an enterprise if I fairly entered on it . . . . My heart's desire for many years past and coming,' he goes on, 'was always to find *any* honest employment by which one might regularly gain one's daily bread! [while hopelessly writing *The French Revolution*, for example, hopeless of money or other success from it] I thought my case so tragically hard; could learn to do honestly so many things I have ever seen done, from the making of shoes, up to the engineering of canals, architecture of mansions as palatial as you liked, and perhaps to still higher things of the physical or spiritual kind . . . . In a word I got into considerable spirits about that Astronomical employment – and after a few days, in the light, friendly tone, with modesty and brevity, applied to my Lord Advocate [then Lord Jeffrey] for his countenance as to the first or preliminary step of procedure . . . and the answer was prompt and surprising! Almost or quite by return of post I got, not a flat refusal only, but an angry, vehement, almost shrill-sounding and scolding one – as if it were a crime and an insolence in the like of me to think of such a thing.' Nevertheless, though feeling himself exceedingly ill-used at the time, Carlyle had friendly and moving things to say about Jeffrey in later years when he was wasting, frail, and – as the writer said: 'grown Lunar, now, not Solar any more'.

It was Thomas Henderson then, in 1834, who became the first Astronomer Royal in Scotland, Professor of Astronomy at Edinburgh University and a brilliant mathematician and observer at the Calton Observatory. An extraordinary man succeeded him in 1846. The career of Charles Piazzi Smyth was long and full of a multitude of interests and adventures both fortunate and catastrophic. At sixteen he was in South Africa where the great Herschel was studying the skies of the southern hemisphere. When young Charles arrived

Halley's Comet was to be seen, this time at its most spectacular. Piazzi Smyth, artist as well as astronomer, made sketch after sketch of the phenomenon including a painting of the comet's long tail then brilliant enough to be clearly reflected in the sea.

Luckily even those totally ignorant of stars can be reminded of this unusual astronomer every day in the city at one o'clock. In 1858 a Time Ball was erected on the column of the Nelson Monument on Calton Hill, to be followed a few years later by a Time Gun mounted in Edinburgh Castle and controlled by the Transit Clock of the Observatory. Nowadays, even the stone deaf may adjust their watches by the sudden flight of hundreds of pigeons from the rooftops above Princes Street on the stroke of one.

More than a hint of something tragic now comes into the story of Piazzi Smyth. Possibly the width of his knowledge and his endless curiosity led him to an increasing interest in the mystery of the Great Pyramid of Cheops. The Edinburgh astronomer came to believe that those learned French scholars who accompanied Napoleon on his expedition to the Pyramid were right in their belief that this huge construction had been built 'to make a record of the measure of the earth'. Piazzi Smyth decided to make an expedition there himself. Box upon box of general stores and photographic equipment went with him and his accomplished wife to Cairo – the astronomer now being an expert photographer, indeed a pioneer in that flash photography needed in the dark, narrow passages of the pyramids. The astronomer hoped to date these pyramids the with help of ancient star positions. Strong attacks were made on his more mystical ideas by the Royal Society of Edinburgh and led also to his resigning from the Royal Society of London. Nevertheless, a great deal of travelling, experiments and photography were still to come, including observations of the effects in the atmosphere of the catastrophic volcanic eruption of Krakatoa in 1874, resulting in the changing colours of the solar spectrum. In spite of the struggles and disappointments at the end of his life, Piazzi Smyth never gave up his sense of wonder and his love of adventure.

It was not so long after this – early in the twentieth century – that other great discoveries of Ancient Egypt were being uncovered. The words cornelian, calcedony, jasper, turquoise, alabaster and lapis-lazuli slipped easily off the tongue like liquid gold. Soon travellers were bringing back copies of every object that had ever been dug up. Back in Edinburgh it was the same. Replicas of gods and goddesses, sacred dogs, cats, birds, snakes, and lotus-flower ashtrays would be ranged along Georgian mantelpieces or on the small bamboo tables brought back from India at an earlier date. Even the old reprobate dentist, while not reaching Egypt itself, had brought back a load of stuff from Africa, falling very far short of anything hoped for by way of ornament, namely – a pile of wizened baby crocodiles which were passed round friends and family with varying degrees of disappointment and distaste.

Ralph Copeland, third Astronomer Royal for Scotland, and the man behind the choice of a new Observatory for Edinburgh, was born on a farm in Lancashire, had his first lessons from a local weaver and was apprenticed to a cotton mill. As usual, Adventure and Astronomy went together. At sixteen he set off for Australia where he stayed for five years in the middle of the gold rush, working as a shepherd for a Scottish sheep farmer. It is intriguing to realise that it was the glittering night sky of Australia that awoke his interest in stars. At any rate his mother was asked to send him a small telescope and he began to study the work of Herschel along with the Bible and Shakespeare. On his return to England he joined an engineering works, went on with Mathematics and for professional training went to Germany to be taught by the top astronomers there. In the tradition of astronomer-explorers he joined the German Arctic Expedition to study the north-east coast of Greenland. Back in Britain he spent a long and successful period at the Observatory of Dunecht where he was to build up its library of rare books and journals.

Meanwhile the Calton Observatory was becoming more and more unsuitable as a useful Observatory for the capital of Scotland. It had been likened to the Greek Temple of the winds. It got the winds all right, but the smoke and dust of the city was its final undoing. After his long studies, his many adventures, it was Copeland who had to find a suitable site for a new building. Blackford Hill, high above Edinburgh, was chosen and the Observatory was opened in 1896.

CHAPTER

5

The city's ancient volcano could be seen for miles around. From such a distance it appeared as a misty, blue hill with a few dim, central hollows. Close up it was a fierce, dark-cliffed mountain with precipitous streams of red and black rocks below which were piled long screes of rusty gravel covered with patches of grass and wind-bent thorn bushes. Arthur's Seat was only one of many outbursts of vulcanism in Scotland. Its dim hollows could now be seen as dark basins where millions of years ago fires had spurted, where thundering ash and molten lava had filled the cavities and poured out over miles of the surrounding countryside. It stood high above the city – a dramatic landscape and a lonely one. Black and red sharp-edged cliffs rose above the path circling the hill, and beneath it, far below the steep scree slopes, one looked down upon formal white crescents, over criss-crossing roads between old houses, over spires and domes, and across to the stubborn knob of Castle Rock – that great plug of hard black basalt which had outlived a whole series of huge, primeval eruptions. Even the moving ice-sheets had not levelled it.

It was up here that Steve and Martin occasionally climbed together at weekends. Steve came to look at rocks, Martin to get a break from a boring Sunday. From time to time they would stop to look down towards the city's centre, and further out to the suburbs where Steve's road might be identified with binoculars. Steve himself spent no time in trying to make it out. He could never wait to get away from the city, to have a few hours of freedom from the garage, from his own house. He was a man who needed some drama, some loneliness, perhaps a certain terror in his life, even if merely at secondhand. It was true only the long-distance travellers to his garage occasionally supplied this. It was they who conveyed the real difference between day and night, loneliness and company, between space and solid earth, between talk and silence. Martin, whose domestic life was one of brisk common sense, and his professional life spent in the necessary, flinching silence of his patients, was sympathetic to these feelings. Yet the garage-man Steve admitted that – though he liked to hear of far-out happenings – he himself was not particularly brave. He was, he knew, rather a coward about human relationships, fearing that the catastrophic emotion, the meetings and partings he heard others talk about, might one day tear his life across. The need to be sensible in all things had been drummed into him as a child – never to be caught out either in business or in human dealings. Nowadays he spoke seldom about personal things. Life with his wife was thin, dry, uncommunicative and uneventful. Peaceful was what some might call it. Once they had been bitter that they had no children. Now they were resigned. He supposed in middle age they had settled down at last. Martin, on the other hand, talked often about his wife and his two children. His wife was an attractive, openminded, active woman and the children would undoubtedly take after her. No, they seldom had 'meaningful talks' about anything. Who did? She too was a dentist, doing part-time work in schools. In earlier days, when dentists' appointments were more to be dreaded, he'd discussed the meaning of pain with her, and how much of it could be endured. Kate, his wife, believed people were different in how they coped. Even men and women down the ages had been different. Women had once endured the pains of childbirth – not once, twice or five times, but often nine or ten times because God or Nature had decreed it must be so, until Queen Victoria herself had decided enough was enough and made anaesthetic fashionable.

'Don't forget the frightful pain men have been forced to go through in wars – not to speak of losing their one and only earthly life,' Martin had replied, 'while women stayed home in the old days, writing songs and sewing banners. Even today they're seldom asked to hold a gun, far less drop a bomb. Where's the equality there?'

'There isn't any,' said his wife. 'They can only work together to stop wars. It's the only equality worth while.' All discussion on pain gradually dropped out as news brought more and more horror

36

stories from every part of the world. Was there any end to it, and had it ever been different?

Martin's wife interested herself in other things besides teeth. On one afternoon a week she took a group of young people into parts of the city they'd never seen before. All had come from difficult, dangerous backgrounds. Often one or other parent had left home long ago or been in jail for years. Many of the young ones had themselves left home some time or other – occasionally disappearing for months on end. Eventually they might be picked up in London or sometimes even abroad. All of them now appeared both very daring and very frightened, looking over their shoulders continually, while at the same time moving forward quickly with a curious, dodging gait. Sometimes they drew attention to themselves by sudden bursts of unprovoked laughter, or by an exaggerated enthusiasm for some common sight which meant nothing to nearby onlookers. Others tried vainly to attach themselves to strangers passing in the street. Often they had no clear memory of the past and showed little curiosity about the future.

Kate, because she was calm, cheerful and graceful, could bring a kind of order and rhythm into these strange walks. Martin admired his wife. She was efficient and also kind. At the same time he considered himself lucky to be in a job where kindness was not the first thing people expected or even wanted from him. In pain, his patients were often hard on themselves and hard on him. Some even saw him and his surroundings as definitely hostile, and came prepared to be very tough themselves. This tough streak, he discovered, made certain people interesting, even sympathetic to talk to. In fact he was exacting towards himself, tense in his work, but away from it – a good-natured rather lazy man who needed the company of undemanding people.

In a way Steve was undemanding – easy to talk to, though not much of a talker himself. He confessed to Martin that he considered it lucky that in his garage he dealt with people mostly inside their metal shells who talked through the slits of rolled-down windows. The dentist assured him that even the momentary window contact of the metal box was no more and no less than many city people experienced with others. It was true that this was the way that Steve had first met Martin and heard about his work, his wife and his friends.

'And the night class?' Steve asked. 'You'll be getting to know them there?'

'In time, maybe. It's a very peculiar thing to be staring out from earth. We're rolling through space together and beginning to feel it too, if that's what you mean by knowing one another.'

'Not exactly,' said Steve, 'but it's as good a way as any.' He discussed the love-hate relationship of drivers with garage-men because one oversight in the garage might hinder a journey or even prevent it for hours or perhaps days. How vulnerable and frail were drivers without their armour, yet loath to put foot on solid ground. Cars he said had a raucous language, a common lingo of hoots, and spluttering oaths along with displays of sudden headlight stares. Indignation was ever on the boil for the mean and tortuous tricks of parking, the humiliation over lack of tenpence pieces, over narrow entrances and barred exits. Above all there was hatred for the yellow race of traffic wardens. He had to sympathise with it, of course. Vehicles, after all, were his livelihood, his garage a cure not only for cars, but for their owners.

The two men went on to talk about books and stars and stones. Steve picked up a heavy pebble to take home with him. He already had a fair collection of things he'd gathered over the years from shores and caves around the coast. Many years ago in the chalk cliffs of the south he'd found ammonites. It was then he'd felt the first stirring of a passion through his bones. Above the cliff that evening he visited the hut of an old man who'd collected these fossils all his life. His place was hung with the convoluted forms of ammonites, some small as buttons, others like cartwheels − but all perfect. The man spoke hardly at all but moved amongst them delicately as if amongst works of art which, with immense care, he'd saved, un-broken, from the picks and hammers and greedy fingers of careless beachcombers who went about their work like vandals in a cave of sculpture. To Steve this man's room seemed a most silent place, far removed from the withdrawing sea beneath. The man had become bone-white himself, his profile thin as a shell against the darkening windowpane. Enthusiastic talk of his particular obsession was out of the question. There was nothing for sale here and nothing to be said or shared – simply a passion for this relic of an ancient sea. Steve had left, having hardly exchanged a word, and almost in fear that a passion for anything could grow so steadily without speech. This man might have a stony heart for all he knew. Now he feared for his own.

For some time now Steve had been exploring the secondhand bookshops for works on Geology. In the generation before him a great Scottish geologist had done the same when he arrived in the city by sea from the north of Scotland. Steve as a young man had already discovered and read most of the works of Hugh Miller, not only because of a dawning interest in Geology, but also because his childhood had been spent in that region outside Edinburgh which Miller had described as being, in his time, an old 'slave village'.

In total contrast to the fearful dwellings he was to see later, Miller had his first sight of the fine, new buildings of Edinburgh as he looked up from the boat at low tide in Leith. 'A flat reach of the New Town came full into view,' he says, 'along which, in the dimness, the multitudinous chimneys stood up like stacks of corn in a field newly reaped; at another time, the Castle loomed out dark in the cloud; then, as if suspended over the earth, the rugged summit of Arthur's Seat came strongly out, while its base remained invisible in the wreath.'

This man, who was working as a stonecutter and mason, was soon exploring the stone quarries and finding in the ancient coal-seams evidence of the bole-like stems of great primeval plants and trees: 'and so the vegetation of the Coal measures began gradually to form within my mind's eye, where all had been blank before, as I had seen the spires and columns of Edinburgh forming amid the fog, on the morning of my arrival'. Miller, who was almost as much a writer as a geologist, described how he imagined himself as a Lilliputian standing under the dark, club-like heads of the horsetails 'tall as the masts of pinnaces', seeing tropical jungles in the tangled grasses and walking under dense, dark forests of bracken. Miller worked without any guide or assistant and without the help of the popular geological vocabulary of later times. This language was, for him, written in the strange fossil and vegetable scribblings on the stones he uncovered. The geologist's perceptions and interests were spread widely across different parts of the country, and stones in particular were for him often related to some personal experience of sea or land. One early stone-story, for instance, was different from any in his later quarrying days. He reported that the sea on the west of Scotland was much deeper and more transparent than the water on the eastern side. When diving on the deep western side, Miller would practise what he called the Indian method. He chose an oblong-shaped stone, sixteen or eighteen pounds in weight, but thin enough to be held in one hand. Jumping with this into the deep sea, he would find himself, in a second or two, on the grey, pebbly ooze twelve or fifteen feet below the surface where he could remain, steadily picking up any object which took his interest, and then – his breath failing – would let go of the stone and rise quickly again to the surface.

During his work Hugh Miller came to know what was left of many mining villages near Edinburgh – places long since disappeared at that time. In the remains of one such village, Miller wrote, a collier was still living who could state that both his father and grandfather had been slaves – that he himself had been born a slave – that he had worked for years in a pit near Musselburgh before the colliers got their freedom. His father and grandfather had been parishioners of Dr Carlyle of Inveresk and were contemporary with Chatham and Cowper, Burke and Fox.

'I regard it,' said Miller, 'as one of the most singular circumstances of my life, that I should have conversed with Scotchmen who have been born slaves. The collier women of this village – poor overtoiled creatures, who carried up all the coal from underground on their backs, by a long turnpike stair inserted in one of the shafts – continued to bear more of the marks of serfdom still about them than even the men. How these poor women did labour, and how thoroughly, even at this time, were they characterised by the slave nature! It has been estimated by a man who knew them well – that one of

40

their ordinary day's work was equal to the carrying of a hundred-weight from the level of the sea to the top of Ben Lomond .... I have seen these collier women crying like children, when toiling under their load along the upper rounds of the wooden stair that traversed the shaft; and then scarce a minute after returning with the empty creel, singing with glee. The collier houses were chiefly remarkable for being all alike, outside and in; all were equally dingy, dirty, naked and uncomfortable. I first learned to suspect, in this rude village, that the democratic watchword, "Liberty and Equality", is somewhat faulty in its philosophy. Slavery and Equality would be nearer the mark. Whenever there is liberty, the original differences between man and man begin to manifest themselves in their external circumstances, and the equality straightway ceases. It is through slavery that equality, among at least the masses, is to be fully attained.'

There was a great fire in Edinburgh while Hugh Miller was there. Many of his descriptions were from eye-witnesses who had come running to his workplace with accounts of the spire of the Tron Church blazing like a torch, a great bell descending in a molten shower, and most spectacular of all – the church of St Giles bathed in crimson, its walls in umber, the red light gleaming inward through huge, mullioned windows and flickering on the stone roof. The fire was a chance for some of the leading divines of the day to turn their minds to hell. Indeed one preacher, looking back to an early Musical Festival held three weeks before, saw it as a judgement upon the city. Edinburgh had sinned, and Edinburgh was now punished. Hugh Miller 'liked this reasoning very ill' and had this to say: 'God did not reveal that he had punished the tradesmen and mechanics of the High Street for the musical sins of the lawyers and landowners of Aber-cromby Place and Charlotte Square; nor could any natural relationship be established between the oratorios in the Parliament House or the concerts in the Theatre Royal, and the conflagrations opposite the Cross or at the top of the Tron Church steeple. All that could be proven were the facts of the festival and of the fires; and the further fact that there was no visible connection between them.'

Hugh Miller was a sailor's son and had lived with workers all his early years. Afterwards, looking back on an eventful life, he was able to make some shrewd comparisons of people he had known. 'During the later years in which I wrought as a mason,' he says, 'I was acquainted with a good many university-taught lads; and I sometimes could not avoid comparing them in my mind with working men of – as nearly as I could guess – the same original calibre. I did not always find the general superiority on the side of the scholar which the scholar himself usually took for granted. What he had specially studied he knew, better than the working man; but while the student had been mastering his Greek and Latin, and expatiating in Natural Philosophy and the Mathematics, the working man, if of an inquiring mind, had been doing something else; and it is at least a fact, that all the great readers of my acquaintance at this time – the men most extensively acquainted with English Literature – were not the men who received the classical education. On the other hand, in framing an argument, the advantage lay with the scholars. In that common sense, however, which reasons but does not argue, I found that the classical education gave no superiority whatsoever.'

Earlier in the century, however, changes had been going on in education which could only have been commended by such a man as Miller.

The Edinburgh School of Arts in 1821 – 'for the better education of the Mechanics in Edinburgh in such branches of Physical Science as are of practical advantage to their trades' was regarded as the pioneer venture of the true Adult Education. Most of the 452 students were joiners and wrights, followed by smiths, iron machine workers and watch and clock makers. A fortnightly 270 books were issued, and thirty to fifty men were found each evening in the reading-room. More books came into the library from the learned of Edinburgh – 'no doubt,' it was said, 'their own publications'. The moral and religious note was often struck in the early days of this venture. It was asserted 'that the objects are not narrowly confined to unfolding scientific principles but rather to enabling the artisan to add to his comfort and happiness in exercising the highest faculties of his rational and immortal nature'. So also a high-flown lecture was delivered in Glasgow some years later by Rev. Robert Buchanan,

DD; 'Lord Rosse's telescope has dispelled the last lingering cloud that hung upon the all but infinitely remote horizon of the astronomer, and the galvanic wire has, in the circulation of intelligence, actually realised the fancy of the poet, and annihilated both space and time. But still it continues almost as difficult as ever to get men to see across the few roods of land that separate the dwellings of the rich from the habitations of the poor.' He goes on to cite Dr Chalmers who drew the celebrated distinction between the 'attractive' and 'aggressive' systems in education. In the first, the teacher opens his school and by the attractive force of its accommodations and the cheapness and goodness of its education, he draws children into it. 'We must lean more on prevention and less on punishment. We must multiply our schools.' Apart from the possibility of opening such schools for children, 'We have, moreover,' said Chalmers, 'instituted popular lectures on various subjects: Natural History, the outlines of Astronomy, elementary principles of Chemistry, Savings Banks etc. and turned our classrooms into reading rooms three nights in the week where mechanics and labourers of the district can read periodicals and news in a comfortable apartment. To make it more useful I am preparing to add a library.'

Back in Edinburgh, Political Economy, oddly enough, had been commended to the Mechanics' Institutes by Chalmers because of its 'soothing effect'. A Thomas Murray, fellow student of Carlyle, was now lecturing in the capital and had attracted about a thousand students. This Thomas Murray was praised by many, though – not absolutely surprisingly – this view of him was not taken by his thrawn old roommate, Carlyle, who recalled him as 'wordly, egoistic, small and vain'.

Hugh Miller had many difficulties in later life. He was a religious man, but he was, above all, a dedicated geologist and came into conflict with men who, at that time, looked on Geology as an attack on what was thought to be scriptural truth. The geologist was a shy, reserved man with a few good friends, but living little in society. His health suffered as he grew older and his many conflicts began to prey upon his mind. Just before Christmas 1856 he shot himself. Miller once said that he not only wanted to know a man by his writings, but he was also curious to find out what he looked like. So it is interesting to read this account of the geologist himself: 'In appearance Hugh Miller was tall and squarely built; he had some conceit of his muscular powers. His chest weakness and studious habits had slightly bent his figure, and he was inclined to be neglectful of his dress: at his best he looked a well-to-do tradesman in his church-going clothes. A grey "maud" or shepherd tartan plaid was a characteristic adornment. His most striking feature was his abnormally large head, set off by hair and whiskers of a reddish hue. In company, though apt to be smitten by a "singular speechlessness", he carried with him an air of mysterious power. Like Chalmers, he pronounced his vowels strangely – but otherwise spoke as he wrote, in a clear, carefully constructed English, nobly unaffected in manner, and unspoiled by success.'

CHAPTER

6

Late one Friday afternoon, Martin went into the city centre earlier than usual. There were crowds in the streets, queues in the banks, and a throng of last-minute shoppers preparing for a holiday weekend. It began to rain. The Castle, floodlit for the event, shone through a mist. But nothing could damp the spirits of this sudden spending-spree. People came from the shops with items for every emergency that could possibly happen within three days – heavy cardigans, thick and thin underwear, a couple of flowery dresses for three dinners in bed-and-breakfast hotels, plus sensible shoes and silly ones. To make the most of one glorious hour's madness, certain shops had brought out SALE placards near closing-time, while assistants began to unpack boxes of flimsy skirts, shirts and blouses. Shop windows, long ago laid out for winter, gambled one last fling on sunshine, placing leftover sunshades with umbrellas, while along the counters inside were remaindered tubes of sunburn cream beside pots of colour for wintry cheeks.

It grew darker. A wind blew slanting rain through the first street lights. Martin was about to cross the road when he heard on his right the screech of brakes, a blare of hooters and the cries of people following the thin figure of a boy darting among cars. His movement was exact and swift as a bat evading all obstacles by millimetres – an angry, side-swerving dance, dodging both metal and the stretched-out arms of those running in to catch him. On both sides of the road people stood and shouted warnings or ran towards a nearby phone box. A heavy man had reached him now in the space where the cars had stopped. For a moment he bent to grasp the boy more firmly. At once the boy stepped back the better to deliver a vicious kick to his rescuer's head. The man staggered and went down, disbelief in his open mouth. When the ambulance arrived, ready to pick up a boy, they found a man laid out in the street, his temple and one eye streaming blood. 'That was the thanks he got,' someone remarked. 'And where's the boy? They say *he* wasn't hurt at all.'

'Never mind,' said the ambulance man. 'We'll deal with this one first.'

The boy was not hurt. Nor was he hiding. Martin crossed to the other pavement and had a good look at him, meaning to curse him to high heaven. The boy was standing perfectly still. Stronger gusts of wind had lifted the whole spread of a torn newspaper against him, one corner plastering his mouth, the rest wrapping his shoulders like a shroud. Martin saw dark eyes, frightened and frightening, sly and bright as a fox, and still furious, staring at him over the edge of the paper.

'Trapped,' said the boy. 'You saw them. They were all trying to trap me.'

'What's your name?' said Martin. 'I'm going to take you home.'

'My name's Niall, and I don't need anyone to take me home!'

Martin saw the boy raise both hands to hold the damp paper away from his body. For a moment he appeared to study the opened pages intently before flinging them behind him. Then he turned and disappeared into the half-dark with the steady, unnaturally delicate steps of a tightrope walker. Martin had never attempted to recall all his patients and he seldom remembered his new ones. Just now, however, he had the sudden picture of a tiresome woman who'd tried to talk to him about her son. She'd walked away with just such precariously balanced steps as these.

Martin picked up the newspaper and studied it for a moment. It was not a white paper, not even a grey one. So dense and close-set were the headlines that evening that its all-over appearance was black and clotted with disaster. Gunfire, bombs, stabbings, rapes and crashes. There were no spaces here to relieve the eye. Martin dropped the paper and watched it – heavy with its dark stuff – blow lightly away up the street to be kicked here and there by the odd shopper hurrying home.

CHAPTER

7

The stone Steve had picked up on the Crags travelled a long way between one week and the next. One night it went to a pub near the city centre — a place where several groups gathered after Evening Class. In there he passed it to a young Art teacher, uninterested in Geology, but ever on the lookout for interesting objects her pupils might draw and paint. From her hand the next day it passed into the school bag of a boy Niall who had no interest in art as a stone, art for art's sake, or the peculiar ambitions of his teacher; but nursed secretly an extreme and frustrated interest in cracks and splinters in glass which had never been properly exploited. Apart from crunching and cracking thick ice underfoot in winter, only one other episode of this kind had ever excited him. With a jagged stone from his own garden he had once made some much more spectacular splinters on a large bathroom mirror when alone in the house one afternoon. The mirror had hung by a window in a shaft of sunlight. This, in a flash, showed him a bizarre face, crazily distorted — one cheek sliced down in an ugly grimace, a snarling lip, a double nose, hideously out of joint, as from a sudden punch-up, his red forehead lit by a star of silver cuts. He wondered at first if he had actually deformed himself and put up his hand to find his face smooth, though burning with excitement. Looking again at the glass, he then began to see himself differently — a much more interesting and alarming character than anyone at home or school had reckoned with. The only pathetic thing about his mirror face was that it lacked the bright, flowing blood of those shattered faces beside newspaper headlines and on TV — faces of persons carried away on stretchers from murders, rapes, slashings and car accidents, with groans and screams, and accompanied by the hoots and screech of ambulances. No. He could still hear birds in the quiet garden below. The cat mewed pitifully outside the bathroom door. Otherwise the house was silent.

Sara Reay knew nothing of this early episode, otherwise Steve's stone would never have been taken to the classroom but simply left on her own windowledge as an ornament amongst all the others – amongst the art postcards, the curious bits of bark and shell, along with small figures and clay heads she had made herself, plus bowls, glass, decorated boxes, paperweights and fragile cups. Her collections of objects, her clothes, even her choice of friends were haphazard and seemed to her to make up in some way for what she considered a senseless reserve in herself and a monotony in other sections of her life, apart from her teaching. For she was a good teacher, knowing and treating all her pupils as totally different characters, each one worthy of the greatest effort and attention possible in a large class which demanded as its right the freedom of water and paint splashing, a constant moving from desk to sink, the right to pin its own paintings to the floor, dropping sharp tin tacks on the way, to try out indelible designs on the palm, the knee, the forehead and the ear, to use the gum to stick coloured paper to windows, to decorate the awful blank of white walls and to disguise and cheer the sad mono-tony of its friends' faces. But these things were nothing. They liked and trusted her. The only boy she'd never really known was Niall Gaffney who now carried about with him a much heavier stone than the one he'd taken from his garden. And she herself had given it to him.

The young art teacher had been a pupil herself for the past weeks. She was taking an Evening Class in the History of Portraits. The heads and stick-like figures she first saw on Wednesday nights were those once scraped by sharp sticks, stones and shells on the sides of caves – heads in white and red, sometimes with black circle eyes like beings startled into humanity by unexpected light. Later the faces were painted on brick or clay, the heads fashioned from the bulging cheeks of ancient jars. There were heads round as boulders and long distorted heads to be metamorphosed aeons after – man into goat, into bull and stag, girl into bird and tree and mare. Slowly over the weeks a total human head emerged, modern, familiar, like someone known to her. The forms on the screen became whole. Great beauties now looked out, known tyrants, warriors, kings and queens, expressly cruel or benign in every bone and gesture. Gradually the portraits and the sculptured heads entered history. They were given names, a genealogy and a family. They took their place as fathers, husbands, mothers, wives and mistresses. Now they were as far from the scratched heads as a known planet from a distant star.

In some ways the class missed the old, anonymous beings hidden in caves and under ledges. Age by age and step by step, without knowing it, even these shadowy fathers and mothers, kings, empresses and soldiers would soon enter newspapers and magazines, find their place on screens and film-shows, lose the mysterious, archaic smile and slap on the tooth-gleaming grimace. The portrait class was unlike any other. From the start those in the dark room had stared at their ancestors in silence, stared at each other when the light came on, looking more closely at noses, eyes, lips and cheeks, touching their own features like tentative sculptors. They wondered how on earth the human face would develop in the distant future. There was no escape from Science Fiction these days. No escape from monstrous heads with bulging eyes on tiny bodies. Yet by the way they tenderly touched their own faces and glanced at one another it was clear they believed a recognisable human head would survive, unless some grotesque brain grew too big for this head, cracking the skull and cracking the whole earth. There were discussions and questions of course, but no one spoke of the possible fate of the lips and mouth and eyes that had taken so long to evolve from the sea and from the forest. 'And before that?' people asked themselves in the dark room. Well, there were theories that everything came from the sky; maybe a speck from some passing comet had started off the whole business. And no doubt they could be left to finish it off themselves.

Sara was glad to leave the turmoil of the schoolroom once a week — the more so as the lecturer soon decided to move on to the third stage of his course and bring them straight into the age of portraits in the city. This was the Golden Age and there was indeed a special luminosity about many of them, as though the city and its people were bathed in a perpetual golden light. It was true that many of the painters of that time had made the Italian visit and brought back a feeling of the warmth and all-pervading beauty of the light of that country. But there was another light being spoken about, and that was the light of reason. This light was seen most clearly in the portraits of that time. It was seen in the confident pose of the sitters. These people were not always handsome or beautiful, but the eyes that looked out of Allan Ramsay's portraits, for instance, all seemed too clear, too absolutely direct and confident to need flattery from the painter or anyone else. Even the most beautiful of the women seemed cool and sure. They were not raising a shoulder in defence or coquetry, but sitting straight-backed, not necessarily even smiling, but simply giving back steady stare for stare. This Adult Class wondered, looking at these intelligent women with the direct gaze, why so few of them wrote about themselves, about the men who looked at them, or about their own city or country. In France, on the other hand, such women were to the fore. The freer spirits wrote books, poems, journals and letters. The wealthier ones had salons and would talk and argue in company till all hours. It seemed that the golden light of this era shone rather more evenly across the Channel on both the sexes. Surely the firm-lipped, clear-eyed Scottish women were not behind the scenes making tea? Were they always called down to join in the talk after the children had been put to bed?

Allan Ramsay was perhaps the greatest Scottish painter who depicted reason and confidence on the canvas. The people of his paintings were usually prosperous, well-set-up persons who knew how to arrange their clothes to best effect, where to place their hands and how to make themselves at ease in a comfortable chair. Many of the men, like the magnificent David Hume himself, appear to have just looked up from an enthralling conversation with the painter before settling themselves patiently and good-humouredly for a long sitting. One of the most beautiful of Ramsay's portraits was of his young wife, Margaret Lindsay. Here a fall of delicate lace, a spray of roses, and hair drawn back from a clear, smooth brow, portrays his feeling for the beauty of this girl and for her youth.

This midwinter Evening Class grew warmer and more tranquil in the light of these paintings. They had travelled far. In a few weeks of coloured slides they had flicked up through History at a dizzying speed, moving from the eerie, ancient faces to the smooth turn of smiling, classical heads. They had glanced with awe at the carved wooden faces – angel and gargoyle, and at the luminous manuscripts and tapestries of the mediaeval world, seen the stiffness and gravity of certain religious pictures of a later age, admired the Royal Renaissance heads, stiff with curls, ruffs and jewellery. They had seen capes, gloves, hats and halos, and tried to find the secret behind sneers, smiles and murderous glances. The skies behind all these heads were different – sometimes black and ominous, riven with lightning and denoting evil, sometimes blue with wingy white clouds, describing virtue.

With portraits of the Golden Age the class felt themselves nearer home and in the company of persons who'd walked the Edinburgh streets where they themselves walked every day. These were people who'd looked from the same windows onto views which were often little changed. Sara had particular reason to feel pleased that her small top flat with its north-facing windows was no distance from the house where Raeburn had painted in a high room looking out at the same view. It was not only for this that she studied him closely and considered him her favourite painter of that time. It was something about his bolder, more relaxed approach that pleased her. Here was a man who, in a rather grey city, had instinctively allowed light to tell him how things looked – light, rather than an acute foreknowledge of how his subjects 'ought' to look. She decided that this more relaxed way of looking was the happier one. At any rate it was an outlook which gave more confidence and freedom to persons like herself – persons too intent on keeping within bounds, within lines, believing that they should always be able to explain the world with absolute clarity. This was perhaps a natural target for the ordinary art teacher. She had tried, without great success, to be an out-of-the-ordinary one. She had wanted to let her pupils become as daring as they wished, in ways she'd never managed herself, exploring new patterns and shapes, putting colours side by side or on top of one another, colours that had once been thought impossible to bring together. Even discovering a new colour. For, above all, Sara felt the need to search for this colour. She felt the gap, the strange sensation that it was there – not a mixture, not a slow shading of one colour into another, but a totally new primary colour which might be somewhere in the universe. She believed that many people felt the gap, felt the need to search. But blindly, as it were. There was nothing rational about it. The need made her neither happy nor unhappy. Nevertheless, it was the continual feeling of missing something tremendously important that she would never reach in life. Or not in this life. She was not a religious person, but she believed in the possibility of other lives, and therefore other colours, other sounds and forms.

Sara worked hard with her pupils, sitting for much of her time at the cramped desks, mixing up paint on a dozen palettes to reveal the dark against light, crimson running through blue into purple, blue and yellow turned suddenly to green, and powerful black and brilliant white mixed to a soft, dove-like grey. These were mysteries all right, and the children sighed and whispered close to her cheeks, watching intently as though in the presence of an alchemist. Even a full brush being washed, winding its strands of colour through a water-jar – this was a mystery.

Niall Gaffney kept his distance through all manifestations of miracle. He himself was something of a mystery to Sara. She believed him to be a difficult though clever boy. He didn't care to be cajoled or complimented, far less to enter any charmed circle. He hated his best efforts to be held up to the light or pinned to the wall. If this was done when he wasn't looking, he laughed derisively at his own paintings, pointing mockingly at their childish defects – the defence-less, spindly figures, the trees whose branches were thin arms with twisted fingers, houses that – in spite of his fifteen years – still looked like childrens' building blocks. Was he as proud as that then? his teacher asked herself. Would he rather have his work destroyed than give it the doubtful honour of the public gaze? True honour or none at all? He demanded much more than she had ever wished for herself. He was a tall, thin boy with red hair and a long, bony face covered with reddish freckles which had spread to make his skin appear almost brown or sunburnt like the sporting types he admired. He obviously felt stronger than the rest of his class, and far stronger than the frail, despised creatures he drew and painted – figures who seemed to him to float always aimlessly along empty pavements, and through parks full of the spiky, spiteful trees.

'It's about time you did a bit of hard drawing and painting,' Sara had said one day after the others had left. 'Have you got that stone I gave you?'

'Yes, I've got it. But a stone isn't for drawing or painting.'

'Artists have always used everything they could lay hands on. If you don't like it we can look at others. I'm taking some of you to the museum one of these days. You can draw anything you like there.'

'Well it won't be stones,' he said. 'Stones are for weapons. They say you're in some kind of class,' he added. 'It's a funny thing for a teacher to go to class. I thought people quit all that as quickly as they could. I'll never go near a class when I get old.'

'Have you got the stone?' asked Sara again.

'It's in my bag. Why?'

'Some of the others might be interested to see it.' Niall brought over the bag, lopsided with its weight. He took it out. 'It's quite hefty and large too, but I can still hold it in one hand.' He weighed it in his hand and stood, balanced easily on his feet as if ready to throw, like a scowling young David judging his Goliath. The unease that made him plain had vanished. He looked sure of himself, thoughtful, even handsome in that pose.

'Where did you find it?' he asked, still brooding on his stone.

'I didn't find it. A man gave it to me.'

'Your boyfriend. Sorry. I mean your lover or something.'

'Don't be foolish, Niall. He's studying stones. Going to a Geology class.'

'Funny sort of gift. Fancy giving you a missile.'

'It's not a missile. He guessed I'd like the shape and colour. I told him some of you might like it too.'

'He knows nothing about us. About me.'

'No, of course not.'

'What are you doing in your class?'

'At the moment — looking at portraits. Very beautiful paintings of people. Two centuries ago. I might take your crowd to the gallery one of these days.'

'No,' said Niall, 'I don't care for that sort of picture. I've seen plenty of portraits. Portraits are too calm and silent. Those people look as though they'd never changed. What's worse they don't want you to change or talk or move either. No, I don't like those silent, staring portraits. They're caged-in. They'll never move again. I like people on racing horses, people in racing cars. I like men with guns and knives. I like the noise. I know what you're going to say, of course, but I like all the late stuff on TV. I like the feeling I'm in it myself and the others aren't. They've gone to bed, you see.'

'How can you know what I'm going to say?' said Sara. 'I wasn't going to say anything.'

'No, but you're looking very kind and calm, and what they all call "caring". That's exactly what I can't take,' said Niall, 'that "caring" look.'

Sara went out and down the stairs slowly, turning round just once to see the unfamiliar, distorted face behind. She'd taught children too long, she began to think. She'd been absorbed, even enjoyed herself, but never stopped to notice time was passing. She had to remind herself that the one behind her was now hardly a child.

CHAPTER

8

A few weeks later Sara Reay brought her small group of pupils to the doors of the museum, and almost immediately lost sight of every one of them. This was only to be expected. From the flat street, they had suddenly entered myriads of worlds – not only those which extended round the whole of the earth's curve, but others which drew them from the grey, Edinburgh sky down into hot depths of rock and up into the freezing depths of space. They went confidently, almost running, along the corridors on either side of the building. Behind them, Miss Reay's figure, in a hall of tall, slow-beckoning statues and calm, seated Buddhas, quickly dwindled. They were escaping, at last, in the most extraordinary way possible for human beings – moving swiftly back in time and space. Some of them took the stairs to the stars, others the lift to the ancient shells and stones. This last was a journey to the deepest parts of the ocean and not, as it felt, nearer to the glass and metal of the high-angled roof. Instinctively they were drawn first to the minerals of the most northerly islands of Scotland. Some of the stones and shells from Orkney and Shetland were unlike those from any other part of the country, or rather, it was as if they belonged to a different continent. Their colour, their icy glitter and shape made them appear like great, crusty knobbled jewels, broken off forcibly from the rest of the rocks. The group leant and breathed upon the glass cases until they became cloudy and had to be polished with handkerchiefs and sleeves. A few of them had pencils, crayons and notebooks. Sara had told them to sketch anything they wanted. Now this seemed ludicrous, like being told to sketch something from another planet, and Niall, in particular, maintained that if anyone tried to put one of the gem-studded stones on paper it would only look like a dirty bone the dog had dug up at the foot of the garden. They were surprised, then, to see that he took out a notebook and started to work himself, and that his cheeks became pale, then red as he went on. Silently they drifted away to other counters and came back again after some time to find that he'd been copying a flat, greenish-black rock with wavy lines across it not unlike the rippling green and white foam-lines against a black sea. 'Serpentine!' he exclaimed proudly. It was a dramatic and careful bit of work and he allowed them to praise it for a moment before crushing it into his pocket. Quietly the others moved on again to see the stones of shores nearer home. It was empty and silent in the high gallery, and not a voice to be heard from adjoining rooms. They decided it was too silent. As they moved slowly round, bending over the glass cases, there began a curious incantation – a chant of magical-sounding words which, starting with one, were echoed by another, taken up by the rest in turn, until one strong, resonant chord was humming along the length of the gallery. 'Serpentine,' said someone softly. 'Tourmaline and Jasper,' came the jealous retort. 'Fluorite, Haematite, Kyanite, Chalcocite, Cervantite, Stilbite,' came the other voices loudly and confidently from all sides. 'Diamond, Pearl, Sapphire, Ruby, Emerald,' cried a sarcastic voice from the back.

'*Precious* stones,' said a pretty girl with a badge on her jacket, intent on order. 'It isn't fair to bring those in where they don't belong.'

'It's not fair but I like the sound and the look of them,' answered the voice. Something about his accuser made him eager to push her towards the Grit.

'Don't worry,' said another. 'He's never seen a ruby in his life, never mind a diamond.' This was indignantly denied. His sister had a ruby and two diamonds in her engagement ring. 'Just come over here and look at this,' said a peacemaker from the other end. They gathered to look at a greyish rock, stuck all over with shining white fragments like great snowflakes that had frozen crystal hard.

It was nearly midday. Downstairs more people were coming in. Steve, who was now a regular visitor to the upper gallery in his free time, looked in around lunchtime on his way back to work. He spotted Sara at once and went over. For a while they looked around the main hall. Nearby a large, gilded Buddha sitting with folded hands, his thumbs placed together, held their attention, and Steve put his hands in the same position. He had large hands and one thumb had been broken years ago at work. 'So that's no good,' he remarked. 'Anyway, meditation isn't up my street. And if it were, who'd leave the street for a meditator's garage? Cars hardly stop for a wheel-change, never mind the thoughts.'

'When I get home after work,' said Sara, 'I sit down for a long time – sometimes even before I take off my coat. I don't know if it's meditating or what it is. It's certainly not sleep and it's not thought. My mind's simply blank as a scrubbed blackboard. Not a letter, not a figure, not a scrawl on it. For about an hour. My mind only fills again when I fill the kettle. So an hour's gone out of my life and I can't account for it. Does it matter?'

'Well, I hope not. You can imagine the time I see wasted in my job, – people cruising around from one place to another. Some can hardly remember where they've been or even where they're going.' Again they stared at the Buddha, trying to guess his advice.

'Helping isn't exactly what he's here for,' said Sara. 'It's just good to see he's serene.' She moved away and looked towards the roof. 'I've got a group up there,' she said, 'and I'd be grateful if you'd go up and have a word with them. I gave your stone to the tall boy with red hair, by the way. He might like to know what it is and where you found it. I'll follow on in a moment or two.'

Steve went to the lift and found himself quickly flashing up through floors of animals, tropical vegetation, astronomical models; maps, painted pottery, tribal dress and historical costume. The first object confronting him as he walked along the high gallery was a small statue of Hugh Miller, standing solid as a rock in his fringed plaid, a stone in one hand and a chisel in the other. Though the thing was no masterpiece, Steve stood long in admiration of the man. But Miller himself was looking inward, weighing his stone and perhaps weighing up the doubts and conflicts of his life. When the garage-man reached the group at the far end they were breathing over a case of sparkling purple quartz. 'I was talking to Miss Reay down there. She said you might show me what you've been doing.'

'Why? Are you a painter?' said one. 'We've done nothing but look around. Except Niall here.' A red-haired boy was pushed forward.

'I believe you've got the stone I gave your teacher,' said Steve.

'Yes, I have,' said Niall Gaffney. 'Do you want it back?'

'No, no,' said Steve. 'Is that what you were drawing just now?'

'Of course not. Yours was rather an ugly stone, wasn't it? There's far better stuff here to look at.' He produced his crumpled sheet and Steve smoothed it out on top of the case. The dark green seascape with its waving foam lines drew a faint gasp of surprise from the man. Everyone heard this, and some came nearer. Only Niall drew back a step as if startled by himself.

'Miss Reay will be terribly pleased to see that,' said Steve. 'Are you interested in stones?'

'Not particularly,' Niall replied.

'Because there are regular talks going on here. You could probably go to some of those,' Steve went on.

'No, I'd much rather see them lying on the ground.'

'Well, that could be done easily enough. There are arranged walks in Geology classes.'

'A class walk! Oh, no thanks. I'd rather go on my own. You can find the out-of-the-way places better by yourself.'

'I'm trying to persuade him to join a Geology walk,' said Steve as Sara came up. 'Failing that the three of us could go up to the Crags one day. How about that?'

'Of course,' she said. 'Don't expect me to pick up stones, but I'll come for the walk.'

'I see you've done a good job in your painting class,' said Steve, spreading out Niall's crayon piece again.

'It's in the family,' said Niall with rather a malicious grin. 'You see, my brother's a very good painter.'

'You never told me that,' said Sara.

'Oh, not *your* kind, of course. He paints walls, ceilings, signs. Let me know if you need your house painted.'

'I certainly will. And thanks for telling me,' said Sara.

Chilled and stiff when they first entered, the group of pupils, now leaving the building, looked back from the steps flushed and elated. It was not an unusual reaction. They had looked into a place which had grown over the years into one vast treasure trove. Everyone in the group had some special object there – some stone, image or animal – which they were determined to make their own. Each time, on coming back again, they would rush to that particular item until jealously familiar with it in every detail. After weeks and months they could truly say it belonged to them.

This building where every pupil, like a bee, could carry off richness from some favourite plot – was once known as the Museum of Science and Art and came to the fore following Prince Albert's Great Exhibition in London which started museums across the country. The most important part of the Scottish collection came first from the scientific world, with the inclusion of the University's Natural History Museum dating from the seventeenth century. Two physicians, Robert Sibbald and Andrew Balfour, had collected together its original material and were also behind the establishment of what was to become the Royal Botanic Gardens in Edinburgh. Sibbald in his survey *Scotia Illustrata* summed up his hopes: 'I resolved to make it part of my studie to know what animalls, vegetables, mineralls, metals and substances cast up by the sea, were found in this country that might be of use in medicine and other artes useful to human lyfe, and I began to be curious searching after them and collecting them, which I continued to do ever since.'

Much later, in the nineteenth century, came the great period of exploration when all sorts of specimens were brought home from polar voyages and from the great overland treks across Australia and Africa. A foretaste of this came in the huge findings of gold and precious stones in the Australian continent. Two Cornishmen, for example, fossicking in 1869 near a small town in the state of Victoria, came upon a huge nugget of pure gold resting only a few inches below the surface. It was twenty-one inches long and ten inches thick – the largest piece of gold of its kind every known. Needless to say, it was not taken back to any museum, but broken into three pieces for easy carrying and taken to a bank nine miles away.

Nothing about discovery could be said without remembering the intrepid women travellers of that time who set off, often quite alone, to unknown places, learning the language on the way – painting, writing, collecting plants and butterflies, decoding national myths, traditions and medical lore, while the letters and diaries that came back were as important and long-lasting as the specimens. Marrianne North was one of them – an unmarried, middle-aged Victorian lady who, in 1871, started off alone on several epic journeys to make a pictorial record of tropical and exotic flowers, eventually bringing back eight hundred pictures to be housed in Kew Gardens.

Rather earlier, Mary Kingsley, also unmarried, and after years of looking after elderly parents, left domestic life at last and set off on her famous travels in Africa. One of the best-known passages of her book concerns the rare forests of this continent. 'As it is with the forest,' she says, 'so it is with the minds of the natives. Unless you live amongst the natives you never get to know them. If you do this you gradually get a light into the true state of their mind-forest.' She dreaded that the native people should be divided from their own culture, and feared the outlook prevalent at that time that the native was 'led to good or bad respectively by the missionary and the trader'. As well as the study of animals, rivers and mountains of the terrain, she wrote in clinical detail about the diseases of West Africa, the wedding and burial customs. To the British Museum she brought back insects, reptiles and fishes, a new snake and new species of fish.

In the middle of the twentieth century Isobel Hutchison from West Lothian in Scotland overcame what was called 'a gentle upbringing' to become a formidable traveller, climber, botanist and photographer. Her two-hundred-mile walk across Iceland and later her year-long stay as first British woman to the then almost unknown Greenland, were not done simply as feats, but to collect rare plants and ethnological specimens, to climb one of the country's highest peaks and to meet with its people. Sheer courage and endurance brought her to Alaska to collect Eskimo artifacts as well as plants. By cargo boat she went to Skagway, overland to the Yukon River and down to the Bering Sea. From all these journeys she brought back quantities of diaries, letters, books, photographs and paintings. She reached Japan and Siberia. She also found strength to write a novel and some poetry.

Soon around the mid-nineteenth century in Edinburgh, a more expansive museum was needed to hold all the collections that travellers were bringing home. It was visualised in these words of Adam White: 'Let it be a nucleus to which the spirited sons of Scotia may give and bequeath pictures, statues, specimens, books and mss. Let it be a place to which your hardworking Sailors, Soldiers, Merchants and Medical men in active foreign service, may delight to send specimens of Natural History or curiosities connected with rude and less civilised nations: let it contain a large collection of casts from the antiques for artists and architects to copy; let it contain models of the Geological structures of your country, which in itself is almost an epitome of the world, let us have specimens ... to illustrate the Mineral structure of the country – let us have a place where students might delight to study and afterwards instruct the world in those most useful and remunerative sciences, Minerology and Geology.'

The other half of this museum was to be an industrial museum under its director George Wilson. An immense number of new materials, machinery and tools were now added on the technical and industrial side, so much so that a large extension to the building was planned. As if to show how magnificently Art and Science could work together, a dramatic perspective of glass, metal and wood was raised to create a perpendicular roof which allowed light to pour into the building from all angles. One of the great contributions this museum had always given to the city was the series of lectures offered at a small charge to working people and artisans. These were given by some of the most distinguished men of the time working in Botany, Geology, Chemistry and other subjects. Although these lecture programmes had many ups and downs, owing to lack of Government backing, they kept going – though not always in the way hoped for – up to the present time.

CHAPTER

9

Sara was as good as her word in arranging that Niall's brother should paint her flat. Even the highest flats in Edinburgh could become a little gloomy after a few years. It wasn't only time that did it. Those who'd been lucky enough to go to Italy, France, Greece or Spain for spring or summer holidays could come home to find their white walls strangely grey, their carefully chosen apricot of the bedroom mysteriously faded, the daring plum-coloured ceiling darkened from ripe purple to a shade nearer black. No amount of window cleaning helped to let the light in. The glass appeared to obstinately withhold transparency. Shadows had entered the room while the owner was away. Sara wondered if this opaqueness was in the lens of her own eye. But the trouble went deeper. These changes had occurred when she returned from Italy in the early autumn. The need for colour had become a hunger for all kinds of things. It was a hunger for the sight of hanging fruit – the small, half-hidden lamps of lemons and oranges amongst dark leaves, for the look of smooth brown skins, for white bread with a tawny crust, for warm red wine and honey. Was it the eye that was famished or the stomach? And what about the desires of the nose? Were they for spice or incense, olives or flowers, hot cooking oil or chilled white wine? She felt, on return, like a person lacking senses. But never, as a proper citizen of this city, lacking the so-called common sense. She pondered on the phrase – always said in commendation: 'She has come back to her senses' and wondered what little meaning this might have for returned travellers. And why had the word 'sense' ever got muddled up with the brisk no-nonsense outlook of half the western world?

Niall Gaffney's brother Iain turned out to be a strong, affable young man ten years older than her pupil and a great deal more forthcoming. He arrived one morning with a boy to help him carry up his ladder, his planks, paintpots, buckets and brushes plus the large carpet cover. This cover, when unrolled on the floor, resembled a huge Pollock painting of blue, yellow and green spots splashed with strokes and curls of black and scarlet, and all lightly flaked with white like snow. Sara stood for a moment looking down at this tangle of marks. Certain familiar forms seemed to emerge and then as suddenly recede again. There was something disturbing about this, like momentarily resolving some intricate problem in a dream, and losing the answer on wakening. She seemed to glimpse animals, figures, forests, grasping hands and staring eyes. She remarked that this cloth made her feel uneasy. The painter agreed, saying he'd felt the same himself sometimes, but he'd laid it on so many floors he guessed he'd got used to it. At any rate he'd seen stranger things hanging on walls. He knelt to pour and mix his paint. The white walls that had turned grey during the summer were to become a warm cream, the apricot walls a brighter shade and the plum ceiling nearer to geranium. The mixing of the paint from white to cream was satisfying to see, the movement calm and smooth. However many times he did it, he said, he liked this part of it. He liked watching the very slow change of colour. Nothing could happen unless the heavy paint was always mixed in exactly the right way, slowly and rhythmically. You couldn't hurry this bit of it. 'But you know about that,' he said, 'being a painter.'

'No, an art teacher – a very different thing,' she replied. She admitted, however, that she knew a bit about colour and how it affected people.

After some time Iain climbed the ladder and started to paint, and for a while Sara remained watching from the door. The morning rush was almost over. It had become suddenly silent so that the swish of the large brush on the wall was now clearer than the occasional car passing in the street below.

'I believe you teach my young brother,' Iain remarked, holding his brush steady for a second in the corner between wall and ceiling.

'I do, and a very clever boy he is,' she replied. 'Good at painting and good, so I hear, at all his other subjects.'

'Oh yes,' Paul answered, turning to paint again. 'Much cleverer than I ever was. He'll go far, as they say. If he gets the chance and if he can bring himself to take it. At the moment he can't take anything from anyone.'

Sara came into the middle of the room and looked up at him. 'Iain, why is he so angry? It seems to me that Niall is always angry, and with everyone. Why is that?'

The sweeping brushstrokes stopped again. Iain came slowly down from the ladder and went to the window. Momentarily he put his forehead against the cold glass as if, whatever else, he would be absolutely cool and neutral in his speech. He sounded flat, almost without emotion. The woman had to listen the more carefully to this dull voice.

'We're only five of us at home – but all the same, a crowd past helping, some would say. A problem family's our official name, I've not a doubt. The thing is we're reckoned to be ungrateful for any help and advice on offer, and there's been a lot seeing my father's been in and out of prison for the last years. Not the violent crime neighbours could at least find interesting. No, just stupid break-ins after bouts of drinking in company with louts years younger than himself who've managed to sprint off first sign of trouble. He's clumsy and slow himself even in crime. I've got very mixed feelings about my father – ashamed and proud. He couldn't do enough for us as children – very gentle and careful. I'm ashamed of the beating-up he gave a boy who happened to catch him out one night. My mother had a very tough deal. Most of the time she was on her own – no time to make friends, to find decent jobs, no time or money to make the house or herself attractive. She was untidy for a start, never mind the house. In those days I was a pompous young prig, about everything – colour and cleanness above all. Our father was a builder, but house-painting got me early. I liked to make other rooms look good even if ours never stayed bright or clean from one day to the next. You asked about Niall. I'd say Niall was always a difficult boy. The thought of a father inside was horrible to a youngster who'd had the idea of total freedom for everyone – half-baked though the idea usually is. That boy could never bear to be held, even embraced or circled inside a game, far less kept within four walls. To be trapped behind bars is his idea of hell.' Iain turned round and leant back casually against the window. 'Did Niall ever tell you he had a young sister, Daphne? She's nearly nine now and at a different school.'

'No, I never heard of a sister,' she said. 'He never spoke of his family, except you. "A very good painter," he told me. "One of the best in the city."'

Iain gave a slight smile at that. He went on: 'Last autumn this small girl set out one afternoon with a friend of her own age to pick blackberries on the Braid Hill. They went off without telling anyone, you understand. Where was *I*?' Iain shouted suddenly to Sara. He covered his mouth and after a long silence started quietly again. 'I was round the back of the house messing about with a pile of wood! I never heard them talking about it, never saw them getting their gear together, never saw or heard them go off. They each had a white plastic picnic box for the fruit. They'd had plenty of picnics, the pair of them, in the garden. They'd both been given small thermos flasks at Christmas, but they hadn't bothered with these that day. Daphne's friend carried a raincoat on her arm though the day was warm. She was a silent, cautious child. They both had summer dresses on – almost identical as far as I could see. They were best friends and at the tiresome identical stage, the same hair-dos the same beads and clips and bows. They wore their best blue sandshoes with long, red laces. They weren't yet at the boyfriend stage when all identicals come to a sudden stop. It wasn't at all a strange place they were in. There are sheltered spots where people sit and read the papers on a Sunday or take their dogs for walks. If you go some way round you find yourself looking down on the dome of the Observatory. We'd talked about that Observatory a bit. Daphne was interested in everything, but she used to say she didn't like that great green dome. She exaggerated its size, for one thing, and the idea that it stared at stars all night made her feel lonely, she said. I thought it an odd notion for an adventurous child who seemed to have no fear of anything. Now, when I look at that dome myself I feel a sort of terror of all unknown things. That day,' he went on, 'it seemed there wasn't a dog or person in sight. Imagine places crowded one day and suddenly deserted the next for no reason at all! There were few blackberries in the spots they went to first. Near the paths everything had been picked. So they went further. Yes, the best are furthest away as they always are, so it's said in all the tales — the most beautiful and the kindest people, the best and highest fruit, the treasure piled deep under the sea or in the earth. Perhaps children had fallen for all that once. As far as I know, that was all done with long ago. Anyway our ones were very practical and down to earth. There were good people and bad, and that was that. They walked on and on. Daphne was determined to pick a lot, enough for her mother to put in a pie or even to make jelly that very night. It grew very silent as they climbed higher, she said. Most of the time they stood with their heads down, searching deep inside the dark bushes where the largest berries were. Yet she was aware after a bit, there was someone watching them from a distance. The man was smiling and very friendly-looking, she said. Evidently the thing that made him seem friendly and almost familiar was that he also was picking and eating a few blackberries himself — not collecting them in a box, but just casually, lazily picking them here and there as he came nearer. This undoubtedly made him a friend. From her point of view he'd got up that morning like them, looked at the fine day it was, got dressed, eaten his cornflakes, toast, marmalade, and drunk his tea, as they had, and then gone out with exactly the same idea in mind. His smiling lips were purple. Probably he was greedy like them and had his mind on a wife or sister who'd be making pies and jelly the next day. It was only strange that he had no box. Her friend must have thought it even stranger. Suddenly she stopped picking and, without a word, turned to go downhill. Naturally the slightest fear's infectious. Daphne also turned, first starting to walk quickly and then breaking into a run. But the man didn't walk, didn't run, he leapt after her. That was the word she used. He changed from this smiling, slow-moving being to something she knew nothing about. He got her by the neck of her dress, jerked the collar off and threw it behind him into a bush, ripped her dress from top to hem and made to kick the legs from under her, but lost his footing on a steep, muddy patch and landed on his knees. Daphne described how suddenly furious this made him, how he babbled and shouted after them. The words, it seems, meant nothing. For some reason this alarmed them more than anything else. They flew on. Buttons and blackberries marked where those two children went.' Iain stopped, again covering his mouth with his hand.

'Is there more to tell?' asked Sara.

'No, they got down the hill. It's not an easy place to manoeuvre. No doubt they knew it better than their pursuer. On the road at the bottom they found a young couple in a car and were brought home in a bad state. Policeman and doctor arrived. At first our two would hardly utter. They acted as if they'd forgotten how to talk. All sorts of words came out but not the ones to describe anything. I suppose we managed to pick up a good deal, and Niall was there too, of course, listening to every word but going on as if he'd never heard a thing. Acting dumb, in fact — asking where the berries were, when the jam was to be made and so on; all this when the rest of us were asking endless questions, arguing, quieting the neighbours and making cups of tea. But it was the young couple who were the best, far better than the rest of us. At any rate, they showed absolute calm, assurance and — yes politeness. I'll never forget how polite they were to those distracted children. At first, naturally, they'd smoothed them down a bit at the bottom of the hill, but now they gave them back their dignity and sense of fitness. Both of them talked a lot. They made it sound as if, in spite of violence and fear, craziness and chaos, there was love and order and a rock-like firmness still to be discovered. I remember the girl did up the remaining buttons of my sister's dress, smoothing the opening where the collar had been torn off and pinning it with a brooch from her lapel, all very slowly and talking the whole time. After that she took out her comb and did Daphne's hair — again slowly and carefully — and as the bow was gone, slid the clasp from her own hair and put it in. Then she took a mirror from her handbag and let my sister look at herself for as long as she wanted — the hair smoothly combed and the opening of her dress neatly fastened with a grown-up brooch. Daphne's no stranger to mirrors, I may say, and she took her time. I can't remember everything the young woman talked about after that. I just know she went on determinedly and rather boringly about one thing or another — whatever came into her head, I daresay: where she'd been on the Saturday, what she'd seen and what she'd bought. She talked about her lunch and what kind of food she liked, the clothes she'd seen and wanted to buy, their shapes and sizes and their patterns — stripes, checks, flowers, dots and whatever. At one point Daphne interrupted, raised her red eyes and asked with a touch of impatience — not to say jealousy: 'Well, what *did* you buy then?' The rest of us were silent, stunned by the idea that drama could be followed by commonplaces such as this. Looking back now, I wonder if I said anything at all. But I've talked enough now. I'd better get on.' From the top of the ladder he said: 'Now Niall's angry at everything, angry that his sister will grow up, that he'll be a man and, even then, not able to protect her from other men like himself. Daphne got over the thing fairly quickly. He's still very confused. He'll get over it, of course. Just now he's the age that knows everything and nothing. Believe me, there's not much escape for him. He pores over every paper, watches the box till all hours. There are things he knows more about than I do myself. He's got more time to watch, to talk, to listen. I've got none. This is the longest bit of talking I've done for months, I can tell you.'

'And I'm glad you talked,' said Sara. 'I'm thankful you told me this.'

They didn't discuss her pupil again, but occasionally the painter spoke of the problems of his trade in the city. Most of the time he worked in the empty rooms of new house-owners. It seemed too that, however hard the times, people must be forever changing houses or if not houses, colours. And these dramatic changes were made not only in small rooms but on the spacious walls and majestic ceilings of the New Town of Edinburgh. Certain people made a strong impression on him. Some time ago he'd worked in the top flat of one of the great Georgian crescents. It was owned by a French teacher and his sister who'd come from France a dozen years ago. Their windows looked steeply down and round onto the backs of other flats and into their narrow gardens. A railed-in stone walk ran behind the gardens, and beneath it a spectacular grass slope plunged down through trees into a dark ravine where the river ran. To the north was the blue shore of Fife, growing black as the night went on, with sudden oil flares from the water and luminous strips of sky over distant towns further up the coast.

Iain felt an affection for the two from France if only because they looked at the city with new eyes. He'd met a lot of lonely people in the huge, freezing rooms where he painted and they were usually glad to talk. The true citizens of the place took their pilasters, their marble mantelpieces and curled cornices very seriously. These icy-white grapes, ivy leaves and frosty apples were the first things guests looked at. Before looking at one another or even at the host and hostess, they studied walls and ceilings. The French pair dared to laugh at this side of Edinburgh society. They themselves looked at people rather than cornices. The woman confessed to the painter that she even missed the glances of men and women who passed in the street. Did he ever feel that himself? No, but then he didn't particularly wish to be looked at. And anyway, he didn't have their confidence, their elegance. She'd explained it was nothing to do with clothes, looks and the rest – simply she liked people to have natural, human curiosity. But maybe they thought curiosity was rude, he'd said. As a child he'd been told never to stare at people, he went on, looking down from the picture rail at this woman who was very well worth staring at. 'Well,' she'd said, 'perhaps certain things in this fine city are rather unnatural.' From above the painter had murmured that his wife was rather beautiful and she was also a very unnatural woman. The French woman had at once asked what was so unnatural about her.

'She has everything she wants,' Niall's brother had replied. 'Two great kids, a nice home, good neighbours. Yet she's always wanting to be off somewhere, anywhere – as long as she gets out of the house. And not just away, but far away and for as long as possible. She has *everything*, yet she wants *away* from everything!'

'And from a good husband too, I've no doubt,' the French woman had said. 'Naturally she does.'

'And if ever she did that – what would I do?' the painter had asked.

'I've no idea. I'm just commending her for still wanting things.'

'Discontent's O K then, is it?'

'Can be. Some women stop wanting anything when they get married. Personally I often want to get away from this city. Being thought the best and the most beautiful tends to make it very smug and dull at times.'

There was one bit of work that Iain had never spoken about except to his wife. He'd once painted in a battery hen-farm. He'd described this experience as some might describe the decorating of a row of death cells. He was not an ardent animal-lover. He had no dog or cat. Far less was he a hen-lover, but for a while his nerves had been shattered by what he'd seen – his dreams full of horrific eye-stabbings, de-beakings, and the vain, crowded clawings of half-broken wings. During this time he wondered how he would ever paint again. He talked endlessly to his doctor and to the few friends who could understand. These were strange talks. He had almost forgotten them now. But sometimes in the night he relived the horror of remembering, the helpless fear of returning to the place.

This painter was a craftsman who'd studied the work of former centuries, and occasionally, while employed on the ins and outs of his cornice grapes, the ivies and fruits of a ceiling, he'd tell newcomers of much older decoration and where it could be found. Had they seen the seventeenth-century paintwork in the apartments of Queen Mary at Holyrood House, for instance, or the painted foxes and grapes on the beams of an old house in the Lawnmarket? And if they went to certain houses further north, there they would see angels with instruments, devils with pitchforks, owls, dogs, flowers, trees and fruits, kings on horses, clouds, crowns, halos, suns, stars, and long Bible texts. If they mentioned Festival decorations, he would say what a come-down it all was – mostly stuff done on the cheap and no great credit to the city; the City Fathers announcing themselves on garish flags and banners and posters advertising Guinness. On fine green slopes certain flowerbeds were decked out with lurid plastic and pebble patterns. Whereas when James VI passed through this city the place was all hung with gorgeous tapestry and painting. He reminded them, of course, that there was still plenty of stuff to be seen, up and down the country, in castles, palaces, churches and the like.

Iain was never surprised when people wanted to watch him mix his paint and hear about its history. Paint had a long history beginning with the red and yellow ochres in ancient caves. But certain things were on their own doorsteps, and he let them in to the secrets of those painters a few centuries back who boiled down scraps of parchment to make the glue size for mixing with the paint. Those dramatic ceilings he had just described were covered first with a thin coat of whiting, the design then drawn with bold black lines and finally filled in with colours. Once in a while, renovating, – when workmen and painters were around – a stone would suddenly drop from wall or ceiling, showing a patch of brilliant painting, good as when it was new.

When Iain had done the main rooms, Sara asked if he would give a lick of paint to the old coal bunker. These were fairly sizeable places in the city's houses – some of them being used as a cupboard or even a small room. In the city, as in every other place, most coal deliveries had slowly disappeared. At one time most of the tall, elegant houses of Edinburgh's New Town had a large coal bunker, built like a solid, wooden trough into a spacious cupboard off the kitchen. The coalmen would come wheezing up the sixty, eighty or ninety stairs, each with the sack on his back. These would be delivered over the head in one tremendous crash, after which the men would immediately turn down for the next load, passing the others wheezing and plodding up. When electricity was installed many house-owners 'still liked a real fire best' and would keep their coal bunkers until finally, years later, these were emptied and cleaned. Under layer upon layer of white paint the black dust was at last abolished. A chic, new, snow-white cupboard could now be shown to visitors – its shelves holding, perhaps, china and glass gleaming under electric light. Anything, in fact, could be done with these old coal cupboards. But exercise was not on. There was no air and no room to stand up straight. Crossleg-ged meditation might be possible but was seldom thought of by common-sense inhabitants. Everything was once carried up the steps. There was a continual passing and repassing and no doubt a continual washing and rewashing of the fringes of long shawls and the hems of flounced skirts. The servants, who did everything, were housed in strange places – sometimes in an upper loft with a window opening onto the hall below. Years before, water had to be carried to the top of every city house. The story of this water was a dramatic one.

The bringing in of a proper water supply to Edinburgh brought many heart-searchings and some violent confrontations. The problem in the New Town was never so severe, but the high ridge of the Old Town with its lofty, narrow, close-packed tenements was a particular difficulty. Now, as well as for domestic use, there was a great and growing demand for water by the brewers, the mill-owners, the paper-makers and the bleachers on the Water of Leith.

The familiar moral tone is again sounded in this era. Bailie James Colston fulminates a little: 'Like many other things water can be abused and wasted. There seems somehow an unfortunate propensity in human nature frequently to undervalue property which is held in common, etc.' On this want and wastage of water in Edinburgh the manager of the Edinburgh Water Company gave his evidence in answer to this grave and soul-searching question:

Q. I believe you know that the habit is prevalent in these common stairs, of people tying up the handles of their WCs and letting the water run? What I want distinctly to understand is this. Whether that practice, to your knowledge, is a prevalent one in Edinburgh?

A. Yes, it is prevalent to a most enormous degree.

A kind of body talk and lavatory language seemed to appear in a piece of cross examination concerning pipes and orifices.

Q. Are you quite clear in your own judgement that having but a single pipe of only three quarters of an inch in diameter is one of the principal difficulties? Will you tell me, is it the fact that your Company put in a thing like that [handing a piece of brasswork to the witness] which is to reduce a diameter to one eighth of an inch?

A. Yes.

Q. So that the diameter of the pipe being one of the principal causes of the deficiency, that is the means you take to get over the difficulty?

A. No, it depends on the orifice.

Q. What is that?

Other Voice. It is called a stricture, I believe.

Q. Where do you get it from?

Other Voice. I do not know. He tells me that that is what is put in. It is something of the same kind, but I do not at all say that the orifices in that corresponds to the orifices we use.

A good many suggestions were put forward as to where a supply of good water might come from – Edinburgh having no large river or loch nearby. One hopeful idea was that water should come from the clear springs of the Pentland Hills. Nevertheless there were other very different ideas which brought out some curious comments from many quarters of the city. There was, for instance, a suggestion that water from St Mary's Loch in the Borders should be used. A doctor writing in *The Scotsman* drew attention to various insects that might lurk in the loch. Any drawback of this kind was instantly denied by two other Edinburgh doctors. In our day reassurance is the chief aid of the medical man. Even at that time these two doctors used it to the full. 'With regard to waterfleas, I need hardly say that they are perfectly harmless insects,' said one. 'I have rarely found them from lake water in the summer.' The other gentleman outdid himself in his love of waterfleas. 'These waterfleas,' he rhapsodised, 'are found in the best and most wholesome waters.'

Notwithstanding, the graffiti throughout the city began to change. Gigantic fleas were scrawled everywhere. Greedy, bug-eyed, crook-legged creatures appeared on walls of houses, at shop corners, on churches, schools, steps and pavements.

In the early days and chiefly in the Old Town, water had been carried upstairs sometimes by the inhabitants and sometimes by the Water Caddies. These Water Caddies were a familiar sight coming from the city's wells, through the narrow closes and up and down stairs. Often they were old soldiers and the wives of soldiers – still wearing their old, red military coats with the water barrels strapped to their backs. The many women amongst them would sometimes be wearing the red coat too with a quilted black and blue petticoat plus a leather apron on their shoulders to protect them from the wet. The women Water Caddies were more than a match for the men in strong drink and stronger language. It was said that any suggestion that the water they carried could ever be mixed with good whisky drew their most withering contempt. Indeed such gossip around these city wells has never been heard before or since. This was augmented by the fierce quarrels that broke out between the Water Caddies and the servant girls. Such were the fights between them that even the meanest councils of the city thought best to furnish the wells with duplicate handles 'to moderate the fury of their ire'.

As well as the springs of the Pentland Hills, a loch of the Moorfoot Hills to the south also supplied water to parts of Edinburgh. The place was Portmore Loch on the borders of Peeblesshire. In 1879 the Moorfoot Water Works set off one morning from Waverley Station on an excursion to this spot. It seemed to be in the nature of a huge Sunday School picnic – an occasion to be described and looked back on with an almost lyrical feeling for the details of the experience: 'The effects of the sun and mist were interesting in the extreme . . . The tasting of the sparkling waters . . . the stroll on the sides of the loch and the general movement to a corner where a picnic luncheon was served.' At last places in the vehicles were resumed: 'The warm sun made the drive exceedingly pleasant and everything around had quite a holiday aspect.' A pipe was to be laid between this loch and Gladhouse Reservoir and thence conveyed into the main conduit leading to the town. 'When the company arrived at the Reservoir prayer was offered up by the Very Rev. James Cameron Lees D.D., minister of St. Giles and Dean of the most ancient and most noble Order of the Thistle and one of her Majesty's Chaplains for Scotland. . . . The turning-on of the Waters was followed by the dinner at the extemporised dining hall near the Reservoir.' It was to be hoped that the diners had not already done themselves too well at the picnic luncheon, for the dinner menu was printed as follows:

Mayonnaise of Lobster.   Dressed Crabs.
Buissons of Lobsters.
Mutton Cutlets in Aspic.
Truffled Game Pies.
Boar's Head.   Roast Beef.
Roast Chickens and Cresses.

Boiled Chickens à la Béchamel.
Yorkshire Ham.   Ox Tongues.
Raised Pies.   Roulade of Veal.
Pigeon Pies.   Veal and Ham Pies.
Roast Lamb, Mint Sauce, Potatoes and Peas.
Wine Jelly.   Vanilla Creams.
Gooseberry, Rhubarb and Apple Tarts.

The toasts, as well as to the Royal Family, were to the Clergy of all Denominations and:

To Edinburgh Water Trust.
Provosts and magistrates of Leith – proposed by a Bailie with the formidable surname of Tawse.
The Old Water Company.
Contractors.
Croupiers.

The return train, though no doubt Getting There even in 1879, 'was unluckily delayed for an hour'.

So eventually Edinburgh had its water supply – water consisting almost entirely of pure spring water from the Pentlands, and water from a loch by the Moorfoot Hills on the Borders of Peeblesshire – a little brown, it was said, owing to a small quantity of vegetable matter, but none the worse for that.

CHAPTER

10

There were times when Sara was intrigued yet worried by Niall's work in the Art room. He no longer wanted to paint objects or anything that might be easily described. A thing that could be recognised and named now seemed beneath his contempt. Occasionally someone would pose or she might set up a Still Life group but — sensing the boy's dislike of the familiar — she would also group certain blocks and cylinders together to form one abstract shape. Even that wasn't good enough. The forms seemed too large, too knowingly placed, too obvious to him. His compositions had become excessively small — a tangle of wiry lines knotted tightly together, usually drawn very carefully in ink with a fine pen or brush. Sara never asked him what this meant. She had the feeling, however, that he was not happy about what he was doing, that he himself would like to be told what the thing meant and that, in some way, he was struggling desperately to find out. One day, while he was absorbed over a dense, whirling coil of spidery lines, the art teacher came up. She was silent, but after a moment he looked up and asked angrily: 'Where's the beginning and end of this? I can't find it.'

'Just keep going, Niall,' she said calmly. 'It's an interesting piece.'

'But I must know where the line begins and where it ends,' he insisted. His expression was not only angry but genuinely inquiring, with some anguish about it.

Now they both bent over the tight coil in order to unravel the problem. Again Sara said it was an interesting sort of puzzle and reminded her of the French artist, Duchamp, who'd done strange puzzle drawings, some based on machines, but others simply complex coils of lines, not unlike this one. The interesting thing, she said, was that he'd put very definite titles to his pieces. 'What would your title be?' she asked. 'No beginning, no end,' said Niall, still frowning and looking worried.

Sara immediately set up a sensible, domestically defined Still Life for the whole class – thick, household jug, cheap, useful bowl, some sharp little ornaments. The class took to it enthusiastically like ducks to water. When she went back to Niall, nearly half an hour later, he was still staring at his large bit of blank white paper.

'I simply can't do that,' he explained, 'and I'm not interested. You've arranged it all yourself. Nothing's so definite, and nothing comes together like that.'

'So you haven't even made a beginning,' she said.

'I can't find a beginning,' said Niall.

She was disturbed a week or so later to learn that Niall worked not only in a small way, but was perfectly willing to splash out if need be.

'He does such minute, complicated stuff,' she said one day to Iain who was still doing some outside painting on the windows of her flat.

'Don't you believe it. I fairly laid into him last week and he'll not forget it quickly. He'd got hold of some of my brushes and paint and started off on the side of our garage in full view of the street. A horrible mess of lines and colour, some grotesque creatures – naked naturally, and wherever he could find space, some outstanding words.'

'Creatures?' said Sara.

'Men and women. He'd taken very good note of the difference. Minute stuff indeed! You could see these nearly a mile off! Red, pink, blue and yellow. I had to paint the whole thing over again with grey.'

'How *is* he?' Sara asked.

'How is he?' He's mooning about as usual, rubbing the paint off his hands. He's nothing but some wild creature with scarlet under its nails.'

Sometimes the boy criticised the work of others in the class. Sometimes he praised it. On the whole they remained good-tempered. He seemed to them someone who perceived things they hadn't yet glimpsed, nor ever wished to glimpse. But they knew he was someone who might conjure up harmony from some mad mixture of stuff pulled from a rubbish heap if he were left alone to do it. And he was left alone. He was allowed to set up his own composition for drawing and painting. On this occasion he chose a clock and some brightly labelled tins, a sheaf of paper from the office and a tennis racket from the bottom of a trunk at home. He brought, with enormous care, a bottle of green liquid from the Science room. He brought a ballet shoe, a climbing boot and a bowler hat from the cupboard of costumes. He had taken different coloured cloths for background.

'Good,' said the science master who'd come in to look. 'So you're going to produce order out of chaos.' Afterwards Niall showed anger at this remark by kicking over half the objects while being careful not to disturb the flask of green liquid. 'Don't worry,' the man remarked later in the staff room, 'he sees that stuff as far too beautiful and dangerous to touch.' Niall, meanwhile, was rebuilding his group precisely as it had been before. He left the room for five minutes after that and was disappointed to see how the class had managed to change his arrangement the moment his back was turned. He wasn't angry this time, only resigned. They had brought blues together with purples and other blues, and ignored contrasts. Symmetrical folds of cloth hung behind the clock. The tins had been placed in a line. They had changed the odd shoes with a matching pair and the black bowler hat had been put on the white sheaf of paper. The tennis racket was nowhere to be seen.

Sara went on conscientiously showing slides and bringing in books of paintings for the whole class, and some chiefly for Niall's benefit, seeing he'd professed himself uninterested in the confident eyes and folded hands of portraits, preferring something questioning and startled in eyes and a downturned uncertainty in mouths. He liked violent contrasts. He admired Brueghel – a painting of white, angelic beings pushing down the bulbous, splayed and beaked, the bat-winged rebel angels. 'The Triumph of Death' he studied in detail, poring over skeletal horses drawing cartloads of skulls from burning towns, a gallows in the distance.

Sometimes Sara let him help with the slide-showing, let him organise the entire layout of the lesson himself. He obviously enjoyed his role of master over a crowded darkened room where others sat silently while he manipulated light and colour. This way – simply by a touch on the instrument – he could elicit the odd gasp of pleasure or of horror. Obviously this gave him feelings of great power and satisfaction.

'I never knew it was so easy,' he remarked to Sara one day after class.

'What's so easy?'

'To make them laugh or scream or just sit and smile in a daft way. You don't have to say anything yourself. There's nothing to it.'

'There's a bit more to teaching, of course,' she'd said.

'I know, but I'd never be a teacher.'

'What would you like to be, Niall?' she said. 'I've never heard you talk about the future.'

'I never see the future,' said her pupil. 'What does it mean? Perhaps I won't have one. Lots of people don't. As a matter of fact our neighbour's son died two months ago. And he knew all about his future – absolutely sure what he was to be. Talked about it most of the time. Bored everyone with this old linoleum shop. I've been there often myself – smelly as a wolf's den in summer. He was to be right in there, you see, whenever his father died, walking on the stuff, unrolling it, cutting it up, asking if people wanted squares, circles or zigzags for their kitchens and bathrooms. But of course it turned out he died before his father – probably years and years before. So I don't look at the future much. I'd thought of something with machinery. I like machines better than people. You can depend on them. I mean either they work or they don't. I daresay you want me to be an artist, though,' he added, taking a quick glance at his art teacher.

'Not at all,' she said. 'I think you're no better and no worse than anyone else in the class.'

'I'm glad,' said Niall. 'I've never cared for artists much – any kind. They're not straight people, are they? They always seem the opposite of what they're doing. As a matter of fact we had a cousin painter in the family. He painted those huge, fierce shapes, yellow and orange tigers eating jagged trees with spikes like pikestaffs, and big white nudes sort of melting in the sun like wax and hugging one another on red beaches. Even then it was all terribly out of date. It made him sad, I daresay, for he hardly opened his mouth. A tiny man, he was, and wouldn't say boo to a goose my father and mother said. Too shy to pass the butter, "and anyway, what kind of butter would melt in his mouth?" they said. Writers and poets are just the same from what I've heard. Beauty, Truth, and all that. Love, Love, Love, but they seem to dislike a lot of people, all the same. When I say "painters" I don't mean you, of course. I know you're not really one. A teacher's different.'

'Well I certainly hope you find a machine that suits you,' said Sara.

'The way they're going now,' said her pupil, 'the machine will find me first. I don't care really. If I'm going to be killed, it had better be a streamlined affair – the newest design of whatever it is. I'd want the best.'

Sara's pupils were intrigued with the idea that she herself could sit in a class like them, looking at slides. But faces? No, they wanted more than that. They shared Niall's lack of interest in calm portraits. Above all, they wanted dramatic action and unknown landscapes and seascapes to escape into. So long as the unexpected came up in some guise it wasn't even necessary to have angelic creatures prodding demons back into hell.

'But some of these paintings might be places you know very well,' Sara remarked one day as she unpacked the box of slides. 'Turner,' she added. There were drowsy murmurs of disappointment and some long, simulated yawns. A languid stretching of arms appeared on the screen like the black shadows of intense boredom. They wanted slides that were not part of their world, not part of anybody's world. But suddenly a large watercolour painting appeared on the screen. There were knowing whispers around the room, a few tentative gasps of recognition, and some grudging bursts of laughter. They found themselves staring at the dark, familiar shape of Salisbury Crags looming from a thundery sky with heavy clouds scudding across the foreground. In the distance a spectral Castle was struck by one pale shaft of sunlight and veiled by a shower falling into the gorge below. A black, broken line of old chimneys climbed steeply up from the High Street.

Robert Louis Stevenson described the scene at a different time of day: 'As the sun began to go down over the valley between the New Town and the Old, the evening grew resplendent; all the gardens and low-lying buildings sank back and became almost invisible in a mist of wonderful sun, and the Castle stood up against the sky as thin and sharp in outline as a castle cut out in paper.' Again, looking back to the atmosphere of France, Stevenson was to write in a letter: '. . . whereas here [in Edinburgh] it takes a great pull to hold yourself together. It needs both hands, and a book of stoical maxims, and a sort of bitterness at the heart by way of armour.'

The distant High Street which looked dim and quiet in the painting, would be a noisy place not long before Turner's time. News-seekers gathered at the Cross early in the morning and shops opened after breakfast. At eleven thirty the bells of St Giles played tunes and there was a great exodus to the taverns for a first drink – apart from the ale taken with porridge at breakfast. Broth with oatcakes and cheese made up the midday meal. With any luck there was meat on a Sunday. Vegetables were sold at every corner by various gossiping, gin-drinking old women. At eight o'clock in the evening a bell announced the shutting of shops. Then the hubbub increased to an unbelievable pitch with the opening of innumerable taverns up and down the High Street. At ten o'clock at night a great roll of drums announced the shutting of the taverns and the emptying of rubbish from the high windows – all accompanied by great brawling and fighting in the street below and ribald shouts and warnings from the windows above.

Sunday was different. Alexander Somerville, whose father was a farm servant, and he himself author of *Autobiography of a Working Man*, thought it a laudable thing to save up for a new suit of Sunday clothes and wrote: 'Dressing up for church was discussed by ministers, one of them dilating on feminine hair styles: "Formerly their hair flowed in easy ringlets over their shoulders; not many years ago it was bound behind with a cue; sometimes it was plain and split in the middle. But who can describe the caprice of female ornament, more various than changes of the moon?"' Country parishes still had the 'stool of repentance' as public censure for members of the congregation detected in fornication. The High Street on any day of the week was as full of heights and depths and hidden corners as its inhabitants. Princes Street which came a long time afterwards was totally different. A visiting friend of Stevenson remarked that 'it was the most elastic street for length' that he knew. 'Sometimes,' he said, 'as it looks tonight, interminable – a way leading right into the heart of the red sundown. Sometimes again it shrinks together as if for warmth on one of the withering, clear east-windy days until it seems to lie beneath your feet.'

Sara showed her class more of Turner's paintings. Some places they had been to on day trips and on holidays. But whether they'd seen the places or not, they'd seen skies. The painter had seen more. He had seen huge, luminous rainbows spanning miles of landscape, or seeming to arch from one mountain top to the other. And there were strange, double, white rainbows which disappeared into the sea or were reflected deep in the water. Some familiar places were wonderfully strange. Everybody knew the Bass Rock and some had been round it in a boat. But no one had seen these mountainous waves or the lightning. They saw well-known places which were all rainbow and all storm, mountains which dissolved in whirlwinds of racing cloud, and great valleys in the process of creation, scoured out by hail and wind. They laughed respectfully but loudly at Turner's commissioned painting, 'The March of the Highlanders', with its ranks of kilts and bare knees drawn up for George IV's appearance in Edinburgh, and they remarked how lucky it was that the storms, lightning and downpour had ceased for that particular Royal Visit. More festivities were to follow. A levee was held in Holyrood. Sixty-three peers paraded, followed by seventy-seven baronets and some two thousand untitled gentlemen. Some of the Highland chiefs appeared with 'tails' of men-at-arms in tartan kilts. Sir Walter Scott, who stage-managed the whole thing, wore a kilt himself and persuaded the King to appear twice in a kilt of Stewart tartan. The fattish monarch wore silk tights beneath it, and the very fat Lord Mayor of London wore a kilt as well.

A Thomas Uwins objected to the 'excess of fancy' in the visit. He considered that Scott made too great an effort to recreate the past and so, 'aiming to throw an air of romance about the matter', had lost a sense of perspective in what he was doing. Scott had been shocked by a placard in the Edinburgh streets announcing court dress for hire. This 'fairly demolished him'. 'It is whispered,' Uwins confided, 'that this courtly and poetic baronet, on whom had devolved the arrangement for all the shows, had got a little check from the Royal Geordie, and that he is not in quite so high favour as he expected. The truth is Geordie is no fool, whatever the folks may think. He knows by experience that court business must be got through in a businesslike way, and that poetry and romance had better come at the end of it.' Nevertheless, the King's visit was a great success and was described in *A Historical Account of His Majesty's Visit to Scotland*, published in 1822. The day the ship – *The Royal George* – arrived at Leith the King wisely decided not to land at once because of the weather. Again Sir Walter Scott came into the picture as he stepped on board. When his arrival was announced, 'What,' said His Majesty, 'Sir Walter Scott? The man in Scotland I most wish to see! Let him come up!' That night the writer had the honour of dining with the King on board. Sir Walter had on his Windsor uniform – a blue coat with red cuffs and collar, and white trousers. That evening the immense bonfire on top of Arthur's Seat was set on fire 'while a large crown on top of the gas-house, illuminated with gas, presented a no less striking appearance to the citizens. The shaft of masonry on which it rested was rendered invisible by the humidity of the atmosphere. Yet, when viewed from a distance, the crown looked like a splendid meteor suspended in the firmament. On the morning of the fifteenth it ceased to rain and the Monarch, as he ascended the deck, beheld the Scottish capital with its towers and palaces basking in the rays of an autumnal sun. The Forth was covered with innumerable boats and vessels, and from many of them arose the strains of bagpipes which floated over the water and were heard in the distance, wild yet pensive, like the voice of Scotland's genius, welcoming her Sovereign to her hospitable shores.' A magnificent procession to Leith was described: 'The scaffold on the drawbridge was filled with the youth and beauty of Leith.' The writer of this account, perhaps guided or under threat from his wife, didn't hesitate to comment continually on the beauty of the Edinburgh ladies, 'our fair countrywomen', the sight of whom caused the King to hold up his hands in wonder and joy – particularly 'at the ecstasies of a beautiful *married* lady in one of the high balconies'. A reception at Holyrood again showed the ladies off to great advantage – 'their demeanour extremely characteristic – sedate almost to demureness, their eyes motionless, yet keen with intelligence, dignified but betraying the invincible modesty of their natures'.

The Assembly Rooms came into their own, this time fitted up in the style of a tent – 'walls and ceiling covered with rose-coloured and white muslin in alternate stripes. The curtains on one side were thrown open, and here the wall was painted with Scottish scenery in the best style of Mr Roberts of the Theatre Royal, which produced a most enchanting effect. On the Saturday there was a banquet – turtle and grouse soup, stewed carp and venison, grouse, and apricot tart. The glasses were in the form of the Scots thistle. The dessert consisted of peaches, pineapples of so uncommon a size as to weigh three and a half to four pounds upwards, as well as apricots, currants, cherries of a peculiar kind, etc.' It is difficult to understand what the dry dessert of 'orange chips' could have been, but the King enjoyed everything greatly. On a later evening he attended the theatre – a performance of 'Rob Roy' where 'the waving of handkerchiefs, the plumed bonnet and scarf added much to the impressive gladness of the scene'.

CHAPTER

11

The class was now madly painting Turners. Great sheets of paper were brought out, and the biggest brushes swirled and splashed recklessly over a white expanse. Turner was freedom. Turner was daring and tumult. The circumspect waterfalls in quiet landscapes that they'd achieved in the past had broken their banks. Torrents now boiled and splashed from rivers eternally in spate. Certain pupils found their best effects came from simply pouring a pool of water from a brimming waterpot straight onto the paper. Others made it by dabbing the surface with a full brush till the liquid bubbled here and there and finally ran off the board. The rainbows, it was agreed, were better and brighter than those of the painter himself, and made full use of the spectrum − red, orange, yellow, green, blue and violet − arching from high mountaintops, often passing one another or colliding in space. The more cautious pupils would take blotting paper from the cupboard to tone down their rainbows or mop up overflowing pools.

Turner's Bass Rock was no trouble. It could be painted as a great seastone among huge, hard-edged waves. Unknown castles and palaces were more of a problem, and all eventually turned into small versions of Edinburgh Castle − their awkward contours carefully hidden in thick white mist.

Occasionally through the swirling mist and crash of waterfalls they seemed to hear Sara's voice saying something. 'Don't forget,' they heard her call, 'don't forget Turner was a *scientist* of painting. Like an astronomer he studied light. *Perspective!*' they heard her shouting to them above the roar of storms and waterfalls. Yes, he worked with infinite time, care, science, perspective, endless trials and errors, repaintings, measurement, optics. They raised their heads momentarily from their streaming papers and gravely took this in. Yet they knew in their bones that genius came in from God knows where, sweeping light and dark, water, root and rock before it like a tornado. Explanations failed to survive this force.

'We're going to see the real thing today,' said their teacher a week or so later. 'Leave everything behind – bags and books, pens and pencils. You need nothing but your eyes.' They were near the National Gallery at noon, having eaten sandwiches and ice-cream in the Gardens. At first the idea of pigeons and nearby statues had occupied them more than paintings. 'So flat,' said Niall. 'Pictures are always flat against a wall. I like to walk round and inside things. I like to put my hand on an arm or leg or measure my foot against a foot. Once I stood on the steps of a Historic House arm in arm with a metal chap in a spiked helmet till they moved me on. After that I couldn't take the house and its pictures. Even the chairs were roped off.'

They moved on up to the gallery. 'Better buy the postcards last when you've seen the paintings,' said Sara as they entered the vestibule.

'I *like* postcards,' said the oldest girl of the party. 'So I might as well sit right here and get on with it. My boyfriend doesn't care if I've seen the paintings or not.'

They left her busy and passed on into the rooms. 'The Turners are at the far end,' said Sara.

'Real ones?'

'Yes, if you look close you'll see the brushstrokes and the oil.'

They looked first at Rome in a golden mist, viewed from a nearby hill where brown and white goats moved – their stiff beards and the small bells round their necks precisely painted. The class went near to see the white brushstrokes in the sky and on the wiry hairs of the animals. On another wall they saw a great house in a park, a lake, and a line of ducks taking to the water. From there some of the girls wandered towards a Gainsborough lady in a plumed headdress, holding a long, white feather in her hand. Her tiny, white-beaded slippers were studied closely and enviously compared with their own sensible, black-strapped shoes. From there they approached an elderly lady by Sir Thomas Lawrence. 'Very like my grandmother,' said one, 'except for the hair-do and the frilly ribbons. That one would stand no nonsense and neither would mine.' They agreed however, that unlike their grandmothers, she'd applied a little rouge to her cheeks, and as likely as not a touch of colour to her lips as well. Up a short flight of steps the boys were standing in front of a painting of James Watt who was shown staring with bright, expectant eyes at the steam rising from a vessel heating on the fire. The boys had gone up close to this picture and were pointing knowingly at the hammer and tongs and various other instruments lying about. They were talking about steam engines. Behind them the girls appeared quietly. They mentioned that James Watt's legs were very stout and his trousers far too tight. On the way out the group noticed an enormous gilt frame – empty and filling nearly one third of a side wall. In front of it and almost inside it stood one of the officials in his black uniform, staring morosely out into the gallery. Niall insisted it was by far the most interesting thing he'd seen in the place. He'd never seen a living person framed like that before. Framed in a window or a doorway, yes. But a great, ornamental gilt frame! It made the man clear-cut, weird, and very lonely. This was the subject he'd like to paint, he said to Sara – not flowers, not Still Lifes, not idiotic imitation Turners like the rest had done, but a frightened man inside a huge, shiny, empty frame.

'What makes you think he's frightened?' she said. 'He's probably forgotten – if he ever knew – that he's standing in front of that frame. Perhaps he's just bored.'

'Well, frightened of the boredom then,' Niall replied as they made their way out of the room. In the vestibule Phyllis was still writing postcards.

'But I thought it was only *one!*' exclaimed Sara.

'Three. The first is the one that matters, of course. But I've got to keep the others as spares in case the first falls through. I'm sending him the skating clergyman. Not, thank goodness, that he wants to be one. But he *does* want to be a champion skater. I'm hoping to travel the world with him.'

'On skates?' Sara was all for ambition and equality.

'On my feet, I suppose. I can't skate.'

Sara sighed. The skater would be lucky to get into the electronics firm where he lived and his girl to get into the nearby shoe factory. From the number of babies around amongst the young couples, skates might only come into their own when pram-pushing.

The school was used to writing essays. Sara was pleased to hear that in the English class her pupils had been asked to write on strange dreams and happenings. Half a dozen had come up with an art-gallery experience. Horror stories and the supernatural were usually considered by far the best for writing. Some wrote of the horror of being alone in darkness with living portraits, one of a vindictive grandmother figure who told frightening bedtime stories, leaving a night of black dreams behind her. Another told of a lady with a feather who used this soft, white plume to paralyse with one stroke everyone who approached. Even the eager-eyed James Watt was described as the originator of all dangerous and explosive happenings in the world. Chernobyl itself was laid at his innocent-looking door. His ordinary iron tools were now written up as the gigantic and lethal instruments of war.

Whatever the outcome of any scientific experiment, James Watt's earliest ones did indeed seem to be of a peculiarly innocent kind. An advertisement appeared in the *Glasgow Journal* of 1763: 'James Watt has removed his shop from the Saumercat [Salt Market] to Mr. Buchanan's Land on the Trongate where he sells all sorts of mathematical and musical instruments with a variety of toys and other goods.' Though Watt knew nothing of music or musical instruments his reputation as a mechanical expert meant there was no limit to what he was asked to do. Soon he was repairing and then making violins, guitars, flutes and even organs. It was not till many years later that he became interested in the problem of steam power.

As early as the seventeenth century the power and pressure of steam was being discovered. A Berkshire scientist, Sam Morland – commissioned to construct some pumps – had published a book in Paris dedicated to King Louis XIV. As in much writing of those days the words have a literary interest as well as a scientific: 'Water being evaporated by fire, the vapour requires greater space than that occupied by water; and rather than submit to imprisonment, it will burst its ordinance. But being controlled according to the law of statics and, by science, reduced to the measure of weight and balance, it bears its burden peaceably (like good horses) and thus may be of great value to mankind, especially for the raising of water.'

A pumping machine for the raising of water in mines was an exciting discovery, but some time later James Watt was to ask: 'Why limit this new power to the raising of water? Why not employ it in the factory to work power looms, and on the roads to impel vehicles and locomotives?' Long afterwards he recorded this seemingly sudden idea of the new power: 'It was in the Green of Glasgow. I had gone to take a walk on a fine Sabbath afternoon. I had entered the Green by the gate at the foot of Charlotte Street – had passed to the old washing-house. I was thinking upon the engine at the time, and had gone so far as Herd's house when the idea came into my mind that as steam is an elastic body it would rush into a vacuum .... I had not walked further than the Golf House when the whole thing was arranged in my mind.'

It is as though to the mind of genius – whether artist or scientist – the sudden revelation exactly fixes and illumines everything around it – streets, buildings, persons, weather, time of day.

CHAPTER

12

Steve, for his own peace of mind, liked to believe that his wife, Ruth, was very content in their immaculate, small house, in their neat, well-kept garden. The furniture was still almost as good as new – the table unmarked, the chairs seldom dented by guests and the spare bedroom closed from one year's end to the next. She'd got away from all the closeness and awkwardness of his own home. 'So she has everything she's always looked forward to,' he assured her friends who might have wished to argue. 'If she'd wanted something else,' he'd say, 'she'd have gone all out for a job.' But he himself, he would add, had been able to give her everything she'd ever wanted.

But they had no children. Sometimes Ruth wept over the strange non-appearance of a child. She'd heard often enough of that mythical double image 'a good wife and mother' and wondered why they were so often paired together. She'd met women who were said to be excellent wives but poor mothers. She'd also met those who were highly-praised mothers but got exceedingly low marks as wives. The unmarried brought out various emotions. Either they were not mentioned at all or were pitied. On the other hand, they could be envied and cherished for their unusual good sense and courage in managing to stay single in a 'doubles' world. She often wondered who could ever be confident or happy enough to achieve the highly-commended 'good-wife-and-mother' image. She imagined it as a kind of eastern goddess with four arms, a head that could swivel in all directions, yet with a fixed, jewelled eye which presumably could never glance sideways at any other man.

She was, she supposed, a faithful, reasonably competent housewife like any other. There were moments when she wondered why Steve had chosen her at all, or why she'd chosen him. Did choice come into it? They'd gone a few well-known walks together in the district, had sat with his family, their friends and neighbours, and kissed occasionally when there was a moment's privacy. It would have been exceedingly difficult to fit in the hour and the place to sleep alone together even had this been thought of in the circumstances. It took her some time to realise that nobody was forced to lie in a bed, in a room, or even inside four walls. She was not a romantic person, but sometimes she'd felt aggrieved that the wood, the secluded field, the lonely beach had not been suggested to her. On the other hand, she remembered she'd taken pains not to notice people making love in any such places. She wasn't proud of this. She thought it more likely that this had been an excessive prudishness on her part rather than tact.

'I'm taking young Niall Gaffney up the hill after breakfast tomorrow if it's fine,' said Steve one Friday evening at supper. 'I spoke about it to his teacher the other day. That boy needs to be taken out of himself.' From deep within her chest his wife screamed silently, 'What about me? Will I be taken out of myself?' Without a word she laid the supper dishes out. 'Will his teacher go too?' she asked. She had a certain jealous interest in Sara — a young woman who'd obviously had things easy in life, who knew nothing whatsoever about Steve, herself, their families or the hard work the two of them had done together to get a life going in this new part of the city.

'No, she can't come this Saturday. She's got all the school stuff to arrange for Monday. It's a bad time of term.'

'How on earth did you meet her?' she asked.

'I handed her a stone in a pub.'

'I see. She's at Geology too, I suppose.'

'No,' said Steve.

'What kind of stone was it?'

'A round, heavy dark one. Rather ugly, some people thought it. She found it interesting.'

'Where is it now?'

'I've no idea. Lost somewhere in school, I daresay.'

Nothing on earth could have brought his wife to ask if she, then, might accompany Steve and Niall up the hill. She felt that a silence following the suggestion, even the smallest hesitation in replying, would finish her for the day. Very little was said the following morning and shortly after breakfast Steve set off. He was to meet Niall at the foot of one of the paths winding up towards the black, burnt cliffs of Arthur's Seat. On all the green slopes below sheep had once grazed. Even this morning it was a peaceful enough scene. Few people were around for the sky was overcast. There was a wind higher up and a mist moving down over the rocks – a mist which now and then thinned out to show a fretful circle of whiter mist behind, or sometimes gathered itself into a darker cloud, dense and swirling at its centre. They had arranged that each should bring a thermos of tea and something to eat. The boy had a bulky bag slung on his shoulder. He was silent on the way up, and showed a cool disregard of anything Steve said, scarcely raising his head to what might be pointed out. He plodded on, staring at the ground.

Suddenly Niall turned and gave Steve one look in which hate and appeal were singularly mixed. Then he started rushing wildly down-hill, stumbling on long stretches of rough ground and racing at breakneck speed down the smooth, jumping the loose stones, the buried roots, and sliding through long patches of red gravel. Now and then he hurled himself through deep clefts of shining rock where, momentarily, he would fall from sight, to reappear instantly, still scrambling, still jumping and slipping. All through this time the boy kept running and staring back over his shoulder. Behind him, wide-eyed – his hands stretched out before him – Steve followed striding and panting. A long distance away a few meandering walkers stopped short in sudden glaring amazement and suspicion.

Niall Gaffney plunged his hand into his bag and flung a stone at Steve who was making up on him. The man raised his hand to his cheekbone. His face, at first blank and white, showed incredulity then a growing fury. He picked the stone up, swinging and weighing it in his hand, looking for a moment as if to hurl it back. Then he slowly bent and rolled it downwards towards Niall who snatched it up and shoved it back in his bag. 'It's *your* stone! *Sara* gave it to me!' yelled the boy as he ran on.

'The devil!' Steve exclaimed, feeling a trickle of blood. He was now alone. The other persons on the hill had quickly taken themselves off, and Niall had disappeared from sight down the shadowy side of the slope. There was complete silence on all sides. Above, the heavy cloud of mist spread closer and seemed as if it must soon descend into the valley to mix with the darker smoke from hundreds of black chimneys below. Gloomy thoughts and forebodings gradually overwhelmed this man and took the place of all other feelings. He remembered a grim story of devilment between two beings on this very hill. Mixed with his bewilderment and fury was the feeling that, in ways unknown to him, he had become a terrifying figure to this boy, like that fearsome shape whose illusory head, enlarged by mist, had formed itself into the diabolical character of James Hogg's tale of the justified sinner in the book he'd once taken from his father's shelves:

As he approached the swire at the head of the dell he beheld to his astonishment a bright halo in the cloud of haze like a pale rainbow. He was struck motionless by the lovely vision; for it so chanced that he had never seen the same appearance before, though common at early morn. But he soon perceived the cause of his phenomenon, that it proceeded from the rays of the sun striking upon this dense vapour which refracted them. George did admire this halo of glory which still grew wider and less defined as he approached the surface of the cloud. But to his amazement he found, on reaching the top of Arthur's Seat, that this sublunary rainbow was spread in its most vivid hues beneath his feet. Still he could not perceive the body of the sun, although the light behind him was dazzling; but the cloud of haze lying dense in that deep dell that separates the hill from the rocks of Salisbury, and the dull shadow of the hill mingling with that cloud made the dell a pit of darkness .... He seated himself on the pinnacle of the rocky precipice, a little within the top of the hill to the westward. 'Here,' thought he, 'I can converse with nature without disturbance, and without being intruded on by any appalling or obnoxious visitor.' The idea of his brother's dark and malevolent looks coming at that moment across his mind, he turned his eyes instinctively to the point where that unwelcome guest was wont to make his appearance. Gracious Heaven! What an apparition was there presented to his view! He saw, delineated in the cloud, the shoulders, arms and features of a human being of the most dreadful aspect. The face was the face of his brother but dilated to twenty times the natural size. Its dark eyes gleamed on him through the mist, while every furrow of its hideous brow frowned deep as the ravines on the brow of the hill . . . . He was further confirmed in his belief that it was a malignant spirit, on perceiving that it approached him across the front of a precipice, where there was not footing for thing of mortal frame. Still, with what terror and astonishment he continued riveted to the spot, till it approached, as he deemed, to within two yards of him: and then perceiving that it was setting itself to make a violent spring at him he started to his feet and fled distractedly in the opposite direction, keeping his eye cast behind him lest he should be seized in that dangerous place.

CHAPTER

13

Steve told his wife the whole story of the morning's episode as soon as he reached home. It was possibly the longest time he had spoken and she had listened for years. 'What, in heaven's name, got into that boy?' said Steve. 'Was it hate or fear?' It was a good chance for Ruth to be sorry for Steve. But she decided against it meantime, even though his hands holding the cup of tea were trembling a little. 'Probably a mixture of both,' she murmured, while he wiped blood off his cheek. 'Absolutely unbelievable!' he exclaimed. 'I've always liked him, whatever others said — never wanted anything but to help that boy.'

'Poor Niall! But does he like *you*?' she said.

As this seemed incomprehensible to Steve, he said nothing. Then he said, 'And fear! What could be frightening about me? As far as I know, nobody has ever been frightened of me.'

'Oh yes,' said his wife, 'your sisters told me they were sometimes frightened of you.' As he made gestures of disbelief she went on. 'You were always very kind, of course, but you seldom spoke to either of them on their own, you see. You treated them as a sort of double. Like two parts of a machine you were thankful to see working efficiently. They thought that unnatural, eerie even. They felt totally different themselves.'

'So to show affection I've got to notice what they're wearing, how they've done their hair, and what they did that day?'

'Yes,' said Ruth, pouring tea.

'The difficulty is knowing what to notice and what not to notice.'

'You've *always* been sensible and *nearly* always right,' replied his wife.

'Niall seems to imagine what happened to his sister is happening everywhere,' said Steve.

'He's not far wrong, is he?' said his wife. 'So what are you going to do about the boy? Oh yes, I forgot. You're going to go on being very kind and very, very helpful.'

A week later Steve went out for his habitual Sunday walk with his friend, Ben Perlman, who lived in the district of Edinburgh called Marchmont. Ben kept a small craftshop with his wife and taught woodwork one afternoon a week to several young persons in the locality. Often he speculated on how the district had changed since earlier times. Nowadays it was thought of as a quarter for students' bedsits and landladies of a rather severe kind. In the previous century it had been a different matter. The letters for and against the building of the new district could belong to those one might read in newspapers of any date. They belonged, however, to the end of the nineteenth century. One who was against it at the time wrote: 'I, as owner of the adjacent property, beg to protest against such shops being put up at all as they would not only be an intolerable nuisance to the whole neighbourhood but would also be detrimental to the letting of my property.' Others left the matter to the 'safe decision' of the Lord Dean of Guild. Safe decision or not, the building began under a huge labour force of men, horses and wagons.

Steve, having an interest in stones, in contrast to his day-to-day work with metals and machines, was intrigued with the excellent stone of this district. It came mostly from the Edinburgh quarries though some of it was taken from the ground around the site. His friend, being a natural craftsman himself, pointed out an addition – an addition of genuine art which was the insertion of carved panels on the face of the buildings – panels inscribed with dates, or the initials of architects, builders, and sometimes with shields, thistles, twined leaves or the knotted rope design. Ben Perlman himself was lucky enough to live on the corner of the crescent. Certain corner flats like his were more ambitiously designed and could boast special ornaments. One broad gable of this particular one supported a stone balcony flanked by twin corbelled turrets of Scottish Baronial style. The whole building was topped by a seated lion holding a shield. Ben was very proud of his flat particularly as it overlooked the Meadows and he could, without leaving his home, watch the comings and goings of friends and enemies from all sides. Mostly, indeed, they were friends, but the history of his race had made him very wary of enemies who could suddenly emerge without warning, revealing themselves sometimes by a mere glance, a passing word not even addressed to himself. His dark, tragic eyes searched the ground as he walked, searched the distant chimneys, the sky, searched, it seemed, the whole world. 'Why should he look so melancholy?' people would ask. 'He has a good wife, a good enough job, one of the best flats in the district.' Melancholy irritated them, especially on a sunny day. 'He has *everything*.' Perlman, however, had not everything. He had escaped into the sun, true enough, by some extraordinary stroke of what some called luck. Before that he had lost his first wife, two brothers, a sister and most of his close friends. His escape into another country – not of his own choosing – had caused this courageous man the most fearful pain and cruel pangs of conscience. He wept often and alone, found that he could not explain or even remember much of his former life, though it haunted his every night for many years. For some time he had attended a doctor who helped him remember and then helped him to let go of certain things it would be lethal to carry with him to the end of his days. Slowly he realised that a few important emotions were still alive though others had gone. The Scotsman, Steve, helped him a good deal by being undemonstrative, being rather douce, not even always understanding, yet always meeting him when he needed company and staying away for short or long periods when he needed to be alone. Steve was often unhappy himself. He needed the other man to bring him out, and at these times Ben came alive and spoke as if there were no distress, however paltry, he couldn't understand. Today he saw Steve from a long distance away and ran down to meet him, only slowing up at the dark bottom stairs which were worn into deep, slippery curves.

They decided, as they often did, to go down to the docks. Steve liked ships and the people who worked around them. It made a change from the neat environment of his own district, the claustro-phobic, noisy nature of his work, and brought him the immediate sound and smell of distant places. There were still fine old merchants' houses along the solid quayside and huge, empty warehouses where once grain from all parts of the world had been stored. Now many waterside restaurants had sprung up. In the evening people down from the city could eat exotic fish with the sound of seawater in their ears. Many young people were moving seaward. Rows of old houses had been rebuilt, refurbished and painted in bright colours which looked good against the blacker, ancient places of the port.

Leith, this adjunct to the city, had a stormy history. The capital had once been very jealous of its port. As far back as the sixteenth century special Fish Laws were drawn up which clearly showed the sensitive nature of the relationship. In 1584 a description of good fish is stated thus: 'that the guid fische were to haif thir qualities, viz "the heiring to be callour slayne, stif, cleir and spawnit, having heid and taill with melt and rawne, weill guttet, saltet and pynet and to be well laid and paket and presset within sufficient stark treyis of guid bind and lichnes" '. There were stronger Acts laid down for serious offences: for instance 'eschewing of fraudulent measures and of false and unjust packing of herring and white fish which is muckle used by unfreemen, fishers and other slayers of the said fish to the great hurt of the freemen, burgesses and the hail common weil of this realme'.

Fish was not the whole of it. A complaint of 1581 was against 'certain maltmen of Leyth for buying and reselling of their beir and other stufe with their owin mesouris and not metting the samyn with the townis commoun mesouris'. And in Leith merchants had also been buying and selling butter, cheese and meal – an offence in the eyes of Edinburgh. Timber import had been a source of jealousy: 'The haill Norway tymmer quhilk is common at Leyth.' In fact, everything about Leith needed looking into. Here is a warning for one, Charles Gatt of Leith who 'came in the townis willis for cutting of ane tow of a Norway manis schip and oblist him not to do the lyke in tyme cuming'.

In the seventeenth century five witches from the Leith region were strangled and burnt 'for intimacy with the devil, dancing with him, renouncing their baptism, being kissed by him though his lips were icy cold and his breath like damp air: taking communion from his hands when the bread was like wafers, the drink sometimes blood, and other times like black moss water'. This was the time when trivial offences were severely punished and many arrests made by military police. To be found cutting a cabbage, boiling a kettle or merely wandering in the streets 'during the hours of sermon' was an offence. In the early eighteenth century some interesting experiments in cures began. Between the Tolbooth and the Shore there was what was described as 'the setting up of a Bath Stove after the fashion of Poland and Germany and approved by all physicians in Edinburgh, remedies to cure all diseases in old and young; with the help of doctors the diseases commonly cured were gout, deafness, the itch, sore eyes, tremblings, ague, the melancholic disease, summer and winter. All days of the week for men. One day, Friday, for women and children.' Every person was to bring fresh linen with him. Also in Leith there was founded in 1788 The Society for the Recovery of Persons Apparently Drowned, – the word 'apparently' seeming to give a macabre, hopeful or hopeless scene set against a black ocean backdrop.

Bell's Mills in Leith had always housed plentiful stocks of meal, oats, beans and wheat, but the winter of 1759 was so severe that the mills were stopped. Later great riots followed a terrible harvest. Early in the nineteenth century the great body-snatching scare arrived in Leith. Chains were fixed across tombs and graves and patrols were formed in every cemetery. Now there were great fights with oars, boathooks and any other sharp weapon that could be found over the ownership of the precious oyster beds. Huge cursings and bloody encounters took place. Oysters were sold at sixpence the long hundred. In Leith the casualties – apart from these violent struggles – were mostly due to fires and shipwrecks, and in 1874 one of the most destructive fires that ever occurred was in Tod's Flour Mills. As one paper described it: 'The mills were totally destroyed. On removing the debris, smoke and flames kept bursting out for three weeks after.' And in 1877: 'A terrific conflagration, the most disastrous in Leith. The fire broke out in a bonded store, filled with Russian spirits, old whisky, brandy and rum, and spread with alarming rapidity. On the roof falling in, the burning spirit overflowed into the streets causing a panic.'

The two Edinburgh friends often discussed why they felt more at home down in Leith. Steve simply put the sea itself as his reason. No doubt it was a dirty sea, an oily sea down here, but it gave movement, even turbulence to the whole scene, unlike the formality of the city which could be both beautiful and rather forbidding. Down here the sky was fretted with the gesticulating shapes of old ships, and near the water were the cracked blocks from an ancient harbour wall. Behind new shops stood remains of the old — their signboards scoured with half a century of salt. Old brass confronted new glitter. Even now Leith was a sombre place divided by strips of water-reflecting light, a black place with bands of newly-painted colour, a noisy place, but still dead silent in the lonely lanes between the vacant warehouses. Steve was also attracted to the place because his great-grandfather had once been a ropemaker in Leith, and no doubt there were various relations of his hidden away somewhere. It was too late, he thought, to find out now, though it intrigued him to imagine that at any minute, unbeknown to him he might be passing some distant relative in the street. More likely they were to be found abroad. The old man, he'd been assured, had fathered children in other countries and had shown no intention of going back to look them up. But the two men seldom talked about their families. Ben Perlman was proud of his three children, but was careful not to boast of them, seeing Steve had none. Wives were spoken of only occasionally, and then with a most unnatural politeness. Today, however, Steve did mention that Sundays could be difficult. Sundays could be quiet. Sundays were a very peculiar kind of day. If you weren't inclined to the Church there was nothing to do but walk and talk. He *had* walked last Sunday and gone back to his wife to talk. They had had a 'difference of opinion' on something he'd rather not speak about at present.

'Of course not,' Ben replied. Steve added that women could get odd ideas if they were left alone for any length of time. The trouble was he had his work to do and couldn't be around whenever anything awkward happened to strike her. After all, she was free, totally free to do whatever she wanted, to go anywhere, visit anyone, take a bus trip or go to a film. In fact, compared to some, she was incredibly lucky, perhaps almost too lucky, he dared say, for her own good.

Ben, gradually convinced he was not to hear more, hailed a bus that went into the city and out again in another direction. Neither of them were ready to go home yet.

But all in all, it had not been a bad Sunday, not so bad, anyway, as that Sunday described by Stendhal in 1840: 'I shall say nothing about the terrible Scottish Sunday, in comparison with which London's resembles a pleasure party. This day designed to honour Heaven is the best image of Hell I have ever seen on Earth. "Let's not go so fast," said a Scotsman to a French friend of his, while returning from Church; "people might think we are just taking a walk."'

CHAPTER

14

That Sunday Ruth was in the house till midday. In the afternoon she sat in the front room stitching flowers onto the border of a traycloth ordered from a local sale. She had a few pins in her mouth which she had removed one by one from the hem with her nails. This made her look rather fierce. She was a true lover of flowers but, as she sewed, she wondered why on earth women through the ages had been expected to put flowers on everything – sewing them on cushions and clothes, painting them on earthenware jugs and plates, splashing them on canvas, pinning them into buttonholes, and, as brides, carrying huge, wired bouquets that hung down to their white-stock-inged ankles. Naturally, it was meant to be a compliment. Women and flowers were supposed to go together. She was inclined to think that was a mistake. Unfortunately women, as they grew older, could seldom be compared to flowers. Children, she conceded, were differ-ent, and occasionally healthy babies might be compared to roses. Otherwise, nothing should be freer than a flower blowing in the wind. But no, it had to be stuck down, pinned down, sewn, painted, wired, twisted and glued into submission. In that case it was much better not to look too closely into the comparison of women with flowers down through the ages.

Thunder had been forecast. The sky was yellow and the place so quiet that the warning bark of dogs could be heard far off in distant streets. Suddenly there was a stupendous blow on the windowpane. Ruth started up to see a huge star of cracks had opened in the glass. Within this glittering star she perceived the pale face of a boy peering in at her. A stormy sun shone behind him. His hair was spiky-wet. She smelt the rain.

'God in heaven, I thought it was a thunderbolt!' she exclaimed. She heard a whistling wind and large drops of water struck the floor. In the midst of it all were the bright eyes of the boy, still staring, whether in fear or joyful malice she couldn't say. 'Well, come round to the door,' she said, approaching, 'unless you mean to climb through jagged glass.' She stood for a moment, staring at splinters, remembering that this should make her furious, yet feeling that this flashing hole might somehow be her means of escape from dull rebellion within this house to the wildness of things outside it.

'You've got it all wrong this time, Niall,' she said as she opened the door to him. She was holding the stone in her hand. 'If this was meant for Steve he's not here today and won't be back for another hour or so. You can wait if you want to see him, of course. But you don't, do you? You'd want to kill him if you could, I dare say. I know nothing about it. You'd better come in and tell me, if you can.'

'I'll bet he told you himself,' said Niall as they went back into the room.

'Oh yes, *his* side of it. I want to hear yours.' Niall gave her a strange look, half-incredulity, half-hope. 'He was after me,' he said. 'He's always wanted to get me. I saw it all along, of course. Around the school, around the museum, even when I was with Sara, even around my own house. But I was never by myself, you see. So he waited. And then he asks me out alone on the hill. The minute I turned my back he sprang. But I was too fast. I had the stone. *His* stone. Did he have blood on his face?'

'He had some blood on his cheek,' said Ruth gravely.

'I mean real blood. Was it pouring?'

'I don't know who you're after, Niall, but it can't be Steve. I happen to know he cares a great deal for you. He wants to help you.'

'Oh, caring!' shouted the boy. 'All this caring and loving – I can't stand it. He was pounding over the rocks like a devil! I got the better of him though – him and his care and his stones.'

'Did you expect to see him here then?' Ruth asked.

'Yes, and to give him back his bloody, wonderful stone,' said Niall with a wild grimace. Ruth turned her back to hide a smile and started to lay the table for two. She went to a cupboard and opened a pot of home-made jam.

'Where are your children?' Niall asked.

'I haven't any.'

'Why not?'

'I don't know,' she said. Some people don't have any. They can't help it.'

She cut some slices of bread, put on the kettle, sat down again and covered her face with her hands. There was silence until the kettle boiled. Suddenly she felt his hard, bony fingers prising her own apart.

'I feel so frightened,' said Niall.

'About the window you mean? I'll explain it to him later.'

'No, I mean all the time.'

'What about then, Niall?'

'About myself. What will I be like when I'm older? I feel so old now, I don't see how I *can* feel older.'

The woman put out her hand and carefully tipped his chin back. It was an unusual face, luminously pale, bony at the chin and with jug ears. When his hair grew he would look better. Just now he had a convict crop so sparse the scalp showed grey.

'You'll be rather good-looking, I should think,' she said carefully.

'No, not how I'll *look*!' he cried scornfully. 'What will I be *like*?'

'I couldn't say anything about that. I've hardly seen you before, have I? It all depends what you want to be like.'

'You've not seen me a lot, but I'll bet you've heard of me,' he replied rather proudly.

'Oh yes, you'll soon be making a name for yourself in one way or another. And personally, I shouldn't want to get in your way.'

He thought about this, staring at the window with wide eyes which appeared to reflect the dark holes and bright cracks of shattered glass. Ruth had poured two cups of tea and cut slices of cake.

'When is he coming home?' the boy asked.

'Probably not for some time yet. He's walking with a friend. Sit down now and don't touch the window. You're going to cut yourself.'

'I *have* cut myself.' Between two fingers a little blood was flowing. 'So that's all right,' he added. 'We're quits now. Me and him.'

'I don't think so,' said Steve's wife. 'His cut was much worse than yours.'

'Yes, you said it bled a lot. Did you get the doctor?'

'No, simply put a plaster on it. Come and wash yours under the tap and I'll put something round it.'

While they were upstairs he told her how he'd once cracked the bathroom mirror in his home. 'Don't start wanting to be a danger round the place,' she said. 'It's a stupid ploy – boring and idiotic at your age.'

'Everybody's doing it,' said Niall. 'Isn't everybody wanting to be a danger to somebody. You see it and hear about it every day of your life.'

'Ah, so you want to be like everyone else!' Ruth exclaimed. 'I heard you were clever. I never thought you'd want to be a cruel young copycat, and stupid, I daresay, into the bargain.'

'It looks as if people were meant to be cruel,' Niall said. 'I've heard them scream with laughter at the flicks when blood spills out. The more shots, blood, bodies, the more yells and screams. One film I saw a man take a knife down the front of a naked woman. It made a straight, red line from her throat to her patch of hair. There was this silence for a second, then some people laughed, then more and more. I sometimes scream and laugh myself. I can't help it. It comes bursting out in the dark.'

'Hysteria mostly, and sometimes fear,' Ruth said.

'I think I'm horrible,' said Niall. 'I absolutely loathe myself.'

'Oh no, but you could become an awful nuisance if you're not careful.'

'I can't stand your Steve,' remarked Niall more genially after a moment's silence. ' "Caring" you said. But he doesn't like people. He likes stones, of course. I enjoyed the Hugh Miller bit – getting to the bottom of the sea with a stone in his hand. That's what Steve wants to do, of course. He'd like to escape from everyone and just go for stones.'

'Not at all. Having a garage means he has to be quite a sociable fellow. No good for business if he weren't.'

'That's easy,' said the boy. 'He only sees passing drivers for a moment or two and maybe never again. And those boys that help him. He likes boys, doesn't he? I've met one or two of them. They laugh at him, of course. He knows nothing about them after they leave the place, and he can't get away quickly enough himself. They all think he skimps his work.'

'Well, Niall,' said Steve's wife, 'you can't have it every way. If he wants to escape from everyone he's hardly likely to go running after you, is he? Ready to pounce, you said! What kind of idea is that?'

Niall groaned, put his head on the table. 'I feel so tired. I don't feel well. I think I'm going to be sick.'

There was a second sprint to the bathroom where Ruth held his head over the lavatory. Afterwards she sponged his face with cold water, and steered him into the spare room – the immaculate, never-disturbed place. She turned back the fresh sheets, tucked a towel under his chin. 'And just in case,' she said as she placed a bowl at the side of the bed. She put a small bell on the table beside him and went out leaving the door half-open. 'Ring if you need me,' she said.

Downstairs, she phoned his home. It was his brother Iain who answered. 'Niall's with me just now,' she said. 'No, nothing wrong,' she added, hearing a sharp intake of breath. 'Just needs a rest. We may keep him overnight. I'll let you know.' She was smiling as she went back to the living-room. She discovered in herself a deep sense of satisfaction she hadn't felt for years. Even as she stared through the shattered glass she was taking deep breaths, as if air and light had entered through the cruel splinters. All the time she listened intently for a bell. After twenty minutes she heard it and ran quickly upstairs. 'You've been sick again?'

'I couldn't be if I tried,' said Niall. 'There's not a thing inside me. I'm rumbling like some sort of drum.'

'A bell, and a drum? Well, I suppose that's an interesting sound.'

'Will you sit down for a minute?' he asked. She felt the bony fingers grip her wrist, forcing her to sit on the edge of the bed.

'What hard fingers you've got. I wonder what you're going to do when you finish school?'

'Everyone asks that. How on earth am I supposed to know?'

'I was just thinking of your grip just now. It felt like a hammer-thrower's.'

But now his hand lay in hers as light as a leaf. He relaxed for a time, staring rather sternly up at her. 'I'd like to lift my head properly and look at you,' he said. 'But I think I'd be sick again. You're not exactly pretty. They say my mother's very pretty, but I suppose I'm too near to see it. I wish I were here though, not there. They're all so busy and anxious over there. They worry all the time about everything.'

'Well, parents *are* anxious a lot of the time,' she said. 'They worry about their children.'

He turned his head away abruptly and murmured: 'Poor Daphne! I suppose you heard my sister was almost raped?'

'Yes, Niall, but as you say, it didn't happen. A man ran after her and her friend. The family must have made it clear.'

'Well, if they did, I've forgotten all the details. Everyone was rushing about in a state and the house was full of people talking, arguing and crying.'

'Well, don't forget what they said. She was frightened of course, but safe and sound, and always will be.'

'Always?' he took her up. 'I've never heard of anyone who was *always* safe and neither have you!'

As if to corroborate this the evening news blared out next door through the thin walls. From where they sat they could hear guns, crashing stones, shouts and screaming voices.

'Will you stay for a moment till I go to sleep again,' said Niall. 'Most nights I have horrible dreams.'

'Of course.'

'What will Steve say when he comes in?'

'Just go to sleep. I'll speak to him.'

Niall smiled and turned to the wall. But Ruth sat on, looking out at a sky now streaming with the black and blood-red clouds of sunset. She wondered what it would be like to have children, to watch them growing up into the mad world. To be a parent, she noticed, was to worry for ever. No matter how whole, healthy, reasonably happy their children seemed to be, the parents worried. Much later the children worried about their parents. It was a strange, unending circle and there was not much that was ever going to break it. 'All the same,' the boy was now muttering, half-asleep, 'Steve's lucky to have rocks and stones. I can't find anything real and hard. I don't know where to look. Things just dissolve. They melt away . . . .' His voice gave out, and now he was lost in sleep.

As she went downstairs it struck Ruth that perhaps the boy might be afraid of the dark. Impossible ever to imply this without deadly insult. What particular darkness this might be she couldn't guess, whether inside or outside himself. Or was he simply within the shadow side of the earth which now night or day, seemed permanently turned towards the dark?

When Steve returned later that evening, however, he found a woman who was unusually serene, staring out into the garden. She appeared so calm, so lost in thought, she scarcely turned her head when he came in. At sight of the cruel daggers on the window he gave a cry as if he'd been stabbed. His eyes fell to the stone on the floor.

'He came back with your stone,' she said. 'He obviously hoped you'd be here.'

'So I see. Did he hurt you?'

'Oh no, he wanted to talk.'

'Only to *talk*. It looks like it, doesn't it?' said Steve carefully touching the sharp edges of glass with a finger. 'Where did he go?'

'He's in bed. Up in the spare room. He felt ill. And he has bad dreams.'

'I've no doubt. He's to go home immediately.'

'He's staying here till he's better. I rang his home.'

Steve was now looking at himself in the mirror on the opposite wall. He was studying the raw-looking bruise above his left eye. 'So I'm to feel sorry for him, am I?'

'I think so.'

'As a matter of fact I *did* feel sorry for him. Not now. He's to be here all night? Hasn't he got a happy enough home?'

'Oh, I'm sure. But he can stay in another happy enough home for a change.'

Steve glanced at her quickly, waiting for further mockery. But he noticed how carefully she did the dishes, putting them away quietly, one by one. He felt he was himself moving about more silently in his own house, keeping his voice down almost to a whisper. 'Are we going to go around on tiptoe all evening?' he said at last.

'Lots of people do when they've a sick child in the house,' she answered.

She got up once or twice in the night, coming back with an expression he'd never seen for years – satisfied, peaceful and slightly amused. 'Sound asleep,' she'd murmured. 'He's settled down as if it's his own home.'

'That's exactly what I'm afraid of,' replied Steve. 'He's such a perverse creature. Maybe he'll come back.'

'Maybe he'll stay,' she said.

In the morning she rang his home again. On his way out Steve paused at the front door to hear her say: 'Yes, for a few days, I hope. Well, why not? I expect he could do with a little change, and so could we.' The front door crashed shut.

She did not work in the house in case of waking Niall, and an hour later he came downstairs looking better, but still with grey shadows round his eyes. Nevertheless his smile warmed the sunless room. Ruth was still fixing down the hem round the border of flowers. He examined it. 'My mother and older sister are the same,' he remarked. 'Always needles around the place, pins stuck into bits of cloth. And the knitting needles! All that stabbing and clicking with the elbow jerking up every second. They look so angry when they're at it. You can't speak to them when they're counting. And when they're *unravelling* – just get out of their way, that's all!'

'But you like the finished things?' she said, plucking at his handsome green pullover.

'Much, much rather have them from shops.'

'You're pretty hard on the lot of us aren't you? By the way, Niall, if you'd like it, we thought you might stick around here for a few days. A short break. Mind you, I don't mean to pin *you* down. But you'll have to stop the stone-throwing and window-breaking. Otherwise we'll do whatever you like. We might go around a bit.'

He considered this while he ate a late breakfast. Then he said, 'What about Steve?'

'He might fall in with the idea or he might not. You know

perfectly well there's no harm in Steve. You made all that up out of your head. And you'll get to like him,' she added.

'Why?'

'Because he needs you. He's a bit out of things.'

'What about me?'

'Yes, you're out of things too. You've never been properly inside.'

'You're talking about circles, clubs, groups and all that sort of thing? I'm not interested. Young people inside those soon try to break them down and get out.'

'We'll talk about it,' said Ruth.

They went out into the garden where a light rain had been falling. Niall stood quietly, his head in the air. 'That's strange,' he said. 'Your garden hasn't got all that much colour. But it has the most wonderful smell.' He walked along one wall, bending between borders of flowers and herbs, and looked back suddenly at the woman behind. 'Why do you look so fabulously pleased about that? I don't mean it's the most wonderful place I've ever seen. It's not brilliantly well-kept, and most gardens, as I said, are brighter. I'm simply speaking from the nose: it's the smell. Has nobody told you that before?'

Niall said he would stay outside and make a start on the place. No, it wouldn't be gardening, but he might pull out a few weeds, rough up the earth with a trowel.

'Well, I suppose he can't do much harm out there,' said Steve when he looked in at lunch time. 'But what are you going to do with him next?'

'You could take him round to the garage for a start. Let the boys have a look at him, give him an inkling how they work.'

'There'll be no work done at all most likely. And how do you expect him to change his mind about me?'

'Changed it already, I should think. Give him another break.' She touched his brow with a finger as if to guarantee protection.

The man and the boy never spoke as they moved off. From Niall's point of view there was nothing to be said. Steve wanted to say a lot but was silent, still thrown by memories of the day before. The two parted when they reached the garage and the boys took over, greeting Niall with scant enthusiasm at first, followed by slowly growing gusto for the job ahead. The moment they laid eyes on him they perceived him as a freak of innocence who knew nothing at all, a poorly designed vehicle simply asking to be knocked into shape, a soft metal that needed the great, childish dents hammered out of it. What better place to learn than a garage? Only garage-language could express the sexual possibilities of life. Here cars were not simply hosed down, overhauled or filled up. Cars were serviced like animals in autumn. In a garage like this you could hope for every kind of bodywork and, given any luck, a partial or even a full stripdown. If something really loose came your way, quick, careful screwing would fix it to everyone's satisfaction. Yes, sometimes there might be overheating after a really fast run. That was easily dealt with. What did he suppose the nearby Exhaust Centre was built for?

After this elementary education in body functions, Niall stayed on for a couple of mornings, mostly learning how to use his ears. He listened for subtle leak sounds, overheard the knocking, rattling and rumbling while the engine was ticking over. He was taught to recognise, acutely as a musician, the light, tinkling sound indicating pinking. Soon he was taught to check all lights – indicators, brakes and windscreen. At the end of every lesson he was advised that his whole outlook must change radically if ever he wanted to find a decent job in the city. He must learn not to be trusting at all, said one young man, giving him a painful kick on the shins for emphasis: never, never trusting in this job, but full of suspicion of the workplace and careful, above all, of its substances. Right here, for instance, lead – the common garage poison – could be lethal whether in fumes or petrol. Other frightful things had happened through carelessness. Only a few years back an old hand here had been blinded, grovelling under a car, changing oil in the dark. So now – icy cold as the place might sometimes be – it was brilliantly lit, brilliantly aired, summer and winter. Following the lesson on suspicion, Niall watched the whole gamut of Thief Detectors being tested under the eyes of nervous customers, some still quivering from some experience the previous night. Steering Locks were demonstrated. Hand-brake Locks and Wheel Clamps, all awkward enough to flummox the most daring car-thiefs. Warning sounds were also demonstrated. He heard the strident horns blaring out across the street whenever door, boot and bonnet were opened. If that wasn't enough to turn a man from evil ways, then an ear-piercing siren might be added, at a price. Finally Niall was instructed in the pitiful language of breakdown – the engine that falters, picks up again, dies down, and repeats this several times before stopping dead. This was more familiar ground. He recognised the description as being not unlike an elderly aunt of his mother's who'd gone through the same falling off and picking up several times before her death. The boys were not at all interested to hear of Niall's family, his school, his prowess in painting or anything else, but on the other hand they pointed out that sharp eyes might be needed on this job for recognising, say, blue smoke from black emerging from the engine. Blue meant major overhauls. Black? They shook their heads. Black was something else and usually something worse. A shadow of doubt and depression hung about the place. While Niall waited for this to clear, a confident young man stepped forward to tell him that if he ever landed up in a garage he must never forget that many of his customers would seem like children, just as their cars were like toys. Unfortunately some people needed to hang up extra toys in the rear window – jumping teddy bears, fluffy ducks, bouncing woolly balls and swaying pin-up females. Occasionally, if he were in this business, he might have to advise the waverers on what kind of car they really wanted to buy, or even to find out how much money they actually possessed. If they were frightened of garages, wouldn't listen, or simply had too many opinions of their own, then he could tell them about computer-buying which cut out the embarrassing face-to-face contact and all vulgar talk of money. There were lots of people who didn't wish to discuss cost or even colour in a garage. Human nature was very secretive, said the young man. Colour might give away something about their character. Just as crimson or green might be worn by certain types of person – so it was with cars. What one could do for these inhibited, prospective buyers was to let them open themselves up and tell all to a computer. This bit of metal was both father confessor and psychiatrist. And lastly, talking about the buyers of used cars, it was necessary to know the temperaments of all the second-hand vehicles on offer. There were ex-director cars, for instance, and one-lady cars, and never the twain could meet. No amount of polish or repair could effect the change-over. The salesman said he thought it was something like souls. The soul of an ex-director was different from the soul of a one-lady, married, single or divorced. There were also old family cars for sale. These were friendly but often inclined to be shabby and, even after extensive scrubbing, slightly smelly. Certain things should naturally be pointed out to customers, while others could simply be left for people to discover for themselves in their own good time. There were pushy, successful cars whose sole ambition was to pass all others on the road, whether on the right side or the wrong. And there were modest, quiet, law-abiding cars who could make themselves a nuisance by not passing anyone. Would he believe it, there were cars so quiet, so unaggressive, they could hardly bring themselves to hoot? They were perhaps most dangerous of all. Finally the salesman mentioned the need for sympathy in this place. How vulnerable were people when their cars were laid up in here for any length of time! How they became super-sensitive creatures without their shells, stumbling about like lost souls as if on foreign, hostile territory. They didn't understand the numbers on buses, where they came from or where they were going to. The worst cases seemed totally at sea and almost unhinged. Perhaps car advertisements were to blame for this, the salesman said, starting at the hoarding opposite: FOR PEOPLE IN CONTROL OF THEIR DESTINY! proclaimed one poster. YOU AND YOUR CAR IN COMPLETE HARMONY! sang out another.

CHAPTER

15

'No, of course he'll not be bored in the Botanics,' said Ruth the next morning. 'You never saw him when he was out there.' She tried to describe his first reaction to the smell of her garden after rain. Nothing like that had been said to her before.

'Herbs?' said Steve. 'Will he see herbs down there?'

'A whole garden of them, if I remember.'

In fact, it began in the seventeenth century with herbs, and in what was called a Physic Garden. The Edinburgh physician, Robert Sibbald, became appalled at the state of Medicine in his own city. He had travelled widely and now he pronounced on the lack of knowledge on medical matters – greater than anything he'd seen abroad: 'few standard drugs and quacks everywhere'. To change all this Sibbald with another doctor, Andrew Balfour, took it upon themselves to make a wide-ranging study of the plants of Scotland, hoping to bring into being, for the first time, a special garden for the cultivation of medicinal herbs. They themselves collected nearly nine hundred plants and eventually found a piece of land for them near Holyrood Abbey. Then, against strong opposition, they tried to gain the interest of other doctors who might contribute to the upkeep of this garden and help with the bringing-in of plants and seeds from overseas. Such persuasion was slow and difficult, but gradually as the idea grew, so did the plants and seeds. Very soon another garden was needed and this was found near the mouth of the Nor Loch at the east of what was later to be the Waverley Station. This became known as the Physic Garden – a place professionally exact in its lay-out of medicinal plants. Balfour was soon considered the most renowned doctor in Edinburgh. Sibbald was the first Professor of Medicine, until forced to resign and hounded from his house because of his conversion to Roman Catholicism. He went to London where, after finally reverting to his former faith, he returned to Edinburgh. Towards the end of his life he was honoured by Charles II, being made King's Physician, Geographer Royal and Natural Historian. He died in 1715, 'A man of pure intentions, of amiable disposition and of generous temper'.

Finally, in 1820, a tremendous feat of skill and enterprise was undertaken by Robert Graham, the then Keeper of the Royal Botanic Garden, who had to arrange transportation of everything from the garden in Leith Walk to the Gardens known today. A transplanting machine was invented for moving every well-established tree and shrub. This tremendous achievement was described by Sir Henry Stewart in *The Planter's Guide*: 'The removals were executed with a safety which could scarcely have been anticipated. Forest trees of various kinds and considerable dimensions – some thirty to forty feet high – were transferred from the old ground to the new. Ten and twelve horses were occasionally employed so that the procession through the suburbs for many days consisted of men and horses and waving boughs, presenting a spectacle that was at once novel and imposing. The citizens of Edinburgh were surprised and delighted with the master of an Art which seemed more powerful and persuasive than the strains of Orpheus in drawing after it along the streets, both grove and underwood of such majestic size.'

In those days Botany and Medicine were very close. Robert Graham himself was appointed Professor of Botany at Edinburgh University. His lectures were not held in a lecture hall, but in a sunny conservatory in the Gardens, and his appearance amongst plants and flowers was termed 'joyous and healthy'. At the same time he practised Medicine and taught in the hospital. John Hutton Balfour succeeded Graham. Like so many people of that time, he had an extraordinary mixture of learning in his background, including Classics and a rather grim Theology. Balfour made an early, courageous decision to study Medicine rather than Theology as his father had done, plus, of course, the scientific study of Botany. A late picture of him shows a solemn, white-haired old man with sunken eyes, but his lectures were said to be like some vigorous climb with new discoveries coming continually into view. Balfour's principal gardener, MacNab, was presented on retirement with the traditional snuffbox and testimonial. Obviously the great gardeners carried off the laurels from all great university men from that day to this, for in his thank-you speech MacNab confessed 'that the moment I begin to hear the sound of my own voice, everything flies out of my head'.

Ruth and Niall set off for the Botanics in the early afternoon. Everything in the Gardens appeared to be mild, sunlit, peaceful. People on benches were chatting and laughing as if this were the one safe haven in the midst of the dangerous city. Children were running around the flowerbeds and a few gardeners knelt amongst the trees. Yet it seemed to the boy that nothing was as it appeared at first sight. All was not well here. The people on the benches were as insubstantial as cut-outs – dark figures mostly, yet hardly thick enough to block out their background. Like animated cartoons they had become curiously jerky in their movements as if expecting trouble. Behind them the tall, white tulips were not soft and innocent at all, but brittle as glass, ready to break at one twist of the stem. Deep under these bushes there was wildness and darkness. The air was very still, but probably not for long. One blast of wind could crack this peace. Trunks, boughs and twigs would snap and drop. He marvelled at the peaceful gardeners scrabbling away quietly beneath the trees as if expecting nothing but a leaf-fall on the grass. The grass. He was appalled at the idea that this grass might be as artificial as the people; for all he knew it might be the bright green matting of the sports shop window. Yet people were exclaiming at the pleasant day. They were acting as if everything were living, growing stuff – soft plants and leaves, petals and bird feathers. Sometimes he lagged a long way behind Ruth. 'What is it?' she'd called. 'There's lots more to see on the other side.' She began to move away more quickly.

Niall was now overcome by the thought that, absolutely by himself, he might have to force his way down through the top layers of this place to reach something real. What this real thing might be he had no idea. He only knew it would be very deep-down, far out of sight. First he would come to the recognisable things large enough to see – worms, beetles, grubs, along with the human stuff such as buttons, coins, hairpins, half-sucked sweets and old bits of rag and paper blown in from the streets. Deeper down still would be only invisible, microscopic life. Nobody could help him. Alone he would have to dig and scratch his way down through the heavy earth and still deeper, bash through stones, bits of ancient wood, globules of melted glass and shards of ancient buildings. Finally he would hack through to what was called bed rock. This name sounded safe and comfortable. But the mattress was melting. Far down below it was molten rock and fire. Steve had once told him that even the deepest mines were hot with the heat of the earth's centre. So everything was on the melt. There was nothing solid at all – neither above nor below.

But perhaps, after all, the grass, the birds, the people on the benches, were real. In that case he himself was the illusion, the ghost. One winter he'd seen a clear, deep pond glassed over with thick ice. Far below he'd watched the fronds of pond plants weaving together. Waterbugs, their legs silvered with clinging bubbles, swam in the depths. He'd knelt and tried to smash the glassy surface with his fist to reach the living things. His blow was too tentative. Instead of clean, sharp cuts there had been a frayed chaos of splinters through which little could be seen except the magnified and fractured creatures swimming below. Niall's fear and fascination had always been with the mysterious tricks of mirage and disjointed perspective. He'd found his favourite reading amongst his brother's books on those Antarctic explorers whose day-by-day trek had led them through an endless mirage of ice blocks: 'A vast, unpeopled city crossed by silent streets and lanes of blue-black water'. Mirage might be beautiful but it was also terrifyingly unreal. Could Ruth cope with this? Could Steve? Could Steve's friend, Martin, who'd promised to let him look through a telescope – 'a magnification of the unbelievable' someone had called it. Could he bear that himself? None of them, he knew, could help him now.

The gardeners here were the ones he wanted to meet. All of them were young men who knew everything about this Garden since its beginning. Niall wandered towards a group who were now clearing a space in the herb borders, and was immediately and even gratefully welcomed as a lost creature who needed succour. One of them, taking a look at his white face and wavering walk, mentioned that he'd come to the right place at last, told him to sit down, calm down, and listen to what he was told. 'Don't bother any more with flowers for the moment,' he said. 'You look whacked. Don't bother even with trees and all those gorgeous rhododendrons – too many in my opinion. And the exotic stuff's fine for children – huge trees, giant waterlilies and the like. But here we've got herbs, herbs where it all began. Herbs are healers. But you're tired. Put your back against that tree while I tell you something about herbs.' The young man began to speak of some of the botanical remedies before the use of antibiotics. Yet there *were* some antibiotics, he said, derived from certain moulds. For instance, a mould have been known by the Chinese since 2000 B C – a green mould used for festering ulcers. 'And take camphor,' he went on. 'That forest plant with white flowers and red fruits was the good old remedy for colds and "congestion". My father used to talk of getting his chest rubbed, as a child, with warm camphorated oil. There was a good smell in the house for hours afterwards, so he said. Nowadays, of course, he'd get a pill.' The herbalist, who was glad to air his knowledge before the gates closed, spoke of the huge tomes on herbs he'd had to study mostly from the fifteenth to the seventeenth century – a weird mixture of Art, Astrology, Superstition and what would be called today Honest Medicine. Had Niall ever heard of the Doctrine of Signatures, for instance? No, probably not. And why should he? What with all the work he had to do in school. This doctrine started with the idea that all plants were created for man's use and had certain shapes that marked them for treating similar shaped organs in the body. The walnut, for instance, was a brain tonic.

'Fair enough,' said the young botanist. 'It was a brainy-looking nut. But other things were stretching it a bit. I mean the bulbous shapes that were supposed to be like hearts, including peaches and citrons, of course, and certain rounded roots, all used for heart troubles. Myself, I like better the notion of pine cones, lily bulbs, the heads of scabias, and anything with overlapping scales being used for scaly skin complaints. Thankfully,' he added, stroking his smooth, pink cheek, 'I've never suffered from any skin trouble. Certain learned people – as they will from time to time – came up with some real bloomers. Most of all I like the old Italian who claimed that poisoned elephants looked always for aloes to purge the venom in their stomachs. The difficulty was that aloes were found only in one island where no elephant had ever set foot. Still the old boy made up for this slip by establishing the forerunner of all learned societies. It was called Men of Leisure, a name probably not appreciated by everybody. Some of your old mediaeval purges were worth something. Forget all those laxatives you were once given – the lovely thick syrups and the fruity, coloured pills. The ones I'm talking about came in three stages: gentle, mild and drastic. "Drastic" would have worked like a tornado in the bowels. "Kill or cure", seemed the idea in those days.' The young man consulted his watch. 'Ask anything you like before you go,' he said. 'You won't be allowed in the library. That's for experts, researchers and a few of the rest of us. There you'd see everything you ever wanted to know about herbs and cures, and a lot more than you ever ought to know about drugs and poisons.'

'The common herbs you'll find right here,' he said, picking a leaf from a nearby bush. He held it out. 'Rosemary, for funerals and flavouring. Have they given you "Hamlet" yet? Not yet? Well time enough. I can see you've got far too much on your plate already. Rosemary's for remembrance too, and less romantically in the present day – a moth preventative. It was said to thrive best in households where women ruled. Who rules in your house, Niall, your father or your mother?'

Niall thought for a time and finally said: 'My mother. My father isn't around so much. Anyway, she talks the most.'

'Doesn't follow,' said his mentor. 'Breath's a powerful thing and shouldn't be wasted on a lot of talk. Maybe she's wasting her breath, as they say. Think of all that deep breathing eastern mystics managed to do in a matter of minutes. After that they could do anything they wanted to do – lifting heavy loads, doing without food or sleep for hours and hours.'

'But I think my mother's a *good* talker,' said Niall. 'She does all the shopping and cooking too, besides growing her own vegetables. She's busy all the time.'

'All right, sorry. What does your *father* do – that silent, well-fed man?'

'He works in a hardware store. Yes, he *is* quiet. If anyone rules our house it's my brother.'

'Ah, so he rules with a rod of iron?'

'No, with a paintbrush. He's a house-painter and makes quite a bit of money since he's one of the best.'

'Do you have a sister?'

'I don't want to talk about my family any more. I'm tired. I'll have to go soon.'

'Wait a bit. I haven't told you the half,' said the other. 'After all, you're here to rest, aren't you?' It was late afternoon and the Garden was sweet with the smell of roses. He sniffed the air. 'Yes, roses were important in mediaeval times,' he said, 'in poetry, in painting and in medicine. Rose petals on the eyes were supposed to clear the sight. Other perfumed flowers, violets, for instance, were mixed with other juices to prevent drunkenness. You'd need to grow whole acres of violets round this city to do the trick these days. You're absolutely right.'

'I didn't say a thing,' said Niall.

'No, but you looked a bit incredulous. Perhaps your father drinks.'

'He does.'

'But hasn't tried the violet-juice cocktail, I suppose.'

'What other herbs were there?' Niall asked.

'Some very dangerous drugs were used in medicine, still are in one form or another. There was belladonna, the deadly nightshade. Those dark purple flowers and white berries look deadly all right. Still, it was used then and now as a useful drug for dilating the eye. That foxglove across there was a heart stimulant, and still is today. More expensive concoctions were used for the hearts of the rich – lapis lazuli, for instance, mixed with herbs and the bone from the heart of a deer.'

'Do hearts have bones?'

'In legend they might. Legends were attached to lots of well-known drugs. Cocaine was once a stimulant for porters who climbed for days in the Andes on just one chew of the drug and hardly a scrap of food. Those mountain miles were reckoned in "cocadas" – the distance covered in one chew. Another poison, strychnine, had been tipping jungle arrows since ancient times. The legend goes that women were shut into a house with the wherewithal to make the poison. The brew was ready after two days, but if its brewers weren't half-dead from killing fumes, the poison was considered very poor stuff indeed, and the women severely punished.

'There were always healing drugs, of course,' added the young man, glancing at Niall's face. 'Most outnumbered killers in every age. They all had different uses. Anise was one. It was supposed to ease headaches and, mixed with oil of roses, cured the earache. Best of all, it could take away what was called "the griefs of a belly stuffed with wind".'

For a moment they watched fat pigeons scraping and fluttering about the benches where people were shaking out paper bags and gathering their things together. Others slowly passed by on their way to the gates.

'Birds often appeared here and there in the old books,' murmured the gardener thoughtfully, 'sometimes as good omens, sometimes as bad. One called Caladrius was a pure white bird. If it looked at a sick man from the foot of his bed, he would recover; it inhaled his sickness, then flew toward the sun where the sickness was burnt out. But if the bird averted its eyes, the man didn't recover.'

'I must go now,' said Niall.

'Come back and see us any time,' said the young man, while the boys murmured agreement. 'The end of the afternoon's best. We go on working when all the rest go. You can relax here,' he went on. 'Didn't anyone ever teach you how? Or maybe you're just too proud; they say proud people can't do it. They're frightened they'll flop like rag dolls with their mouths wide open and their feet turned out. Open your hands! Don't uproot the whole place!' For one moment Niall had lain back, grabbing the grass with white knuckles and his eyes tight shut. He got up slowly and the boys watched him go.

'He's found his feet again,' said one. 'What was wrong with him?'
'He's seen some horrid sight,' said another.
'On his way here? An accident?'
'Inside his head more likely,' said the older gardener. 'Nightmares.
He's the age for dreams and nightmares.'

The gates were now shut. Silence fell gradually through the
Garden and on the group of boys who were left. They were
imagining night falling here, the new sounds and shapes as the place
slowly darkened. Then they thought of the quick return of light, of
lonely, separated benches and the outlines of unfamiliar trees against
red sky. Some thought of the boy with his white knuckles and his
knock-kneed walk. One or two worried aloud over his nightmares and
his dreams.

'But it *could* be a belly stuffed with wind,' murmured a voice from
amongst them. They rolled about gently on the grass, while one, by
long and sustained effort, managed a triumphant fart.

Wrote Rousseau in *Letters on the Elements of Botany addressed to a Lady*:

The principal misfortune of Botany is, that from its birth it has
been looked upon merely as a part of Medicine. This was the
reason why everybody was employed in finding or supposing
virtues in plants, while the knowledge of plants themselves was
totally neglected: for how could the same man make such long
and repeated excursions as so extensive a study demands; and at
the same time apply himself to the sedentary labours of the
laboratory, and attendance upon the sick: which are the only
methods of ascertaining the nature of vegetable substances, and
their effects upon the human body? This false idea of Botany, for a
long time, almost confined the study of it to medicinal plants, and
reduced the vegetable chain to a small number of interrupted links.
Even those were very ill studied, because the substance only was
attended to, and not the organization. How indeed could persons
be much interested in the organical structure of a substance, of
which they had no other idea but as a thing to be pounded in a
mortar! Plants were searched for, only to find remedies; it was

simples, not vegetables, that they looked after. This was very right, it will be said. Maybe so. Hence nevertheless it follows that, if men were ever so acquainted with remedies, they were very ignorant of plants: and this is all I have here advanced.

Botany was nothing; there was no such study; and they who plumed themselves most upon their knowledge of vegetables had no idea of their structure, or of the vegetable economy. Everybody knew five or six plants in his neighbourhood to which he gave names at random; enriched by wonderful virtues, which he took it in his head they possessed; and each of these plants, changed into an universal panacea, was alone sufficient to render all mankind immortal.

CHAPTER

16

Open Days were held from time to time, in various establishments in the city. There were Open Days at the University, in certain factories and workshops, in newly-built housing-schemes, in theatres and in schools. Anyone involved in this 'openness' knew these places were being displayed in their ideal, unknown state. In places of education exhibits of learning and research were put on show, sometimes under lock and key. In the libraries portraits of the great were hung on prominent walls, and old, illumined books placed under glass. Well-groomed examples of educators hung around to be questioned in all departments. There were Open Days for the sale of new-built houses. Being a city rather renowned for talking across doorchains, people thanked God their own house would never be having an Open Day. In the new estates people viewing were warned not to wear down the plush even in the lavatory, not to dent the brand-new sofas and armchairs, finger the lampshades, nor crumple the curtains while comparing the view from front and back windows. No one, however, could stop them from thinking of crush parties in the kitchenette, imagining perfect love in the bedroom or ideal dinners in the dining-room. In the centre of the city well-known workshops would show pottery and glass-making while certain high-class bakeries demonstrated the forlorn, forgotten art of wedding cakes to elderly crowds who'd cut their own one forty or fifty years before.

The most popular Open Day was at a theatre. All day from nine o'clock till five theatre-goers moved about the place from box to upper gallery, from gallery to basement. They looked behind the scenes where the heavy curtain was manipulated. Most electrifying of all, they were shown the switchboard where the lights were operated. It was a revelation that light and the mixing of lights could effect a change of place, of mood, of time, from the meloncholy blue of winter moonlight to the yellow midday sun. None of the visiting public could bear being caught on stage in a beam of white light. Some tried to hide from it and were followed about till finally they ran off into the wings, confused, as if a laser-beam had pierced their brains, uncovering secrets. On the stairways behind the stage was all the clanking machinery of scene-changing, and dozens of small store-rooms holding props and costumes. Away from lights and voices, there was a strange drabness about these rooms. Dust and greyness were reflected here in long, gilt mirrors. Standing beside the prompter behind the curtain, and looking out upon rows of empty seats, the visitor felt a frightful tightness in his throat and a weakness in his legs at the very thought of breaking down on stage. It wasn't so bad, the prompter reassured them. For the most part actors helped one another in these crises. It was different, they began to see, from ordinary life. They were not usually helped as they floundered in conversation, never prompted as they hesitated for words. 'Thank heaven we're *never* in the limelight!' cried one. 'As a matter of fact I've never felt at my best in anything I've ever done, either in light or dark,' said a tired-looking businessman.

There was a tendency for people coming out of this particular Open Day to look around for drama in the streets. But they came out into an even, grey light where people were moving slowly about their business. Most of them looked sad, not tragic. Nobody was around to prompt the silent.

All Open Days established their own style of doing things. Certain schools, in particular, joined in the fashion. Niall's school was one of the largest and its preparations had been long drawn-out. Parents were to see it as a perfect place and not as the hideous institution described by sons and daughters. A band of cleaners arrived early in the morning with dusters and polish. If there *were* any skeletons in the cupboards they were going to shine like ivory. Joiners were still fixing crooked shelves, nailing loose floorboards. A final glitter was applied to stoves and sinks and cutlery, while in the Gym next door the older boys had searched the place for any flaws in safety, examining ropes and vaulting-horse and testing wall-ladders. Finally the sweaty, dusty place was fumigated and the windows opened.

The kitchen was the most popular place. Today the cold, marble counters for rolling dough had been cleaned and glazed like altars, and rows of white ovens were displayed against white walls. To give this white place some colour, yellow and pink iced cakes, made the previous day, had been taken from refrigerators. They were all for show, but not for sale. Certain determined mothers, who'd made a point of bringing bags, spotted their daughters' work and tried to remove it. They were restrained.

'But what are you going to *do* with it, if it can't be sold?' was the question from all sides. 'Surely better it should be eaten than go stale!'

'No, no, it's sent to several hospitals.'

'Sent to several hospitals,' was hissed respectfully around the room.

'But *are* cakes devoured in hospital? Many a time I've been in hospital and never saw a cake in my life.'

A few well-dressed mothers forgot how well they had been brought-up – taught, amongst other things, never to snatch at cakes, never to haggle at counters. The few fathers present attempted in vain to end these arguments. 'But darling, she can bake as much as she likes at home. *We* can eat whatever we want.'

'No, these cakes will soon be good for nothing – not even hospitals. They'll all be wasted.'

But the politeness and stubbornness of the teachers was terrifying. 'Nothing is ever wasted here. Every scrap will go back to the fridge until it's time to move it.'

The parents passed on silently to see the Gymnasium. About fifty boys were giving a demonstration against the wall-bars and up and down the ropes. Others were vaulting and balancing in acrobatic movements on the horse. The sound of effort filled this place. There was the sudden squeak of rubber shoes on the floor, heavy panting, and the occasional cry and groan during an awkward landing. Finally the gymnasts stood in regimental rows in silence. There was no chance to grab hold of sons any more than at cakes. Each had a dreadful horror of being recognised, encouraged, praised, touched, or even named. Glazed, forward-bulging eyes forbad it. The parents backed out and looked into the doorway of a small hall where the girls were singing about love, happiness and youth, and the flowers that wither all too quickly in the storm. They glimpsed an elderly accompanist striking chords in the bass with her left hand, while with her right she still attempted flowers, youth and the fearful effort to remain upright. Again the parents passed silently on and up the stairs into the Geography room. At first sight it seemed a relatively simple place – a world divided into different shapes and colours, letters and numbers, with nothing more disturbing about it than a neat naming of parts. The only reminders that the earth was a strange object in a wild universe were the large polished globes that could be made to spin at the touch of a finger. This gave an unfamiliar god-like sensation to fathers and mothers who had not felt god-like for years. Fiercer and more unpredictable were the models of unfamiliar moun-tain ranges and volcanoes, of unfathomed seas and the great holes in the earth made by primeval meteors. They were slightly shaken by this view of Geography. For some of them it had once been safely hidden in the pages of huge atlases, or rolled down from the wall on poles in the shape of a cracked and gluey-smelling yellow map.

Even the History display was made of sterner stuff than they remembered. Drama had been replaced by Politics. A rollicking Henry VIII and his fated wives were missing from the walls. Execution scenes, bloody battles, armies of axes, spears and arrows were out. So were gorgeous costume pieces and processions. There were more explanations and writing now, complicated questions of right and wrong, of loans and treaties, diagrams of frontier changes and financial transactions, the take-over of countries and the forming of new ones. This History had come of age. There was no question of skirmishing for ever amongst knights and their ladies. The parents must pull themselves together. The homework was going to get harder and harder.

They saw the new room where Mathematics was taught. It was an austere room – bare, angular, lit with a brilliant white light. Round the walls were some small computers, and above them examples of their intricate designs – interlinking spirals, squares, triangles, pages of dots, crosses and questioning curls. This was the sign language that spoke for every part of the world. Here Maths came close to Art, Art to Science, Science to Music, Medicine, Atoms and Stars. They were intrigued, amazed, seduced, awed and delighted. Finally they felt frightened for themselves, for their clever offspring and for the future of their descendants.

The parents continued cautiously on and up into the Art room. Here several pupils, including Niall, had come early in the day to get the place ready. A search for the best of the year's work had been made by Sara and her pupils. Old paintings had been taken down and new ones selected. Niall knew his family would be around before the afternoon was out, and saying nothing, quickly retreated into the depths of the spacious cupboard and watched intently, like an animal in its hidden lair, for their arrival. He had turned off the light and it was dark in there, smelling of paint and turpentine and years and years of spilt glue. The floor was blotched with blue, red and yellow where crayons had been trodden down. There were huge blots where whole bottles of Indian ink had been upset. Occasionally, when in here alone, he'd been rather afraid of these strange blots. Some of them looked like grotesque heads, others like prancing animals, kicking with hoofs, claws or talons and with flying tails and ears.

Before long a group arrived, including Niall's family. He saw them, as it were, from a great distance. Sara was greeting them, taking them round the room, pointing, smiling, explaining. Explanations had always angered him. Someone would ask a question, and after a long or short pause, an answer came back. But what exactly was happening in the long silence or split second? Was this where some bit of truth lay hidden in darkness and dumbness – something that might never be shown or uttered? As far as he could see this was happening everywhere – in houses, in streets, schools and colleges. Questions were asked and were answered on the dot or not at all. Either way, some mysterious essence was left out. This, he imagined, led to the furious frustrations between husbands and wives, fathers and sons, brothers and sisters and even between close friends. Far back in his dark place he saw his family as he had never seen them before, both magnified and unfamiliar. In embarrassment he heard his mother asking some question about painting and was angry to hear Sara answer without a moment's pause, while smiling with forbidding confidence. His tough mother, who alone had managed to keep everything together through thick and thin, now appeared stupid and rather timid. His father, who had been weak through every escapade, was overdoing it at this moment in blustering bonhomie. Daphne, a sad and inward-looking girl who'd once needed all his reassurance, was giving her views vehemently about the room, about the paintings, about the whole school. Iain, because he alone had met Sara, was clowning around the place and, in the eyes of his young brother, making a fool of himself. Was this the only way, then, to see others clearly? By peering through the slit of a door from a dark cupboard? Sara herself seemed hardly a teacher at all now, but simply a non-stop talker, a bit of a show-off and a flirt into the bargain. But now he tried to imagine what might be thought of him if he were to be viewed from his hiding-place. He seemed to see himself – grey, undefined, an ungrown youth, still without substance – a mere ghost.

The room was changing imperceptibly. With a last close look at the paintings, a few more questions, more explanations, his family began to drift away, one by one. He saw Sara take up her handbag and look at her face closely in a mirror. She'd spoken so often of faces in the classroom, he wondered what she made of her own. He saw her smile – not a real smile, but a stretching of the mouth to help her apply lipstick. Then she left the room closing the door quietly behind her. Now it was silent here – only one tap slowly dripping and a scrap of paper moving in the draught from the corridor. He heard footsteps pass the door, footsteps going down the stairs, growing more and more quiet as they reached the bottom, and from there moving along distant passages below. He imagined people having a late tea or watching a last demonstration in the Gym. Cautiously he came out of the cupboard, testing himself as if stepping from prison or a haven. Once he was out he lost his ability to perceive things sharply. At once they took on their usual cold, flat appearance. He felt exposed and shivered to see the sky so much greyer than he'd imagined. Very gradually he realised he wasn't attending to sounds at all but listening to a profound silence in which the tap dripped on and on into the sink. He turned this off, and knew he was alone.

Niall felt a moment's panic, then forced himself to think of all the solid things around him; the two massive tables pupils had worked at through the years – cut and scrawled over like fantastic showpieces – the heavy boxes of paint piled on the shelves, and in one corner an angular wooden figure which was there to demonstrate every joint in the human body from neck to fingertips. He was grateful for the weight of all these objects in what he sensed was a vacuum opening up around him. This was the highest room in the building. He went across to look out, and for a minute the sight of moving traffic and people walking on the pavement below calmed him. There were open doors and open windows down there where people were escaping. There was no sign of panic. Nevertheless he couldn't put off his own attempt to escape. He opened the door of the Art room and stepped out. A huge silence buffeted him. Slowly and very cautiously he walked down the first flight of stairs to the passage below. On either side were open rooms showing exhibits of one kind or another. Here was the Science lab with an unnaturally tidy display of bunsen burners and bowls, shelves of glasses and coloured chemicals in bottles. A row of empty scales glittered under the windows, one gently swaying as if recently touched by a finger. Down another flight, and still alarmed by his own footsteps, he went into the Craft room. Here there was something reassuring about the sight of halffinished stuff where not long ago warm hands had been working. One small loom showed a loose wool strand wavering in the draught. The modelling clay, carelessly uncovered, was still damp. The unfinished head of this boy drew his attention. He stopped to stare. The face was friendly, the eyes steady and amused, and for a moment Niall took comfort from a companion in the deserted room. Nevertheless, he swerved from the handmade mirrors reflecting his pale face, and passed on through ragged, hanging rugs, through pictures made of strips of cloth sprinkled with shells and polished stones. He touched clumsy hunks of wood – bits of oak and beech which had been chopped and sawn into a semblance of animal shapes. He stopped at a rugged, butting bull with smoothly-sanded horns. He imagined all the noise that was going on here only half an hour ago. Nevertheless, through all the imagined chatter and hammering of this workroom, the silence of the building began to penetrate like a deepening fog. The normality of a crowded school had vanished. He found himself walking stealthily from this room as if not to disturb whatever might be lurking down there on the floors below. Each sound was unfamiliar. Even his damp hand produced a faint squeaking on the polished banister, his rubber shoes a soft, anxious padding on the stairs, more like a hunted animal's feet than his own. He glanced into the unlit Gymnasium and tried to remember it at any ordinary time with its shouts and thuds, its cries of scornful laughter and its bursts of praise. It was not easy to see in here. The wall-ladders went up almost into darkness. The ropes dangled like a hangman's noose from a black ceiling. He came out quickly, wondering whether to run right up again to the familiar Art room or to go down to the ground floor and the locked doors. First of all he walked the length of the dining-room and came to the pantry where a few mutilated cakes were waiting to be gathered up in the morning. At once he started a greedy, desperate attack on the centre of a large yellow cake, and was almost immediately sick into a bucket which contained a bunch of withering dahlias. For a while he sat looking in disgust at the yellow-sprayed flowers and thinking of Ruth holding his head and sponging his face at a sweet-smelling basin. He was disgusted again when tears filled his eyes, and he got up quickly, accidentally kicking the bucket at his feet. Immediately upon this there was another sound that made him jump in terror. A door had opened beside him and through the slit an old man was peering from a small room behind. Niall had a glimpse of a coal fire, a lamp on a table, and a folded newspaper stuck against a bottle. 'Now what, in God's name, are *you* doing here?' exclaimed the man in an angry voice. 'No one comes down here. This is my place. You should have gone long ago. Everyone else has left.'

'I've been *forgotten!*' cried Niall. The word had an anguished sound. In the cramped space it was reminiscent of derelict houses, empty playgrounds, and all the wind-blown scraps of paper rising at night above unfamiliar squares. The old caretaker had seen all these in his youth. After years in this snug lair he still recalled them.

'Forgotten?' he replied. 'Oh, my goodness, no! They haven't forgotten you. There'll be one hell of a row going on at home right now. They'll all be pounding on these doors in no time. Wait till I do a bit of phoning. Come in and give me the number. There'll be lots of noise and trouble ahead for both of us. I've never seen you before, and I don't suppose I'll want to see you again in a hurry.'

Niall sat down at the fire while the old man poured a spoonful of fiery stuff from the bottle into a glass. The boy swallowed it, gasping and grimacing. 'That's right,' said the man. 'Don't get a taste for it.' He spoke into the phone for a moment. 'Safe? Of course he's safe,' he ended. 'They're very pleased just now, of course,' he said when he came back to Niall. 'Just now – yes. But later very angry indeed, I've no doubt. You're too old to be stupid, you see.' They sat for a while, and to a question from Niall the man replied, 'Yes, I'm the caretaker of the place. Fair enough. A good name. It's only the building I'm supposed to take care of, but sometimes I have to take care of the inmates as well. Very much more tricky than seeing that windows go up and down properly or the door hinges get oiled. I take the work seriously. Not only boys and girls come to me, of course. The cooks, the cleaners and teachers as well. Oh yes, indeed – teachers. One – and I won't say her name, though it's years ago now – came to me. Crying, as a matter of fact, and afraid to talk to the Head. She hadn't a clue what controlling a classroom meant. Thought it meant speaking politely to some great hulking brute in the back row. Too much TV and the newest Educational Methods. Well, I was a great hulking brute myself once, so I happened to know all about it. From the inside. She went upstairs feeling better, accompanied by myself. And once in a while I'd go to her classroom again without warning, just to tighten a screw, you understand, or see to a windowcord, promising to come back if the screw or the cord ever gave trouble again. I was a fine, strong man at that time, and looked as if I meant business. Anyway, she never had trouble again. I'm just giving you an idea what caretaking involves. What's your particular trouble? You don't look too happy yourself.'

Niall talked for a while. The trouble was finding anything solid under his feet. Finding anyone he could actually trust. Hating people he was supposed to like. Liking people he was supposed to hate. Not knowing how far down you could go into the earth or up into the sky. How far you could go with anyone or anything. In fact, finding any limits at all.

'Don't bother about all that,' said the caretaker. 'It all feels horribly unsafe now, I expect. In a year or two you'll find your feet, as they say. Those are good words! You'll find where the solid rocks are to take you through bogs and floods. I'm talking about some of the people out there, and damnably hard those solid folk can be, I admit it. But never mind. Let's climb up again and I'll show you one of the best views of the city before the others come.' Together they climbed the stairs to the Art room where the old man put out the lights and took Niall to the long windows. They saw the last streak of a fiery sun and the first appearance of the moon. Underneath were streets and streets of dark houses with lighted orange windows, and behind great curving crescents already faintly moonlit. A wind was twisting the smoke through lines of black chimneys.

'When I look out these days I think of other kinds of caretakers,' said the old man, 'caretakers not just of a house or school or whatever, but of the whole city — the people who planned and built it, preserved its stone and monuments, cleaned its decoration, looked after the hidden squares and green places. Along with them you get destroyers moving in — greedy men who can't wait to make a fortune out of ugliness. That's how one gimcrack hotel went up, looking like a piece of yellowish cardboard, surrounded by its new square — once promised as "one of the finest squares in Europe". So that cuts out Venice, for a start. But you're perfectly free to take your choice, of course. You can name the others. There's the bridge, dead straight and hard as a cement ruler that cuts the old street down to Leith and the sea. Now you can hardly see to the corner of that street. For a while there's an outcry, of course, then everything grows silent again and the work begins. Skylines. There's another word that's debated. Some people don't know what the word means, or think it's neither here nor there whether there'll ever be a skyline again in their lives or in their grandchildren's lives. This city's supposed to have rather unusual ones. No doubt that's why our City Fathers – do we need more Fathers, by the way – why these so-called Fathers saw fit to reduce our view of this ancient skyline by this large modern market which, who would believe it, has replicas of pretty Dainty Dinahs or Lavender Ladies, whatever they are, with baskets over their arms. Girls in flimsy dresses in Scotland, poor dears, shivering in the east wind and looking so damnably silly it seems hardly fair to stare at them as you go by. But the worst thing. Shall I tell you the worst thing?'

'What's that?' asked Niall.

'Lots of other things of course. But the worst is people get used to everything in time. After a bit the letters stop, the anger fades, polite good nature comes swilling back like warm beer over the fury and the outrage. Once up, the thing then stays for years and years, maybe for centuries, who knows. We haven't mentioned that white contraption yet, big as a sailing ship in the Gardens – the Tent. What's it for? I don't know. I haven't looked inside. But you can bet, like the rest of these things, – it's for the good of the People. A patronising view you might think, and believe me, I've heard these same People curse and mock at the thing as they go past on top of a bus. I could go on. But what I'm trying to say is there are caretakers and caretakers. Your friends are *your* caretakers.'

'What friends?' cried Niall.

'I'll say it again. Your friends. And with any luck your family, your teachers, your doctor and dentist and the man who mends the roof. I suppose the list's endless. But so was the old Scottish sermon. So I'm going to stop now. Shall we go down?'

There had been Lord Provosts who'd been true caretakers of their city. In the middle of the eighteenth century George Drummond was one of them. As it was said at the time: 'The chief magistrate is devoted to the service of the city, and its glory is his greatest aim. Disinterested are his views; his noble plans proclaim his merit, and his memory shall be dear to posterity.' He it was who gathered in funds for the building of an Infirmary which started in a house fitted up with beds. A few years later a new Infirmary was built, Drummond being one of its chief promoters. In his diary he wrote: 'Forwarding the building of the Royal Infirmary is my only amusement . . . . I am distinguished and called the father of it, with which, alas, I have too much pride and vanity not to be pleased.' A contemporary, Thomas Somerville wrote: 'I happened one day . . . to be standing at a window (in the old town) looking out to the opposite side of the North Loch, then called Barefoot's Park, in which there was not a single house to be seen. "Look at these fields", said Provost Drummond; "You, Mr. Somerville, are a young man, and may probably live, though I will not, to see all these fields covered with houses, forming a splendid and magnificent city. To the accomplishment of this, nothing is more necessary than draining the North Loch, and providing a proper access from the old town. I have never lost sight of this object since the year 1725, when I was first elected Provost."'

The drainage of the North Loch was a stupendous and truly Herculean task. Over the years every kind of stuff had been tipped into it from the slaughterhouses, fleshmarkets, tanners, skinners, and all the manufacturers who worked along its banks. This was not to be wasted, however. When the Loch was drained the stuff was offered, free:

'The Magistrates and Council of the City of Edinburgh hereby intimate to all gentlemen farmers and others, that they are at full liberty to take and carry off dung and fulgie of the North-Loch immediately, and that without payment or other gratuity therefor.' This was, it might have been added, if you were a strong man with a big barrow, and a very weak sense of smell.

'And don't forget the hidden caretakers,' Niall's companion went on as they turned from the window. 'Some of the most important ones. Night workers. People who restore the bowels and entrails of the city when you're in bed – all cleaners of the underworld. And there's the folk who set the pages of the morning papers. Include your surgeons and nurses in the company. Come what may, their work goes on all night. Even if the roof falls in – which happened many a night in wartime – they have to go on. We'd better go down, though they'll take their time coming round, they told me, now they know you're safe. I admit I thought that odd. Myself, I'd be rushing round. But I'll get ready for them and we'll talk about it.'

They walked down to the warm room in the basement where the caretaker put out cups and plates. 'Tell me about them,' he said as he sat down. Niall explained why his father wasn't always at home, though just now he was having a good long break with them. 'But I think he gets bored at home,' he added.

'Is that right?' said the caretaker. 'So he gets bored "outside", does he? Though mind you, I've never believed those modern prisons were as sociable and interesting as we like to make out. People get a glimpse of a picture on a cell wall or see a half-decent chair and think all's wonderful in there. A real home from home. So why, they ask, should a thief or a murderer have such a cushy time while they're working their hands to the bone? And your mother?'

'Bored with my father. He hardly speaks at all.'

'You have an older brother?'

'He's a house-painter.'

'A fine job. Better than a landscape painter, I sometimes think.'

'Yes, he is good,' said Niall. 'But why better?' he added, remembering Turner.

'Because he can lift a low, grey bit of city up nearer the sky in a few days' painting. I've seen it from the very room we've just come from. You can't do everything, of course, even with a brush of colour. For instance there's a newish building out there where students are taught to be teachers – not one of the most beautiful in town, to put it mildly. They'll go out from there as "finished" teachers, poor dears. O K. Fine. But one day when these teachers start talking about Art, Thought, Beauty, Learning, Love, Education, Intelligence, Artificial Intelligence, and what have you, some people are going to say, "Look, you were taught how to talk in a great, undistinguished block of a place which cuts out half of a green hill behind. Be quiet about all the rest for just one moment, and tell us what you're going to do about it. Can you take the thing down, brick by brick, in the night? No, of course not, because you'd be arrested." Well, it's a funny thing but the ones who've taken down some of the finest buildings in the city have never been arrested. The same goes for the clever ones who pulled down half an eighteenth-century square, and never saw the inside of a prison yet. For all I know they were given honours and medals and write-ups in the paper for making a really thorough job of it.'

Sir William Chambers who, before the middle of the eighteenth century, was one of the best-known architects in Britain, in his *Traditions of Edinburgh*, has some fun over George Square: 'It was formerly considered a great affair to go out to George Square to dinner; and on such an occasion, a gentle man would stand half an hour at the Cross, in his full dress, with powdered and bagged hair, sword and cane, in order to tell his friends *with whom* and *where* he was going to dine.'

It was indeed the first true square and Chambers recorded it as 'built in a superior style both as to size and accommodation'.

In earlier times the most respectable and wealthy Edinburgh establishments would find themselves cheek-by-jowl with brothels, lords with ironmongers, judges with their wig-makers. Though this proximity lasted well into modern times in the New Town, a good deal of its liveliness and variety was gradually ironed out, giving its face a smooth, elegant and rather chilling aloofness. It became self-conscious of its beauty compared to other parts of the town, demanding fine lamps, fine doors, and an exclusive entry to its gardens in order to exercise its dogs.

Downstairs the man and the schoolboy were still discussing destroyers and preservers. 'Of course it's not always so easy to spot the city's caretakers,' said the man. 'They do things quietly, on the whole, – washing, painting, scrubbing and straightening. There doesn't seem much drama about that till you think of the silence in an operating theatre. On the other hand, people stand around to watch destroyers, as long as they're not hit by a flying stone. It's the splintering crash, the dust and the shouting that attracts them, and the strangeness of seeing a huge, great dingy hole in the ground where once a tall building stood.

'I believe you've a young sister who came in for a bad experience not long ago,' said the old man, watching the boy carefully. Niall fell silent for a moment. 'No one took care of her the day she went out,' he said. 'She was almost destroyed.'

'"Almost" is the word to hang onto here,' said the other, 'but sure enough you've got to look after the young ones every time. As for the rest, either you stop them going out at all, or you let them go and risk this, that or the other, being knocked down, knifed, raped, murdered by maniacs. It's called freedom, I suppose. But I still think parents are the bravest people. Thank God my ones are all grown-up with lives of their own. Don't think I don't worry about my grand-children though.'

There was a sudden hubbub on the steps outside, tramping feet and arguing voices. 'Here they come,' said the caretaker. 'You never told me they were such a noisy crowd. If they get going on you I'll make some tea to calm them down. And a few hard scones, not as fresh as they should be, are a wonderful way to stop the tongue. I've tried it on a few teachers in my time. I even have a piece of cake in a tin.'

Now there was a loud rapping at the door and Niall's mother came in first. Agitation and anger filled the place like a high wind. 'Oh, what a stupid thing to stay behind when everyone else had gone!' she cried. 'And then to sit eating down here as if nothing had happened, when we've all been worrying ourselves to death!'

'Not at all, madam, since I phoned we've been sitting here quietly talking,' said the caretaker. 'Niall was very worried about the rest of you worrying.' The word 'worry' was being thrown about like a brickbat when Niall's father advanced to the table. He accepted a cup of tea gratefully and sank into an armchair.

'Oh, if you only knew what we've gone through!' exclaimed Niall's mother again.

'What *did* we go through?' his father asked. 'For myself, I knew he was a sensible lad and would be perfectly safe.'

'Why you might have gone away and there he'd have been, all alone in an empty building!' cried Niall's mother, turning to the care-taker.

'I never go away,' he said. 'I live here. That's what caretaking means.'

Niall's brother, Iain, was the last to come in. He arrived, smiling, and could be seen through the half-open door running a comb through his wet hair.

'And Iain has been half out of his mind,' said Mrs Gaffney, 'imagining the school getting colder and colder and darker and darker.'

'I didn't imagine anything of the sort,' said Iain. 'I happen to know that there's always some light and heat in part of the building all through the night.'

There was an argument about fear, locked doors, light, heat, and the extraordinary mischief-makers who'd thought up Open Days. Finally it veered toward the question as to whether teachers, care-takers or parents were the more caring. The old man ran for the cake-tin. For a while there was silence amongst them until, from the street below, a bell sounded nine hours. In all nearby windows the blue flicker of the TV news appeared. The visitors were now all ready to leave and the old man went out with them to Iain's car. 'Take care!' he shouted to Niall as they drove off. He saw the boy smile and wave through the dark.

The caretaker went back to his room. He cleared up the plates and cups, put the cake back in its tin, set the chairs and table straight, drew the curtains and wound up the clock. Then he stood and looked around at the tidy room, listening intently to the scraping of a mouse behind the cupboard. He'd never given a thought to loneliness in his life. He believed it to be the sort of indulgence he couldn't possibly afford, like eating an entire cake by himself at one sitting. Tonight, however, without having eaten a crumb of any cake, he felt in-expressibly alone.

CHAPTER

17

'What friends?' Niall had cried to the caretaker, while staring down a few nights before, from a high window. As if the cry had found an echo in different parts of the city, a few of these friends, young and old, were already gathering together like a safety net to catch a falling body. There was a long weekend's holiday in school, but Niall had been off a few days before and some of his class arrived to find out why. Nothing was wrong with him, so they were told, nothing that company couldn't cure. But the friends had bigger things in mind. A Young Persons' Exhibition of Work from all the schools was to be held in aid of a children's hospital in the city. They had planned a series of Saturday painting picnics where paintings could be sold, hopefully, on the spot. Niall was asked to mastermind these expeditions. The first Saturday afternoon was spent crouching in the old Grassmarket quarter of the city, listening to the rain under the shelter of a rusty roof. From here they made some drawings, ate their sandwiches, and promised one another to start afresh next week, at the same time vowing to backsliders that the emphasis would always remain on picnics rather than paintings. The next Saturday proved better. They sold a painting on the spot to an American about to return to his own country. Their spirits rose. 'He's the right kind to look for,' said one of them. 'He doesn't know any better. A few more like him and we'll be in business.' Next week it was fine. They painted in the Gardens, looking up to the famous Edinburgh skyline. Niall preferred to paint a joyful circle of tall dancers whom he imagined as skipping half-naked around the trees. It was bought up at once by a severe-looking cleric going home with his black briefcase under his arm. 'Yes, you've got to count on the mad ones if you're fund-raising,' said Niall. 'At this rate, who needs an exhibition?'

They were all cheerful that day. It seemed they could see the framework of a splendid hospital rising against the sky. While still in the Gardens Niall tried the portrait of someone sitting on a bench – a young man who turned so angry at the result that the artist had to defend himself against blows by retreating to the War Memorial. The marble place with its dark lists of dead felt freezing. He tried to imagine the leaping living and the sprawled dead from these names. It was no use. This was a clean, unmelting block of stone as remote from terror, outrage and deadly pain as a great Antarctic ice-block from a pit of blood.

They painted a few historic buildings – one being an Old Persons' Home where they were invited in for tea and cakes with the Matron who promised to buy the finished painting if they returned the following week. They were shown into a ward. Here there was some muddle amongst the inmates as to who exactly they were. Finally it was decided they were grandchildren or even great-grandchildren who'd come back at last from the ends of the earth to visit them. The boys seized this chance to travel and described the most exotic countries they'd ever heard or read about, the most unlikely ever to be seen. Each contributed something to the landscape – white beaches, palms, volcanoes, caves and purple seas. They described fabulous cities they'd seen on film or in the pack of photos some seasoned traveller had brought back. One moralist in the group was heard to murmur an accusation about lying. 'All Art's been described as lying some time or another,' said Niall loftily. Another – treacherous to the cause – started to question whether words, after all, weren't better than paint. Niall said no. Words seemed exact and cold compared with paint. Even this room of ancient people was full of colour. A row of knotty white hands lay on pink and black quilts. Here and there red-striped woolly socks hung at the end of beds and underneath was a glimpse of green slippers. From the window you could see across the road to a black wall with a yellow poster. If only he could paint! 'What are thin words to pressing out fat tubes of colour?' he said.

'What have you been doing all these years, dear?' asked the old woman in the nearest bed. 'You're not a great letter-writer, are you?

Your mother was never a letter-writer either. This is a very kind place I'm in, but I'd really like to go home with you now. Could you look out my clothes over there in that cupboard? I've almost forgotten what they look like, but I'm certain there's a black skirt, a purple jacket and a pair of new black shoes. They like to think I've forgotten all about those shoes, of course. In case I put them on and try to get out of here. But I haven't forgotten. Oh no. In the night I can remember every single scrap that's in the cupboard there. And I'll know if anything's missing. Even if it's only a button or a bead, I'll know. The people that look after us love us, of course. And they love anything with buttons too. Anything with buttons, buckles or beads goes missing right away. Just ask the others and they'll tell you what happens to their coats and dresses and their belts with buckles. If you know anyone coming here, young man, tell them to bring plain coats, plain belts, and above everything else, plain shoes. Shoes they love here most of all. But we've got to hold onto our shoes, haven't we? How could we get away without shoes? Tell them to bring plain shoes. You're safe with them. Only buckles and buttons catch their eye. You have to go, dear? Well tell them outside what I told you. And don't forget to write.'

Down the long row of beds arms were raised in a wavering, white pennon of farewell.

It was late afternoon when the group left. It had been a good enough day. Yet they noticed as they went past the High Street shops again, that the real money must lie in the hundreds of paintings and drawings of the Castle. There was the floodlit Castle, the Castle in the snow, in the sun and in the rain. Some had disguised a large lack of talent by painting it in a heavy mist. It had been painted as a black Castle against a moonlit sky, a red Castle against stormclouds and an ethereal Castle floating like a cloud above solid rock. Most of the boys knew almost nothing about the place though it had loomed above their heads for years. There was an argument on the best way to tackle it. 'We'd better read it up first,' said an idealist in the group.

'No, no, the less you know about anything the better for painting,' Niall advised. 'Better to look and know nothing at all. History's the last thing you need. Romantic facts are fatal. Sometimes I wish the words "romantic old Edinburgh" had never been invented. I'd love to look at every person and every thing as if I'd never seen or heard of it before. Real artists do that. None of the rest of us can.' Nevertheless they divided up, sat down in pairs, head close to head and began on the Castle.

One of the shop-owners who'd come out to look at the sketches said he'd hang one or two in his window and sell them at a price with calendars and guidebooks. An elderly man whose tenement window looked up at the same view bought one without waiting.

'How much does your hospital need?' asked the shopkeeper. They named the sum.

'So you've made enough for a roll of first-class bandages already. Only a couple of hundred thousand pounds to go.'

Perhaps there never was a Castle that dominated so completely every street and every corner of its city – a Castle so placed that people, staring from distant and obscure angles, might, by craning out, catch a glimpse of rows of lit windows, a turret, a flag or two, a splinter of reflected light in a far-off puddle. Luckily, it could never be called a merely magic Castle. Too much had happened there that had nothing to do with make-believe, but with a mixture of legend and history, terror and bloodshed, with pious deeds and brave ones. The more established story began with Queen Margaret the Good. Not only was she good, but also a beautiful woman who wished to bring some splendour and civility to the rough Scottish court. Evidently she did not believe piety must be presented as grey and sober. She was, it was said, 'magnificent in her own attire'. She increased the number of persons in attendance on her King, Malcolm III, and saw that he was served at table with gold and silver plate. In the twelfth century the North Loch was a place where tournaments were held. But it was a risk to go far out of one's way: 'Deep pools and wide morasses, tangled wood and wild animals, made the rude diverging pathways to the east and westward extremely dangerous, though lights were burned at the Hermitage of St. Anthony on the Crag and the spire of St. John of Corstorphine, to guide the unfortunate wight who was foolhardy enough to travel after nightfall.'

In all the jewellers' shops of the modern High Street brooches could be bought, the design incorporating a stag's antlers with a cross laid between. This was based on the legend of King David who, while out hunting, suddenly found himself alone in the thick forest at the base of the Crags, and was attacked by a huge, white stag 'maddened by the noys and din of bugillis'. At the moment of his greatest danger, a hand emerged from a cloud holding a sparkling cross which was placed in the hand of the King. Startled, the stag ran off, while the King made his way back to the Castle where, in a dream, he was told to build an abbey on the spot where he'd been saved. This became Holyrood Abbey for the canons of St Augustine. King David was written of as one of the best kings of Scotland. 'I have seen him,' said one close to him, 'quit his horse and dismiss his hunting equipage when even the humblest of his subjects desired an audience.'

At that time most of the houses around the Castle were still built of wood from the forest, and the roofs thatched with straw. But near the beginning of the fifteenth century there was what could almost be called the first Fire Brigade. At any rate, strict laws were passed to force magistrates to keep in readiness seven or eight ladders twenty feet in length, along with three or four saws for common use, and six or more 'cliekes' of iron to draw down timber and roofs on fire. No kind of fire was to be carried from one house to another, unless in a covered vessel or lantern. There was also great severity in the reign of James I for any fanciful clothes, especially in women. All but the richest were forbidden silks or furs or borders of pearls. 'No labourers or husbandmen were to wear anything on work-days but grey and white; and even on holidays only light blue, green, red, and their wives the same.' Advocates in Parliament were 'to have habits of grene, of the fassoun of a tuneike, and the sleeves to be oppin as a tabart'. It was said that, though laws were passed for everything in Scotland, even to the shape of a woman's cap, it was perhaps one of the most lawless lands in Europe. In the reigns of James III and IV Edinburgh Castle became the repository of great treasure – jewels, ancient relics, gold and silver goblets, precious plate, and military gear of every kind. Under James IV Edinburgh itself became celebrated throughout Europe as the place for music and dancing and, above all, for the great tournaments of knights held beneath the Castle Rock. The court of this King was also the centre for men distinguished in the Sciences and in the Arts. Under the fifth James the great defences went up. The Castle became a great bastion defended by walls twenty feet high. Four hundred soldiers were there constantly 'for keeping the samyn frae Englishmen'. The city itself had its great wall – The Flodden Wall – traces of which remain into the present day. The limit in defence was reached in the Parliament of James VI with the rule: 'that no Scotsman marrie an Englishwoman without the King's license under the Great Seal, under pain of death and escheat of moveables'.

CHAPTER

18

'*What* will you do for that boy then?' said Martin's wife one day, knowing that Niall had been in trouble.

'What can I do? I can tell him how we work, but dentists' surgeries are hardly the places to console and calm. And I don't like my instruments touched. I don't like them even looked at, for that matter. From what I hear he's probably a born wrecker.'

'Bring him here for supper one evening,' said Kate. 'I'd like to talk to him.'

Martin called for him and brought him back two days later. It was almost dark when they arrived. The sky was clear and would soon be full of stars. Niall mentioned his group's painting and how he was planning where they should go next. Martin talked of his Astronomy class, the telescope, and what he'd seen in the last few weeks, in particular a nebula and the clearest planets. 'So you *did* see the Orion Nebula!' Niall exclaimed. 'Of course I saw it,' Martin replied. The truth was rather different. He had lain on his back for a long time on the freezing, hard floor of the viewing room and vainly scanned the sky for the dim, misty patch in the constellation. Finally he'd got up from the floor and brushed down his backside. 'It was fantastic,' he told the boy. He was aware that Niall knew perfectly well he'd seen nothing of the kind. 'So you actually *saw* it?' the boy insisted. Martin asked himself whether this repeated question was a simple lack of tact or a stroke of positive malice.

Kate, coming in with a steaming fish pie, noticed a peculiar coolness in the atmosphere. The two were standing near the window. But now, unknown to her, they were not only separate in age, but divided in honesty and in experience. Suddenly Niall turned round. 'Did he tell you he actually *saw* the nebula?' he said. The man decided it was positive malice.

'No, he didn't tell me,' said Martin's wife as they sat down at table. 'But then I know nothing about stars. You'll have to tell me yourself.' At the end of the evening she asked if he'd care to help her on one of the children's walks around town she had been arranging.

'Why do they need to be helped?' Niall asked.

'Well, they aren't quite like the rest of us.'

'I don't know anyone who's quite like anybody else, do you? I mean you and Martin are terribly different. It's quite funny that you live together at all.'

'Well, after about ten years or so, it can suddenly seem very odd. After twenty, if you're lucky, you can settle down again.'

'Settling down,' interrupted Martin who was still at the window. 'Is that what we're doing?'

'Forget it,' she said. 'Anyway, keep in touch, Niall. Come along for this walk some Saturday. Just let me know.'

They went to the front door. The stars were still bright and steady, but the positions of the planets had changed. Even the broad, misty band of the Milky Way had moved marginally above them. Niall said it made him dizzy to feel how the earth moved with its planets, how their great Galaxy moved, and how the distant galaxies spun like fiery whirlpools far out in space. 'I shall probably be an astronomer,' he said, 'and I don't see how an astronomer can ever settle down, married or not.' Martin pointed out the bright Jupiter overhead and said how the huge planet with the other great Saturn had influenced the sun at regular periods in time, tugging at its centre and upsetting its equilibrium. The sun's disturbance had affected the weather in certain centuries. 'So better get your skates on,' said Martin. 'The weather forecast for earth is a distinctly chilly one right now. Ice and frost and fur linings might be on the cards for longer than you think.'

On a fine Saturday afternoon Niall went along to their house to join the walk. The eight children had already arrived and were standing in the garden with Kate. At once he was struck by the great differences between each one of them. Not seeming to take much notice of one another, they were individuals in a way he hadn't noticed amongst his own schoolfriends who were mostly intent on hiding themselves and their differences in order, it was said by the staff, to get away with murder. It was true a few of the girls hung together, appearing smooth, neat and very placid. They spoke quietly, standing still with their hands folded as if passively awaiting a command. If a command did come — or even the quietest of requests from either Kate or Martin — they became very agitated, looked around as if lost and held onto one another tightly until the excitement passed. A few boys and girls went past Martin into the house and made themselves at home, the boys quietly examining small objects on mantelpiece and windowsill, while the girls went to the flowery curtains, holding them up appraisingly like long garments. All looked sharp and clever and eager to be entertained, some in high spirits so that the slightest hitch in getting around the crowded room, some mishap to themselves or others caused loud bursts of delighted laughter. Yet in their midst others stood darkly frowning, giving not so much as smile or gesture.

'Where will we go today?' Kate called out to no one in particular. At this sudden question a strange frisson of fear seemed to run through the whole group, flowing forward swiftly and ebbing again. 'I've decided where I want to go anyway,' said Niall firmly as the silence continued. 'I'd like to go up to the Camera Obscura. Years ago they took me there, but I was too young to be bothered with it.' 'Better go while the sky's clear,' said Kate. They set off. A few girls hung tightly to her, some by a pocket's edge or to a bit of belt. The Camera Obscura, on the street up to the Castle, was housed in a room at the top of a twisting stair, narrow and dark. There was no hope of hanging onto anyone here, but soon they were out into space and light. In one room a few people were already waiting. They divided into two groups. A couple with a baby, a middle-aged woman and her mother were joined by Niall with three of the children. All went in for the first viewing. Kate and the others waited outside. The first group stood holding onto a railing, looking down at the large, white circular table and up to a small reflecting aperture in the roof. Suddenly the light was snapped off in the bright room and the middle-aged woman fell back on the ground as if shot. There was a good deal of confusion while she was carried through and laid on the mat in the adjoining room. The baby, being supported with its feet on the rail, looked puzzled, vaguely irritated, superbly un-concerned. '*He* never gives trouble,' the mother remarked proudly. 'Probably a bit of claustrophobia,' said the young guide. 'Some people go like that when a small room suddenly goes dark.' From the next room came the faint sound of sobbing. '*Our* baby never cries,' said the mother again.

But now, with sunlight striking the aperture above, the miracle began. A living, moving city sprang up before them on the table. A procession of cars glittered slowly along Princes Street and miniature figures passed by on the pavements. Not far away they saw soldiers lined up on the Castle Esplanade. They saw flags waving on nearby poles and the white wing of a gull flying between roofs. It was even possible to make out a sign or two and the flash of glass from windows close by. On one side, part of a church spire rose up, menacing and close, its sharp stones shining like a spiky skin. Occasionally a cloud crossed the sun and the green gardens grew pale, the flags faded and disappeared. But a second later colour returned brighter than ever. They saw people move into a courtyard to hang up clothes. Niall experienced a moment's panic that he'd suggested bringing these children to this room, perhaps for them the most disturbing – a place of total illusion, a mixture of real and unreal, of near and distant things all able to be effaced by passing cloud. Centuries ago the frightening eclipses had been watched through primitive, makeshift cameras. The moon had been studied, supposedly bringing madness if one stared too long. Perhaps their own fragmented lives might sometimes be like this. But the figures hanging out clothes had reassured them. They could just make out a red jumper, a nightgown, a pair of striped pyjamas kicking on the line. The show was over.

But there were other rooms below. For the children the holograms were more disturbing than the camera. Here brilliantly coloured images, three-dimensional and laser-lit, appeared to turn and twist in their frames – smiling mouths changing to puckered ones, smooth cheeks to wrinkled skin. Even Niall moved more quickly past the spectral green skull which seemed to gape and laugh by turns. His group looked at familiar things with amazement, staring at a solid green kitchen tap, apples in a dish and flowers against a dark wall as if they had never seen such things before. In a side room were stunning photographs taken from a satellite passing millions of miles from the two great planets – Saturn with its spectacular rings and Jupiter's blazing red storm-spot. For Niall this was the most extraordinary sight in the whole building. Now they went down another stair to the ground floor and waited at the counter for the others. This place was full of books, pamphlets, postcards and gadgets for tourists. But not a word here about the extraordinary man – Patrick Geddes, who began it all – a man thought of by many from that day to this as a genius. When he acquired the old Outlook Tower nobody knew what he wanted it for, except perhaps, it was thought, for some devilish ploy. In fact, he saw it as becoming a museum which would bring together the problems of workers in all fields – educational, social and industrial. It was also to be a laboratory where he himself would express and gather in the thought of all ages. People in his time were hugely divided about it. Most visitors were none the wiser about the place when they left it. Others thought it a triumph of intellectual experiment: 'It is so unique and original that the conventional man would be hardly likely to appreciate it, but every intelligent man and woman, deeply interested in Science and Education, will see in the Tower a new departure full of untold possibilities.'

Geddes was not the easiest of men: 'Ideas are the important thing. Any fool can beg, borrow and make money. It takes a clever one to know what to do with it afterwards.' Geddes couldn't have achieved what he did without a strong romantic streak. Artists and scientists were the 'forgotten children' he said – children who remained at the windows of life, looking out, while others had to stay in study or workshop. He was also lucky enough to have a wife who stood behind him through the experience of huge debts, through the triumphs and failures in his work, and the deaths of two of their children.

Geddes himself wished for a Tower with a view over everything in life. He had ideas on Townplanning, Botany, Geology. He had plans for an Art Institute, an Outdoor Theatre and a Concert Hall. About the revolt at that time against Impressionist Painting he wrote: 'A child in sunshine sees the violet shadows upon the dusty road just as the impressionist paints them. It is only the mis-educated grown-up who has been trained from old pictures or still more from printed descriptions of them, who persuades himself that the same shadow is brown.'

Geddes's papers were no doubt well-preserved somewhere, but they were not well-known. He could be satiric, not to say savage in his utterances. It would be interesting to know which of these expressions would come uppermost had he foreseen that there would be now simply a very small picture of him on the dark stairs of his Camera Obscura.

CHAPTER

19

The Italian tailor, Viscosi, though he sometimes accompanied Martin to the Astronomy class, was too busy with his work to be up at the Observatory regularly. In the winter, as well as his everyday tailoring, he was often called in to make clothes for players in amateur and sometimes professional theatre. He enjoyed this work. It meant that, though a foreigner, he was never an outsider. The players he dressed were acting out all nationalities, all trades and professions, and he was one of them. While he cut and stitched and pressed their clothes he could be from all countries, from all times, and in any trade in the world. This way, though he might sometimes lose his identity, he also lost his loneliness. Usually the larger companies had their own costume-makers and more often it was in an emergency that he was called. But he was pleased to come in at such times. It meant he could do his job without becoming too involved with the actors themselves. Their disappointments and failures could become very disturbing to him, for as often as not they discussed this with him – though naturally not blaming him in any way. But the phrases 'not happy in myself', 'not easy in the part' seemed to suggest that they had not been happy inside their own bodies, and that this had a good deal to do with the right or the wrong feel of the costume. This happened more often to amateurs than to the ambitious ones who hoped to take up acting seriously. He worked on the parts of noblemen and clowns, of sailors and tramps, farmers and fishermen. Indeed he thought of himself as a philosopher of disguises who could change people's attitude to themselves both on-stage and off simply by placing some garment over their shoulders. After that it was a matter of adjusting the cloth here and there and discovering the way they might move and think more naturally in their disguise. This was always a tricky occupation. It was important that their own characters were not entirely lost under folds and patterns.

Sometimes Martin looked in on his way home from the Observatory. Signor Viscosi was always delighted to brew up coffee and listen to spectacular accounts of either teeth or stars. He was fond of children and listened sympathetically when Martin spoke of his own, and of young Niall whom he and Kate saw fairly regularly. He would like to see him sometime, he told Martin one evening. The boy might be interested in what he was doing. If he was interested in plants and painting he would certainly be interested in colours and fabrics. He opened cupboards as he spoke and Martin had a glimpse of scarlet robes, black cloaks and the sparkle of a beaded gown. 'These are just the spectacular ones,' said the tailor, 'the show-off parts with not too much to say. Masked robbers, fairy queens and the like. Child's stuff. But the bigger parts need subtler colours and designs so that no one can guess who's villain, hero, the lucky lover, the unlucky one, the genius, the fool etc. The better sets need a longer, calmer look than this.'

Martin said how unfortunate it was that he seldom got to the theatre nowadays. Once his patients were gone and he'd had supper, all he wanted was to put his feet up and read the paper. Every part of him was becoming lazy. Except his hands, he pointed out. His hands were as young and agile as ever. He might get fat, but his hands would remain thin. 'We are the same in that then,' said the tailor. 'Whenever I take up a needle or a pair of scissors I'm young again. It's the sharp tools of the trade and years of know-how that help you to keep young. The same with surgeons, I've no doubt. There's something about having to use these sharp and dangerous tools week in, week out, that keeps you spry, makes you intelligent. One slip and you're finished. The young man scything a field of grass, for instance, usually looks exceedingly intelligent and concentrated partly because he's got a highly dangerous tool in his hand. Of course I know what you're going to say.'

'What am I going to say?'

'That the tools can become weapons. That the people carrying weapons can look not intelligent at all, but often brutally stupid.' The tailor sighed. 'If only I could get away with one perfect theory that can't be contradicted before it's scarcely out of my mouth. Have a drink before you go.' They sat on for a time, looking across to one of the theatre entrances where already a few people were gathering. 'A play about a man who strangles his wife,' murmured Viscosi, 'chops her up and takes her by choice portions in a boat and dumps her out at sea. But would you believe it? In the excitement the fact of tides had totally slipped his mind. One of the brutally stupid ones, as I've been saying. Look in with your young friend sometime. And mind you take care of those hands of yours!'

The tailor watched Martin as he crossed the road, saw that his suit was well-cut and possibly expensive, but that he walked with more than a slight stoop. He noticed that the top half of his body didn't match the rest. The legs were youthful enough, but the back spoilt the cut of the thing, spoilt in fact the look of the whole expensive get-up. 'I can make them fine clothes, but if they can't keep their heads up and their backs straight, what can I do about it?' he said to himself as he turned away. All the same, he did a lot. And people were not simply there as mannequins to show off the skill of first-rate tailors. The world, as he saw it from his window, was full of tired, hunched-up persons, limping or throwing themselves along, their necks rigid, awkward arms stretched out, backs bent. These reeling, rigid, clumsy people were the people he worked for. Sometimes he would, with luck, make them feel less awkward or even – for a few moments perhaps – graceful. This didn't happen often, but when it did, it gave him enormous satisfaction. At these times he knew he could create calm and even beauty out of chaos.

Viscosi went back to his table where, before his visitor had arrived, he'd been cutting a long strip of thin white stuff. He looked ironical yet stoically determined as he studied the cloth. It was destined to become the coat of an angel in the Christmas play of a well-known amateur company. It had been written by one of the group and had been well-advertised and highly lauded in the press. The tailor had a leaning towards either high comedy or darkest tragedy. Dressing angels was not his favourite ploy. He wondered why they paid him to make this difficult garment when a decently hanging sheet would have done as well. Once he took up the strip and, going to the long mirror, held it against his throat. This made him laugh aloud. His face looked so dark, so melancholy and so deeply lined above the white folds. Long ago he'd been an exceedingly handsome man and he never apologised for remembering it. Women, married and unmarried, had fallen for him, and all were thankful that though already an excellent tailor in those days, he was not an angel. One of his chief pleasures from early years in Italy up till the time he'd settled in Scotland had been looking at pictures. All painting interested him, but in particular he would study in minute detail the garments depicted by the Old Masters. He followed the way straight folds hung along the body, the way straight hair resembled these folds, and curled hair the softer lines. He admired the way the voluminous garment of a seated figure would be spread like a huge, frilled flower upon a rigid flight of steps, without damage to composition. Also it was only in painting that he could appreciate angels, their hands emerging from immaculately laundered folds, holding one perfect lily. True enough, the stuff on his cutting table was also clean and white at the moment. Once on the stage, however, it would become scruffy, slightly frayed and grey at the edges, and, as the show proceeded, a little less angelic every night. He often had to see his careful work spoiled and torn in this way, just as amateurs could trip and actually tear their way through parts. He was not a particularly cynical person but it seemed to him that the best of relationships became spoilt over the years in one way or another, darkened by misunderstandings and frayed by constant doubts.

Now he folded away his work and all his tools. He had to be neat or he would land in chaos. He wondered as he looked toward the window again, what spectacle was being acted out over there – what chaos of hatred, what fear and murder, what madness and heights of love. Afterwards most of the actors would go quietly off to drab digs in the suburbs round the city. He closed his curtains leaving only a strip of light from the street and the occasional ruby flash from the theatre door.

Martin brought Niall round late one afternoon, introduced him to the tailor and left quickly for a meeting of his own profession. The tailor and the schoolboy took to one another instantly. Viscosi saw Niall as a good-looking young person no more easy in his skin than in his clothes. Niall, for his part, saw the tailor as one who knew everything about concealment, who knew how to create the best disguise if need be, and also how to undo it if it became too burdensome. Niall felt safe. This man would know what was real about him and what was not. First of all Viscosi gave him a look over his entire workshop. He drew out bales of material from the shelves and threw them across the table to let him see how various weights of cloth hung differently. Niall touched them all to find how silk felt on the skin, how wool, suede, cotton, satin and velvet felt, and how mixtures of stuffs had different textures again. Viscosi showed the boy chests of old costumes ready for refashioning and mending, and cupboards full of new ones still to be tried on. He brought out the long strips of shining needles – every size from giant ones for shoving through canvas to minute ones for dealing with frail silk. He opened boxes of pins, boxes of buttons, and drew out an old cabinet with smooth-running drawers full of silk and cotton reels of every shade. Niall was fascinated that red reels had been used more than the other.

'Yes, red,' the tailor agreed. 'Red is the big drama colour, the royal colour, of course. Shakespeare, for instance, is full of red; blood and kingship and the fiery sky seen from a dungeon window.' He then took several red costumes from the cupboard and draped them on Niall's shoulders. 'Far too long, of course,' he remarked. All the same, the boy straightened up. For a second he was regal and proud, dictatorial – a ruler of men. Even his face hardened a little. His lips were firm. Niall peered deep into the cupboard and brought out black. 'Yes, black,' said the tailor, 'the next most common colour, if we can call it that. The colour of darkness, supposedly the costume for evil men and those of dark deeds, thieves and murderers, deceivers and liars, the dye of death and of mourning.' Niall was holding up a short, black tunic against himself. His face looked paler, his eyes more deeply shadowed, his lips red. He seemed rather afraid of himself as he stared in the mirror. 'Don't be afraid of it,' said Viscosi. 'I am myself one third deep black.' But Niall had discarded it for another. He put on a short green cloak.

'How do you feel?' the tailor asked.

'I like this,' Niall replied. 'Now I'm out of doors.'

'Yes, you're probably in the woods,' said the tailor. 'You could be hiding deep in green leaves. You may be shooting or being shot, of course. But I think you're safe enough.'

'I like disguise,' said Niall. 'I wish there was one for the city. No one can feel safe and happy in the streets, of course.'

'Not easily,' said Viscosi. 'You can only be yourself.'

'The first time I met Martin it was in a street,' said Niall. 'He was very angry about something, but I couldn't help it. The people were after me and the cars too.'

The tailor was silent for a moment, then he asked: 'How about this one?' He brought out a silvery blue and green silk shift from the cupboard. 'This was a play about an unhappy youth who was walking by the sea and was turned into a fish creature.'

'What happened to him in the end?'

'He became a happy sea-being who caught humans in a net. Their husbands, wives, brothers and sisters came to the shore to search for them but there was no one there. Some critics found it a disappointing play. Well, it began with an empty beach and ended with one. But do you see,' he said closing the cupboard door, 'that you don't have to live in the same old garment or play the same role. You can change every week of your life if you want, be a totally new person.'

'Is it safe?' Niall asked.

'Not at all. But it's exciting. It's experience.'

'How will I choose what to be?'

'It's not exactly that. It's making sure that whatever you are, you can choose to take on different colours, different shapes. You can try things for size, discard them and take up others.'

'Money?' said Niall.

'No, it's nothing to do with choosing careers or making money. It's a question of having eyes and seeing that whatever or wherever you are there are still choices, − ways of looking at things, looking through things and seeing the strange colours on the horizon − getting into new garments for the next play if you like. Your friend Martin for some reason has begun to tire of the teeth and the white coat, so now he dons his heaviest overcoat every week and goes to look at stars. And as for looking through things, you can look through blackboards, over shop counters, across work benches and even through prison walls. Yes, prisons,' he repeated as Niall gave him a questioning look. 'One man I knew very well devised a method and used it every night of his five years inside to keep himself sane. He tried to remember every bit of that particular quarter of Edinburgh where he lived; every house and flight of steps, every church plus steeples with cocks and crosses, each close, corner, lane and shop, pub and monument. The trees he remembered, the gardens and what he called garden furniture, including gnomes, slides, swings, bird-baths and garden benches. In other words he walked most of the night. He never had to ask the way. All the same, he told me he did get lost once and found himself in a close he'd never seen before and had to stand in a doorway till his memory came back. He was in a panic for the first time since going inside. But when he came out he had a memory like a street-map — could direct you to any part of the city and beyond it. You never need to feel totally trapped, inside or out,' the tailor said to Niall.

'Sometimes being trapped and being looked after can feel the same,' said Niall. 'People come very near. They want to make a sort of circle round you, and there's no way out. You'd need to fly to get out.'

Viscosi seemed to approve this idea of flying. It meant you could escape without breaking the circle or hurting your helpers. 'Our saints, or so the paintings make out,' he said, 'tended to fly up in the air rather than going in the normal way. They liked to leave their followers staring up at the sky with their mouths open. It's the same in the theatre,' he added. 'Exits and entrances are terribly important.' At that instant Martin came along the passage, knocking down an umbrella stand on his way. 'That's what I mean,' said the tailor. 'He's never been on stage. He doesn't know how to go out or in.'

'Don't ever worry about being trapped,' he said to Niall again as he saw them both out. 'Always remember you're a flyer, an escapist. Be proud of it.'

The man and the boy walked silently together down the street and past the theatre. Niall was wearing his old school waterproof, a dusty brown in colour. Nevertheless he didn't envy the actors on stage. Long after the theatre was closed for the night and the players gone back to their digs he would still feel in himself the possibility of being all creatures and all persons. More than that, he was also an escapist, a Houdini who could break through the tightest circles of this stony city.

As well as theatre work, Signor Viscosi in his travels had interested himself in all national costume. When he arrived in Edinburgh he noticed above certain well-established old shops the tarnished and almost obliterated word: KILTMAKER. The tailor looked into this particular national costume and set himself to make it. He was determined that one, at least, must be found on his premises, if only to show that even a foreigner could fashion this extremely complex garment. This difficulty was denied by one kiltmaker: 'We are not going to measure at all when starting on the pleats,' he wrote comfortingly, 'but use our eyes and our common sense.' Yet he conceded that nobody could be fitted to one simple pattern, far less a Scotsman. It was as well not to grow bigger or smaller, taller or shorter or fatter between the making and the wearing. Twenty-three to thirty free-swinging pleats had to come to the exact centre of the knee. This exact length was important as the precious tartan had to be torn across at this particular footage, with special attention paid to where the square would appear when the costume was put on. The tailor made his kilt and found that he must explore old shops and even jumble sales for the buckle, belt, straps and chain needed for the finished garment. Finally, special tailor's canvas for stiffening had to be bought and some very strong lining material to withstand the kicking legs of dancers. The tailor, like any artist, was exhausted and on edge when he had finished his work. The making of the fringe down the right-hand side of the kilt had been a most difficult and delicate scissor operation. After the labour of the kilt itself, the sporran was nothing. Whatever it had been made of in the old days, now it could be made of anything one could find around the place, preferably rabbit fur. The tailor never sold his kilt, though Highland dancers came in to look at it. It was kept with his other national costumes, more than anything else to exhibit his skill, and even to show off the extent of his travels in different parts of the world.

Scotland, in early days, produced many materials, especially linens and woollens which were the main export to England and the Continent. The exports were described: 'The commoditys and staple wair which they carrie out are for the most part salmond, coarse woolling cloath, callit playding, linning cloath, stockines etc.' The luxurious velvets and silks were mostly imported. But the Burgess Roll of Edinburgh records that Alexander Kirkwood was admitted Burgess in 1388 'in respect that he is well expert in weaving silks'. There was an economical strain even in the best-dressed Scottish ladies. Much later, in 1719, it was written in a tailor's account, that a laird's daughter had her gown and coat 'turned'. Dying clothes was also common from this time onwards. William Creech made some characteristically caustic remarks about women's costume in an Edinburgh newspaper of 1785: 'Spinal tenuity and mammary exuberance have for some time been in fashion with the fair, but a posterior rotundity, or a balance was wanting behind, and you may tell the country lasses if they wish to be fashionable, they resemble two blown bladders tied together at the necks.' He recalls that in 1763 maidservants dressed decently in blue or red cloaks or in plaids 'suitable to their station' while in 1783 it was difficult to tell servants from mistresses.

In 1784 James Beattie bought fifty yards of linen and three of cambric to get fourteen shirts made. He paid one pound four shillings for the making. By then the tailors were beginning to sew the ruffle inside the sleeve of the coat for economy's sake. Creech speaks satirically again on boots in the Edinburgh of 1785: 'Boots in the forenoon, with persons who have no horses to ride, is thought very fashionable.'

In preparation for the visit of George IV to Edinburgh in 1822, two girls — the Grant sisters — describe a visit to an Edinburgh milliner to select caps to wear at the ceremonial entry. It was decreed that caps must be 'as gayly decorated as can be'. The sisters each bought caps of pearl-white silk with feathers. Their dresses were made by a London dressmaker who, they were careful to note, had a

Scottish name. The dressmaker was very particular as to how her creation should be worn. 'The feathers are to be put on a becoming distance from the face, the hair to be dressed in bows at the back. The dress over the white satin petticoat to be first put on and then the train to be *hooked* in the lace of the stays as that will be quite safe from slipping.'

Probably the best-known costumes of Edinburgh in the mid-nineteenth century and well beyond it were those of the fishwives. The full, early dress included a cap of cotton or linen surmounted by a strong napkin tied under the chin; a broad belt that crossed the forehead and supported the heavy creel; a woollen pea-jacket, that concealed the upper part of the body, was relieved by the folds of a large handkerchief at the throat. Finally came the vast amplitude of skirt and a petticoat of bright colours, often of striped yellow material.

Having survived many setbacks in taking his trade from one country to another, the tailor was proud to bring out his single kilt. The kilts too had survived great setbacks in their own country. In 1748 men and boys in the army were forbidden by the army to wear tartan, though it was allowed to some in the north who were adherents of the Government, and the Highland regiments had always kept their costume. On the repeal of the Act tartan came in again, though not to a great extent. The kilt was seen at ceremonious occasions or in hunting, and in modern times at Edinburgh gatherings where citizens and visitors, who might or might not set eyes on the Scottish Highlands, would dance the Highland Fling.

Let Queen Victoria and Robert Louis Stevenson give the last word of warning: 'Victoria is greatly distressed that John Brown is suffering from dreadfully lacerated and swollen knees, caused by the flapping of his sodden kilt during the journey. He can hardly walk. The doctor is summoned. He is told he must rest.'

'It is unwarrantable,' says Robert Louis Stevenson in 1850, 'to imagine Scotch extraction a sufficient guarantee that you will look well in a kilt.'

CHAPTER

20

The tailor heard a great deal from his clients, both men and women, about the difficulties and flaws of their own bodies. Even before he measured them they told him that they had always known their arms were too long or too short, and the same went for their legs. Their necks, when they looked around them, were very unlike the average neck and their shoulders were too narrow or too broad. 'But what does "too" mean here?' he would ask. 'And there's no such thing as average. If there were, our job would be a very boring one.' This never convinced them. They were all right when looked at from the front perhaps. But from the side! He must have noticed the rounded back, the protuberant stomach or bottom. They had always been realists about human drawbacks. They knew, however well he cut his excellent cloth, there was very little he could do about it. There were times, they assured him, when they didn't mind being very small, short and fat. It had its uses when getting through crowds at rush-hour. But standing in a crowded drawing-room full of tall, slim people looking down on them was a totally different matter. There were many jokes about such things and they had heard them all. The tall ones – the men who looked most confident – told him how much they disliked people always looking up to them. It put them at the disadvantage of seeming to be superior when actually they felt nothing of the kind, usually the reverse, in fact. In addition they had to be careful about lampshades and even chandeliers. The 'tall and handsome' bit had never applied to them, they said, even if they'd never been called downright ugly. Real, overall fatness was one of the worst difficulties Viscosi had to deal with. There was no way of making clothes that could possibly hide it. They had to tell him that from the outset. They didn't want to insult him, but how could a slimmish man like the tailor really feel for their problems. There was the problem of tight buttons, of unexpected creases that hadn't appeared at the fitting, of the difference in their appearance depending on the time of year, and the presence or absence of good food. Even a change of wife affected the waistline like nothing else.

The tailor tried to tell people that his whole training had been to bring out the best in appearance and to hide or diminish what was less good. He very seldom used the words 'tall', 'short', 'fat', 'thin', and he never maintained that any one of these was better or worse than another. In fact, they all could play their part in a varied and interesting life, just as it was possible to see many rôles being played out in the theatre across the street. There were even people who considered themselves too thin. 'But how lucky you are!' he'd exclaim. 'I've just had a customer who's complaining about a weight problem.' Some of them, however, had strange theories about their thinness. They felt it went with a sort of meanness, as though by not nourishing their bodies, they had gone on a kind of spiritual diet as well. They saw themselves as not only thin in body, but as having thin, pale, undernourished souls. It was in this way that the tailor learnt from the start of his career that very few people liked themselves and that they also found it hard to believe that anyone else felt differently. The few beautiful people he had seen were certain that the slightest flaw or mark took away entirely every other good feature.

Final fittings were often like final rehearsals for entering the outside world again and were sometimes marked with a good deal of nervousness as if the person were going out on stage in a new part for the first time. But he had, however, a few more seriously disturbed visitors.

One day a young man came for the final fitting of his smart new suit. Viscosi was very pleased with it himself. The jacket and trousers were elegantly cut and made of fine grey material. However, when the young man came out from behind the screen where he'd been trying it on, he was pale.

'It looks fine,' said the tailor, 'and seems to fit perfectly.' The young man was standing motionless in front of the mirror. 'Yes, you've done a very good job,' he murmured after a long time, 'but how will I ever manage to feel good in it?'

'You think it doesn't suit you in some way?' said the tailor anxiously. 'It was done, every inch of it, to your specifications.'

'Yes, it's perfect,' said his customer, turning from the mirror. 'But I have this great burn on my back.' For a second the tailor was shocked to the bone. At first he wondered if something had happened to the cloth, some defect he had missed. But no, the cloth was perfect. The fit was right. The young man admitted it was the finest suit he'd ever owned. 'But if you could see this great burn-mark on my back,' he went on, 'you'd understand why I can't wear it. How could I ever feel right in this fine suit? Everyone will compliment me on it, of course, while only I will know I'm hiding this hideous scar.' The young man took and paid for the suit, thanking the tailor politely and assuring him that he'd no doubt sometimes wear it in private. He would deceive no one that way. The tailor wrapped it up silently and sorrowfully with none of the pleasure he usually took in the finishing and handing-over of a well-made garment.

Viscosi brooded a long time about this that night, wondering how many people imagined they were hiding ineradicable blemishes. The tailor asked himself whether he was helping them or hindering them from coming to terms with their life-long burns, scars, cuts, bruises and closely-guarded lacerations.

There were few such extreme cases as the young man, yet his long mirror was nearly always approached cautiously and from the side as if the reflected one was an enemy or, at best, a complete stranger who might need to be placated and certainly could never be touched or spoken to. When he'd first arrived here the tailor had always placed this mirror in the brightest possible light so that people should see every line of their new clothes. But this clear reflection could put them off. They were dismayed to see themselves for the first time in this hard, flashing light. Even if the suit or dress was smooth and fine, they saw their own faces were not. The sleeves might be well-stitched, but their arms, they noticed, were hanging clumsily. The shoulder pads might be perfectly fitted but their own shoulders, as they knew, were not really straight and never had been.

As for the clean-cut trousers and skirts, they were simply a disguise for unshapely knees and thick thighs. Viscosi had not often met this dilemma in his early years, and occasionally he wondered whether this strange lack of confidence occurred more often in this country than in his own. Apart from the young, did people ever compliment one another here, did they touch one another, stroke the hair, touch the cheek in public? Did they feel and discuss the soft and rough materials? Did they study one another's clothes, choose colours and fabrics together? He was remembering certain narrow streets, barred with sunlight, where people walked under the continuous billowing movement of white sheets and pillowcases, red, blue and yellow blouses, nightgowns and dark workmen's overalls, all strung together between open windows where women leaned on their elbows, gossiping or shouting insults and compliments down into the street below. He still missed all this. He certainly wasn't used to the stern honesty, the tight privacy and stifled quarrels going on around him these days in various parts of the city. He himself lived in a district of pubs. There was, he noticed, a certain searing realism about persons here, even when staggeringly drunk. What eventually dawned on him was that people in this part of the world didn't much care for themselves, drunk or sober.

More often now his friend, Martin, would look in soon after his work. They talked of books and journals they were reading, the travels they had made and the rôle of clothes in other countries. One evening the dentist brought with him Thomas Carlyle's *Sartor Resartus* and described how at one time Carlyle had actually hoped to become Astronomer Royal in Scotland. The great Scottish writer's interest in seemingly everything, including stars and the philosophy of clothes, fascinated the tailor. It also gave him a new insight into the strange mixture of interests that might be brewing inside the skulls of these dour and undemonstrative people he was now living amongst.

Even in the city, if it was dark enough, the stars could sometimes be seen. Viscosi finished the book on a glittering clear night, sitting under a lamp at his window, looking up now and then to watch the well-dressed and the dowdy pouring out of the theatre across the street. At the end of the book he came to the chapter entitled

'Tailors' where Carlyle's imaginary German philosopher of Clothes, Professor Teufelsdröckh expounds: 'The tailor is not only a Man, but something of a Creator or Divinity . . . a man is by a tailor new-created into a Nobleman and clothed not only with Wool but with Dignity and a Mystic Dominion, – is not the fair fabric of Society itself, with its royal mantles and pontifical stoles . . . of the tailor alone? What too are all Poets and moral Teachers, but a species of Metaphorical Tailors?' The Italian tailor under his lamp hung on for dear life to the long, involved sentences, and came at last to the final paragraph: 'When turning a corner of a lane in the Scottish Town of Edinburgh, I came upon a Signpost, whereon stood written that such and such a one was "Breeches-Maker to his Majesty"; and stood painted the effigies of a pair of Leather Breeches, and between the knees these memorable words, SIC ITUR AD ASTRA. Was not this the martyr prison-speech of a Tailor sighing indeed in bonds, yet sighing towards deliverance and prophetically appealing to a better day? A day when the worth of Breeches would be revealed to man, and the Scissors became forever venerable.'

Sometime after Christmas, on a freezing afternoon, the tailor slipped and fell in the street, damaging his ankle. Niall heard the news from Martin and at once went over to see him. Viscosi was about to visit hospital and was waiting for a taxi. His door was open when Niall came in, but for a moment the boy didn't see him. The tailor was sitting hunched in a corner beside the fire. He looked very old as he sat waiting there, his skin appearing dull and lined amongst all the smooth, coloured cloths unrolled along the nearby tables. His eyes brightened when he saw the boy. 'So you're in time!' he exclaimed. 'We can go to hospital together. But I've been warned I may have to stay the night and that means I need your parents' permission. You see, I'm asking you to come back to this flat while I'm away. Maybe only a night. Maybe two. In full charge. The couple across the passage will come in if there's any difficulty at all. They've heard about you and you'll meet them when the taxi comes.' He now rang Niall's house. There were sounds of argument in the background and then his mother, who'd met the old man, quickly gave her assent. Soon the taxi was heard below and the next-door couple who'd been staring from their window arrived. The four of them went laboriously down three flights, the husband and wife on either side of the tailor and Niall at his back. Niall alone accompanied him into hospital.

The Outpatients was crowded with leg injuries, and they joined the long row where people sat with sticks and crutches, their stiff, plastered limbs stretched out in front of them. Some had brand-new plaster, gleaming white, and some old hands had long ago decorated their yellowing plaster with intricate coloured designs – dogs, cats, tigers, birds and grinning monkey faces. The daring ones had outsize oaths followed by leaping exclamation marks, like shouts of pain. Whatever else they had, all boasted rows and rows of signatures in coloured inks. To outsiders the number of these friends was unbeliev-able. Unbelievable it might be to the owner of the leg as well, but the signed, stiff limb was powerful enough to stop the swiftly-striding, doubting visitor in his tracks, if need be – trip him up. The row chatted amiably together, and each one sat staring fixedly down the length of his leg as if surprised that the distant toes could exist so agreeably detached from the painful limb. Many patients had come from the wards and were impatient to get back again. There was a good deal of competition in producing effective orchestration from the plaster, some patients managing to produce a sound like a regular drumstick accompaniment with their sticks, crutches or any other thing they had about them. Others managed a lighter tambourine-type percussion with their knuckles. There was a certain discretion about these sounds, and each time a nurse approached to take one or other to the doctor's cubicle, the gentle, complaining tapping died down for a short time, rising again as the long wait stretched out. Soon it was the tailor's turn to be led off. 'Back to your work now!' he cried over his shoulder. 'I'll let you know what happens.' Niall was proud of these words: 'Back to your work!' Several persons along the line glanced at him with interest.

When he got back the sun was shining and he set to work tidying up. Viscosi had done nothing the previous day and the usually tidy place was in chaos. First Niall gathered up the lengths of cloth he'd been working on, folded them carefully and laid them away in the long drawers. Pins and needles were sparkling in odd corners of the room. He picked these up and stuck them into the big, black velvet pads hanging to the table. Carefully he gathered up buttons, fasteners and hooks, putting them into the wooden box where the tailor kept the odds and ends of his trade. He was rather alarmed at the confusion here. It was as if the tailor had fallen about in desperation and struck out wildly at his ordered place. Niall then brushed the floor and put the chairs in place. For the first time he noticed on the wall behind the table a large cork board where the tailor had pinned tickets and orders, addresses and phone numbers along with odd pages of letters, theatre notices and even different-coloured scraps of cloth. Niall went near and examined every part of this board. It was like reading a part of a life that had seldom or never been spoken about. There were also several photos here: one of a women in black with a child on her knee, behind her in the distance a row of poplar trees. There was the photo of an ornate white church with a golden cross, and one of Viscosi in a blue boat, holding up a silver fish. A small crayon drawing of a black-haired girl carrying roses had been placed near the centre close to half a dozen scrolled labels from wine bottles. Under all this were some thick, foreign words followed by the drawing of a grotesque downturned mouth. Where did this fit in with the boat in the sunshine, the silver fish and the girl with the roses? The boy decided this could only be some dark cry from the room's tenant set down on this board in the last year or so.

  There was little in the house to eat. Towards midday Niall took the shopping bag with the purse Viscosi had left for him, and set off for the supermarket along the street. The day had clouded over and a louring sky pressed on the roofs. It struck him that this must be one of the darkest parts of the town. The tall tenements with narrow, black lanes here and there, had never looked so forbidding. The city, capital or not, had never held the palm for cleanness down the centuries. Places further north and west were cleaner far than this. A strong wind blew the greasy papers about and plastered them against wet walls. Sometimes a paper bag would puff up to a high windowsill where it might be drawn into some dark interior by a hand at a sink or else flipped out again into space. Litter swam in the gutters, and small dogs happily laid turds on the pavements, watched by complacent owners. This was the busiest time of the day and the shop was crowded. Women pushed the piled-up trolleys, a child on either side and often a baby perched at one end. There were collisions as the trolleys jolted through the narrow alleyways, demands and loud screams as the sweet-stands came in sight at the payout exit.

When Niall got back he put the provisions away carefully and set about washing the place. First he mopped the outside landing between the two doors. It seemed to him, as the dark grey stone grew paler, that he was cleaning the city itself. At long last he was finding the light under the dark. Inside again, he started on the floor, going back and forth to tip out the pail and refill it. It was the first time he'd cleaned like this. He was surprised that he was staggering and panting as if he'd run an obstacle race. As he sat down finally to his meal, he looked across to the long mirror. Niall was very much surprised to see what he looked like after his work. This was a red-faced, sweaty youth with lank hair, his damp sleeves rolled up from skinny, sleazy arms. Above all, he was taken aback by this angry face when, in fact, he felt not angry at all, but simply dead tired. In a flash he saw how like he was to his mother. Here she was, staring out of this mirror with a frowning, red face, her mouth turned down at the corners. So this was what genuine tiredness looked like – not pale, drooping, pathetic, not weak, gentle or faint, but simply, unknowingly angry with an anger unconnected with anything in particular. He'd never liked her when she looked like this, of course. Yet she'd managed to look after them all for years on end. Possibly when she failed she turned this anger upon herself. Half an hour later he looked in the mirror again and saw himself as grey and pale. Some darkness from the street outside had drained his face.

The phone rang suddenly. A man gave his name and asked if his jacket was ready. Niall looked at the tickets on various clothes in the cupboard. 'I'll be around in five minutes,' said the voice. He turned out to be a tallish man with a peculiarly timid manner. 'So you must be the grandson,' he said on seeing Niall. The boy explained why he was there while the man tried on the jacket and looked at himself in the mirror. 'So you're in sole charge,' he remarked. 'You must be pretty good at the job. I was never left to do anything at all at your age. I was never trusted.' His eyes turned to the mirror again. 'Yes, the shoulders are a bit better, but of course the sleeves are still too long. I meant to tell him to take special account of my short arms.'

'Your arms are average length,' said Niall, rolling up the tape-measure.

'No, no, don't think for a moment that I *mind*!' said the man. 'Naturally I've heard all about the great and the famous who had short arms, starting with Napoleon, of course. It doesn't make any difference to me. I've never cared for those great generals and soldiers. All ruthless killers when you come down to it.'

The tailor came back from hospital the following morning and while Niall made coffee he sat and talked about it. After his ankle had been attended to he'd had time to look at everything. He spoke about the whiteness of it all: the white walls and the bedcovers, the doctors' coats and the nurses' uniforms. Even the newly plastered limbs, heavy and painful as they were, looked brilliantly white at first before they were scrawled with coloured signatures and graffiti. The real colour came in from outside in the stream of visitors with their flowers, he said. He'd suddenly seen colour differently and how good it looked against all this whiteness. Even a plain old woman in black carrying a red umbrella looked good.

His young helper listened enviously to this paean of whiteness and colour. After a while the tailor stopped talking and glanced at Niall. The boy, though he'd been delighted to see him, now seemed strangely silent and downcast. So how had it gone, Viscosi had asked. Niall told him about the man who'd imagined his arms were too short and the tailor laughed. 'Short arms are nothing. If you were here for a week you'd hear about short legs, necks too thick or too thin, big bottoms and round backs. I once had a customer who simply said, "I'm all wrong. What can you do about it?"'

Still the boy didn't smile. Viscosi looked at him hard. 'What would I have done without you? You've taken care of everything for me. But you were depressed here all by yourself? Is that it?'

'No,' Niall replied, 'I didn't stay in all the time. I went out to the

170

supermarket. Everything was dark outside. I've never noticed it so much. The sky was dark grey, the buildings were black and so were the wet pavements. People's faces were grey and glum and their clothes were like dustcloths. I was thankful to get in amongst the yellow packets and the piles of oranges and red peppers.'

'The lemons and the grapes as well,' added the tailor, nodding.

'But even there the air seemed dusty,' Niall went on, 'and when I got back here I saw my own face get grey after a while. Yes it was dark too. It was exactly like a painting I once saw in a gallery. A man, much older than me, of course, and with a dark, yellow face. A bad face. I felt frightened. Well, I don't think I can look in your mirror again; I've never liked it anyway.' Viscosi immediately rose, took up a coat ready for mending, and threw it over the mirror. 'Don't worry about mirrors,' he said. 'Lots of people can't stand them. I've seen the most beautiful men and women turn away, shocked. They'd had the image in their heads so long that it didn't match the glass. Rather plain people, strangely enough, aren't affected so much. Probably they imagine they're gradually growing worse through the years and then find things aren't as bad as they thought. I sometimes think people have a superstition about tailors' mirrors – that they're the truest and the clearest ever made, as well as being full-length and made to swing back and forth to give every weird view of the body.'

The man and the boy went on with their coffee quietly, but Viscosi watched Niall, waiting to hear more. 'My clothes seem so uninteresting, so grimy, amongst all your bright things,' said the boy after a while. The tailor listened most carefully to this part. He wondered whether Niall came from some darkly religious background going back for generations. It wasn't the first time he'd met this here. There were indeed some desperate people who came to him wanting brightness. He'd known some who even demanded whiteness. Atonement, he thought. Pale greys, blues, pale yellows, weren't good enough for these unhappy people. They probably wanted the spotless whiteness of angels. He couldn't give it to them. He made only a few whites for theatrical purposes. Sometimes all they needed was someone to talk to, someone who could assure them they were normal, decent citizens. God be thanked his own people had never demanded the terrifying whiter than whiteness he'd encountered here. He believed it was because they were more used to angels in their paintings, on their altars, crowning their domes and galleries. Besides, these angels of the south wore robes of blue, violet and rose-colour. They had a feeling for music. Many were playing flutes, viols, tambourines, and some even managed an organ. There were singers and dancers too. Here it was different. In the last years he'd even met several persons who were all ready to fly off to heaven, when the call came, in their white nightgowns and pyjamas, leaving far behind all those who had opted for the more casual off-white or a deliberately sinful dark in their deeds.

Viscosi told Niall about some of the old painters of Italy and showed him several books of portraits. 'Yes, I know,' said the boy. 'Sara has told us about them. She even goes to a portrait class herself.'

'So she paints portraits, does she?' the tailor asked.

'Oh, I don't know about that,' said Niall. 'But she has a way of looking at faces sometimes – looking rather severely, I think, as if she's measuring distances.'

'Distances?'

'I mean from one eye to the other, from eyes to mouth, from ear to ear, and that kind of thing. She talks about faces. I've never seen her actually paint one.'

'Do you mind people staring at your face?' the tailor asked.

'Yes. I don't like my thoughts, and I don't like them being looked at.'

'As if people can tell your thoughts!' exclaimed the other. 'I certainly can't, and I've been looking at you for quite a time.'

They spoke no more about painting and soon Niall got up to go. He protested, but not too loudly, as Viscosi tucked two ten-pound notes into his pocket 'for his splendid assistance'.

From his window Viscosi watched Niall as he crossed over and walked down past the theatre, pausing a moment to look at the posters there.

There had been a variety of entertainments in the old days, but while attendance at the scaffold was regarded as a perfectly respectable way in which to spend one's leisure, the opening of the first lending library to be established in Scotland brought down the most severe censure. Allan Ramsay, father of the portrait painter, removed in 1725 from the bookshop he'd founded in Niddry's Wynd to Screech's Land where he opened the library which was to become the centre of Edinburgh literary life. At first this attempt to provide reading for the public met with great disapproval and Ramsay was condemned for procuring 'all the villainous, profane and obscene books of plays printed at London, and let out for an easy price to young boys, servant women of the better sort, and gentlemen . . . '. The same happened to a Tony Alston who tried to found a theatre in the city, and the Society of High Constables made every effort to suppress the performance of these 'abominable stage plays'. Yet a strange result of the '45 rebellion was the sudden interest by Edinburgh people in the theatre as though their sense of drama had been heightened by the true dramatic events around them.

In 1756 the Edinburgh Playhouse became the centre of national debate over the production of the tragedy 'Douglas' when it was discovered that the author was Rev. John Home. The angry elders of the Kirk expelled him from his ministry and published pamphlets against 'those implements of Satan, the actors, who had led aside this lost sheep of the flock'.

CHAPTER

21

A few days later the tailor went up to Niall's school. He met the caretaker on the stairs. 'I'm looking for the Art room,' he said. 'It's the Art teacher I want to see. A young friend of mine, Niall Gaffney, was speaking about her. You know him?'

'I know him all right,' said the caretaker, 'but he doesn't come to see me now. I met him once at an awkward time, and maybe he's trying to forget. How is he?'

'Not bad,' said the tailor, 'though he's got an odd feeling about his face – thinks it's a dark and forbidding one. "Frightening" I think he said. Now he can't stand mirrors.'

'Don't tell me – that pink and white face frightening!' cried the caretaker. 'His family were a dark enough crowd, if you like. The parents: noisy, bossy and discontented. But don't think I blame everything on parents. It's the TV that's into that particular game. I mean those well-primed murderers who tell us they've never been cuddled by their mothers. In that case I'm well on the way to crime myself. Seldom kissed and, believe me, never, never cuddled. Mostly I was asking for something else again, and usually got it. What's more, I've managed to hold down this job for years and years though I could have murdered a child or two with one hand tied behind my back. So it looks as if I'm not the caretaking killer I might have been according to current Psychology.'

'I'm hoping his teacher might help,' said the tailor.

'Sara? She might, I suppose. But what could she suggest? She's not all for brightness, mind you. Bright and dark's her thing. Contrasts.'

'Contrasts, I don't mind,' said Viscosi. 'They're my line of country. It's when everything gets dark I start to worry.' He went on up. He found Sara in her room, tidying up. She was sitting at a desk near the window, going through a pile of portfolios.

'I've come for some advice,' he said as she got up. Behind them on the wall were rows of paintings – bright houses, figures and faces, flowers and blossoming trees, pink monkeys leaping behind yellow bars, black cats sleeping on scarlet cushions. 'Is everything always as bright as this in your room?' he asked, walking round.

'Yes, usually they take the brightest paint they can lay hands on. The bills for this place are astronomical. And most people don't know that different colours cost different prices. White's one of the worst.'

'It's not white I'm concerned about. It's black,' said the tailor.

'What are we talking about?'

'About one of the pupils in your class. Niall is one of yours?'

'Yes. What's he been up to now?'

'Nothing. He's simply going through a depressed stage. Common enough, of course. But I find it disturbing. He's got the notion dark is everywhere. Houses and gardens and streets are dark, people's faces and clothes, and, most of all, himself, of course. He describes himself like an old, weathered man. Naturally it's nonsense. As your caretaker says he's just pink and white and dirty like all the rest. Actually he's rather a fair boy, though with none of the things that should go with the word.'

'What *should* go with the word?' asked Sara. 'Are we talking about the virtues of a white skin?'

'No, but the fair ones are often talked of as rather light-hearted, serene and even amiable. When Niall's off his guard he can be all these things.'

'And when he's *on* his guard?'

'On guard he has a dark and scowling look. He likes to walk in shadow. You're interested in portraits, I believe,' the tailor went on. 'I had the idea that if you were to paint him – even the quickest sketch – he'd recognise the lighter side. It would surely lift his spirits.'

'Yes,' said Sara, 'I *am* interested in portraits, but I don't paint them. More important though, I don't believe an intelligent boy like him would thank me for the pink and white bit as our caretaker calls it, with the sunny background. Better for him, to paint the darkness, the fear and the resentment. That boy wants it recorded and then, with any luck, discarded. Whitewashing wouldn't help. Nor endless benevolence and patience, even if I had that in me. But I'm very willing to try this portrait and some of the others too. He needn't feel he's been made a special choice.'

The tailor talked for a while about his own job. He discussed the effect of colour upon his own customers and upon himself. He told her how often people disliked their own bodies, and how in spite of compliments, mirrors, measuring tapes and the like, they refused to see any part of themselves as normal or even average. Though seemingly reassured of legs, arms, stomach, feet, they could make out a case for unmatching eyes and even outsize ears as soon as his back was turned. He spoke of his own country and brought out photos for her to see. Sara recognised certain well-known buildings, but was more excited to see the oranges and lemons in the trees and black-skirted women carrying baskets of leafy vegetables to the market stalls around a fountain. 'No,' said Viscosi, 'the men and women are *not* all beautiful. That's just a romantic notion the British carry home with them.'

'Poor souls,' said the teacher. 'Why shouldn't they keep their illusion for a day or two longer? What harm does it do them?'

While he spoke about colour, the tailor was reminded again that Niall had declaimed vehemently about the darkness of this city. 'I wonder if he's seen the clean-up jobs going on in certain streets?' he said.

'Probably not. Mostly it's got to be done under sheets, like people being washed under waterproofs.' The tailor went off, promising to be back in a week or so to see what was being done about the portraits. On his way down he saw the caretaker again, putting back desks and tables in the Science lab. 'How on earth do you keep this whole place straight every day of the week?' he asked.

'Oh I have my helpers. There are a few boys who volunteer to stay behind and clean up. They have to be brave, of course. A boy tends to get laughed at if he holds a wet washing-up cloth in his hands too long. Brooms aren't so bad – a pole at one end and bristles at the other. They can be used as weapons. "Helping" has a bad press amongst certain boys. It makes them feel positively weak to be seen at it, unless it's mixed with fighting.'

Some days later Sara told her class she was going to try a few portraits. She started with some quick sketches of three or four of them. The girls, who happened to be pretty, were pleased with the result and the boys were grateful to be depicted frowning into space with their arms folded. The tailor looked in to see the results a week afterwards. He complimented her. 'Thanks,' she said. 'I only wish I could take your compliment, but I'm not much good at this. I've simply given them what they wanted at this moment. The girls, as you see, are all pretty and rather delicate looking, with their hands folded docilely in their laps. They are not asking for much just now. In a few years it will all be different. I've painted most of the boys in the way it pleased them too — grim, strong, frowning and one hundred per cent macho. They are looking aside out of the picture. They have nothing to say to the girls and probably never will have, whether they sleep with them, dance with them, eat with them. I'd have to be a genius to show these things in paint, and I'm no good at it.'

'Then you don't want to paint Niall?' Viscosi asked.

'Yes, I'd like to try. I have a sort of sympathy for that boy.'

Niall sat three times for the painting. On the whole, he was pleased with it. It seemed to confirm everything he felt about himself. The face was shadowy and the eyes hidden and rather sullen like those of an animal looking out from the back of a cage. It seemed to him that he looked old. Strangely enough Sara had made a part of his hair lighter than it was in reality as if some invisible skylight was setting a smooth, blond cap on him. She did more work on this head. The face grew slightly darker, the eyes more forbidding, and the strange, blond cap of hair brighter. He asked where this light came from, seeing it was a dark day, the sky cloudy, and the surrounding buildings high and black. Sara said she didn't know. Light was a strange thing and came very unexpectedly into many dark paintings. She's seen this herself and wondered at it. She reminded him that his brother Iain knew a lot about the source of light and that he would have to direct people's attention to the size of their rooms and the position of the windows. He himself would have to be constantly judging the direction of light. It was all part of the trade of good craftsmen, whether they were painting people or houses.

The portrait sketch was nearly finished and they took a few minutes' break. Niall wandered about the room, occasionally looking back at the easel. He was surprised that, though she talked so much about colour and light, Sara had understood the darkness of his face. Nevertheless he still felt the soft cap of light around his head like a warm plume. When they were on the last sitting Niall remarked that it was odd he didn't now mind being stared at, but he still hated staring at himself. He hated mirrors, for instance. 'I suppose most women like mirrors,' he said. 'At least my sister, Daphne, and even my mother look into mirrors whenever they can find one. And if they can't find one they look at their reflections passing shop windows. I suppose even a pool of water would do if there was nothing else. My sister's pretty, so that's understandable. My mother isn't pretty, but that doesn't matter. I expect they think mirrors will suddenly change everything.'

'You're pretty hard on people,' said Sara. 'You're hard on yourself, of course, but that's up to you. Mirrors themselves are even harder. There are lots of legends around them, rather cruel legends too – people walking into them and through them, for instance, hoping to meet themselves at last and getting shattered on the way. Water is kind compared to mirrors.'

Niall sat still for the next half hour hearing the steady stroke of the brush across the canvas board. It was not one sound but several, going from a stroke, feather-soft and slow, to something brisk, strong and quick as a cleaning brush, calming and irritating by turns. Once or twice Sara would rub around with a rag as if obliterating one side of his face. Then he would feel he was melting, that his hard substance was dissolving like wax. He wondered, in some panic, if she would be able to recover his bones and sinews. Would he become simply a ghost fading into the gradually darkening room? Lost too quickly to be found again? But then she would suddenly build him up, first tentatively and then boldly. He could breathe again, breathe and talk.

'Have you always lived in this city?' he asked.

'No, I lived and trained in Liverpool, taught first in Glasgow, and now in Edinburgh.'

'And you liked it best here?'

'No, I liked Liverpool best. I had lots of friends there and in Glasgow too. When I arrived here I was told how lucky I must feel to be here at last after those other cities.'

'And were you?'

'In some ways, naturally. But friends are more important than skylines. I'm not sure where the chill of the place comes from. Even outsiders can't explain. It's not from the famous east wind. From the splendid terraces and crescents, perhaps, and from those white, unbending statues – public benefactors most of them, but with little love for today's company. And I honestly don't blame them.'

'I like the place all right,' said Niall. 'It's the darkness I can't take.'

'Surely it's not all dark.'

'You mean all the new coloured stuff going up? It may not be dark, but lots of it is horrible.'

'I don't mean the new stuff,' said Sara. 'I'm talking about the old buildings that have just been cleaned. Centuries of blackness coming off.'

'Well, I haven't seen it.'

'Better start looking round then.'

'Everyone's telling me what to do,' said Niall. 'It gets tiring.'

They were silent for a long time. 'That's as much as I can do at the moment,' said Sara suddenly, getting up. 'Do you want to see it?'

Niall sauntered across. He wasn't discouraged by what he saw. The sketch was like him. He could sympathise with it, even grow to understand the person there. True enough, the face was dark, but not gloomy. The eyes were inward-looking, not particularly friendly, but they had an expectant gleam. The pale fringe of light on the head had expanded a little and almost touched one ear. From certain angles it took on a larger shape and colour like a lopsided skullcap of gold.

'I'm still puzzled about that,' he said, bending to touch it.

'Yes, painters are often puzzled themselves about how things turn out,' said Sara. 'When you look at some old paintings you can't imagine where the light falls from. Even certain colours are mysterious. You can't believe you've ever seen them before.' Sara took a book from the shelves by the painter Winifred Nicholson – a passage about something the painter had long felt, but not seen put in words. Sara read it aloud: 'About the circle of colours – red, orange, yellow, green, blue and violet,' the painter had written, 'we must not think of this as a finite circle, but as one where there is a gap of unknown colour that is necessary to harmony. We have not yet learned to fire past the gap in the circle of our scale.'

The phrase 'firing past the gap' made a strong impression on Niall in a different context. He had an explosive need to jump the chasms that divided one person from another. He knew everyone felt this, but it was seldom expressed. People might have huge life-stories to tell. Most were lucky to get in a few meagre words in a lifetime. That day Niall didn't avoid the caretaker as he went out. He went down the basement stair to his door and knocked. The old man, his face shining with pleasure, welcomed him in and put him down at table, setting out a familiar-looking cake which was only a little stale on top. 'So how is it going?' he asked. 'What have you been doing all these weeks? You're looking more cheerful since our last meeting.' Niall said he'd been in various interesting jobs since then. He'd been painting and selling pictures, for instance, visiting hospitals and nursing-homes, assisting in a garage, guiding a tour round the town, helping to arrange things in the Botanic Gardens, helping in the tailoring trade, and many other things besides.

'That's an amazing list all right,' said the caretaker. 'You've fairly been exerting yourself. What exactly were you arranging in the Botanics?'

'You could call it advising, I suppose,' said Niall. 'Where to plant the herbs and suchlike. What flowers need thinning out – things like that.'

'Well, well,' said the old man. 'So you've been throwing your weight around. I should have made it plain that caretakers are more often called meddlers, obstructionists and do-gooders. But of course you were none of those, were you?'

'I did other things,' said Niall proudly. 'In the tailoring I met a man who thought his arms were too long, the longest arms he'd ever seen. I measured them for him. They were O K. No longer than my brother's arms when he's painting at full stretch. I told him so. That was the best thing I ever did, I think.'

'I believe you,' said the caretaker, 'and I forgive you for your great knowledge of herbs. Those herbs were planted years and years ago by experts.'

'I've got to know a lot more people since I saw you last,' said Niall. 'This dentist, Martin, for instance, who introduced me to the tailor. I like Martin very much, but he's a liar, of course. Pretends to know all about stars. He got down on his back all right and looked through the telescope, but I could tell he never saw what he described.'

'Ah, so he's a *liar*, is he?' exclaimed the caretaker. 'Do you tell me that now! And *you're* a student of human nature, as well as all those other things. Yes, you've fairly come on since I saw you last.'

CHAPTER

22

During the following summer, when he was at a loose end, Niall roamed the city trying to look at the place with new eyes. This, after all, was what every first-time visitor was seeing. Just before the Festival ended he'd find himself in groups where people were still exclaiming or pointing out buildings he'd been looking at all his life. But it was something different he now needed. As an inhabitant of the city what he was looking for in its streets was not history, not nobility, nor the memory of great men and events. He was simply seeking the return of lightness to its stone, looking, in certain quarters, for that incandescence from buildings cleaned and made new again, no matter how thick the layer of soot and grit upon them. For something had darkened this town for years. And he himself was part of it. 'Every one of you must make your own city!' was the headmaster's rallying cry at the end of each year. Even the caretaker had implied the responsibility was his along with everyone else.

But where, before long, would be clean water to wash any place or object on earth? What escape from the gigantic engine of progress as it rolled overland and through the sea, spewing, on its way, bottles, tins and cartons, rusting cars, old radios, sewage, rotting garbage and rags, the fish, seals and seabirds all sickening in rivers of black oil?

Martin had said that at any rate it was lucky that the air around earth was clear enough to see out into space. They had spoken at the Observatory of the old French scholar, Flammarion, who had tried to describe what it would be like if the planet earth had been surrounded by thick cloud and dust like certain other bodies. Man would then have been closed in on himself, knowing nothing of stars or neighbouring planets.

One evening Niall was walking home after meeting his friends. It had been a splendid day and even the blackest chimneypots were capped with a curl of red sunlight. He was reminded of the painting of himself. Sara had given him some solidity, fixed him, prevented him from fading, and − speaking of likeness − she said she believed she had 'caught' him. The idea of being caught was not one that particularly pleased him. Yet it was not such a bad thing after all. Finally she had capped his dark head with a streak of shining paint like the chimney in the last light of a summer day. He walked on and on into the city and noticed that a whole crescent of old houses had recently been cleaned. So this was how part of the place had once looked − pale buildings gleaming like pearl against a darker sky. He also saw that, amongst the newly-cleaned houses, there were a few, still stubbornly dark, standing like recalcitrant children between their white neighbours.

In the garden of one dark house he found an irritable woman pulling up weeds. Incautiously he asked her why her house wasn't like those on either side. 'Isn't *what*? I suppose you mean isn't white like theirs? What cheek!' she exclaimed, straightening up. 'Advising me about cleaning my own house! Don't you know that it costs the earth? They don't just take a washcloth to it. And while we're on the subject you'd be well advised to take a scrubbing brush to yourself. Yes, my neighbours *did* have their houses cleaned and a great mess, dust and noise it made too. I had to have my doors and windows closed for weeks, and every crack sealed up but, even so, the dust got in. I took my curtains down, of course, but every passing person could see in. In fact "passing" is the wrong word. Some of them stood and stared as if they'd never seen inside a decent house. I don't suppose my neighbours realise that whiteness won't last for ever. A few years and it'll be blotched and stained again.' Niall felt some sympathy for this bitter woman who'd stubbornly managed to keep dark amongst the lighter crowd. He'd learned something about the cleaning of houses himself. His brother Iain had a friend in this trade. Niall asked about it when he got home that evening.

'House-painting's hard enough,' Iain said, 'but this man's work is dangerous. There's no escaping once you're on the job. You get yourself up like a soldier ready for battle; the toughest clothes, the tightest helmet, breathing gear, and goggles against flying grit. You've even got your gun directed on the stone – granite, sandstone or whatever. Can you imagine the noise when they're all on the job? But the noise is nothing. It's the dust that's the killer in this game if it gets to your lungs. Silica. I wouldn't take the job myself for any money.'

'It's odd never to see it being done,' Niall had said. 'The thing suddenly appears overnight. One day black, the next, white.'

'Well, it's not exactly magic and miracle,' Iain reminded him. 'You've seen the great plastic sheets hanging round scaffolding. They're not there to tease and annoy spectators. It's public protection.'

'There must be easier ways to get dirt off,' Niall went on.

'Yes, obviously. Easier and safer ways. With any luck you can move some dirt with water. Not much good, though, if it's been ingrained for years, maybe centuries. There are chemicals too, hard brushes, steel wire, abrasives – each one has its dangers. This whitening of streets is no easy task, I can tell you. Simply give *me* a smooth wall and a quiet brush.'

'That wasn't so simple either,' replied Niall. 'You once fell off your ladder and cracked your knee.'

'If you knew what those blasting accidents on walls are like!' was all his brother said.

CHAPTER

23

Another Festival was coming to an end. On the last night Steve, Martin and Niall had gone down to the Gardens to watch the fireworks display. Martin's wife had been laid low with three weeks of solid visitors and endless pleasure. Steve's wife said the cat went mad on fireworks nights and needed company. Niall's family said they could see as much as they wanted out of the corner of the kitchen window, if they craned far enough. For a while Niall himself resisted the whole affair as childish. He was amazed at Martin's anxiety to get out on the streets to see the show; Martin, who could climb up any night to the Observatory and see a whole sky of stars and even the odd meteor shower, was acting like a child at the thought of a display of coloured sparks. Tonight the whole wide street from pavement to pavement was a dark, murmuring ocean of people converging towards a central point opposite the floodlit Castle. It was a warm night. On the slopes of the Gardens groups were sitting, listening to the orchestra below. Without warning the music ended. Suddenly the floodlights went out and a moment of black silence followed. Hundreds of people held their breath and let it out in a concerted gasp as the first cracks and flashes exploded overhead. A great cascade of green and red sparks flew up behind the Castle followed by the stutterings and thunderclaps of bigger and higher rockets. Occasionally one single red flare rose far above the rest, bursting and hissing into sprays of colour at its furthest point, then slowly descending, spark by spark, against the black sky. When this happened whole lines of pale faces were turned towards the sky like white flowers opening swiftly and quietly wilting — only to lift and droop again as the next solitary spark went shooting up and slowly sank to earth. Mostly there was silence amongst onlookers, but sometimes when a particularly fiery spray would open and descend, there was a strange sound from their midst – a groan of love and pain as if a scorching bullet shell had burst and exploded in the heart, hearts not tough enough to take the wound.

When all was over the Castle was again floodlit, and people began to move slowly away through the streets. Only a few days ago these streets were rumbling with carts and lorries going back with loads of theatre props. Even the irrepressible Fringe had been pressed back into its Pandora box. Too late now to keep it down. For occasionally this irritating, tangled, clawed and dangling Fringe could remain in the memory after Ballets, Operas and Book Festivals were forgotten. Only a few hours ago the stations were echoing with goodbyes. However much the city loved its guests, there was nothing like this heartfelt goodbye. It was the sheer pent-up tiredness that did it, coming out in a great sigh of relief – relief plus regret for things not done, not seen nor said, for sights not pointed out in time, for buildings never dated, for distant beauty spots unvisited. In the last three weeks the pointing-out had never ceased. The teaching had never ceased, including the story of the Scottish Kings and Queens, the History of Architecture, the Church, the State, Law, Education and Banking in the city. During these weeks of guests a long night's sleep had been essential for their hosts, a silent breakfast taken absolutely alone if possible, followed by an hour or so of solid swotting.

But now the jamboree was over. The shuffle of hundreds of boots and shoes moving homewards could be heard down the main street like the sound of the tide drawing out from a stony beach. Yet some people were actually staring at the sky again. A full moon, unnoticed till now, owing to sparks and floodlight, was at last coming into its own.

Niall made his way through the crowds, through lines of visitors holding hands across the street, past couples embracing and fighting at corners, past people still practising their acrobatics or singing their songs in doorways. Parents with their sons and daughters were making for various houses and hotels in the city. At the end of the street the boy came face to face with a mother and her daughter who told him they were trying to get home. 'Where's home?' he asked.

186

'The real home is Los Angeles,' said the mother.

'Where are you just now?'

She named a hotel.

'I loved your fireworks and your floodlit Castle,' said the girl politely. She was exceedingly pretty and appeared to be dressed in colours befitting a Festival night, though they were more on the side of the rainbow rather than the fireworks.

'We've something better than floodlights and fireworks here,' said Niall. 'If we go round the corner I can show you.' He took them down to where the moon was shining on a pearl-white crescent. The fluted pillars, the balustrades and the steps, all newly cleaned, gleamed like marble. On the smooth pavement in front, the shadows of iron railings lay black and sharp as spears. He led them from place to place, showed them down dark closes between brilliantly illumined walls. They went from shadow to light, from dirt to lustre. By turns Niall's face became pale and then dark, his lank hair spiked with moonlight and shadow as he moved. Outrage and love for this city made him stammer a little. He declaimed his resentment at both old and new, at inhabitants and incomers alike. He led them past new atrocities and gave them time to take in every part of the ugly damage. He took them down into deep courtyards surrounded by high, lit windows. 'I guess it's like a Festival stage-set,' said the girl. 'If I stayed here long I'd think I was in a bit of theatre. I'm not sure what I'd feel about that.'

Niall said he knew a great deal about theatre. 'In fact, I've made costumes for the stage,' he added. It was a night for lying and showing off, and being proud of it. They climbed up again into the newly-white crescent. Groups of young foreigners were gathering here around a hostel.

'Of course I like the place, but in a few years' time I'll leave it, and good riddance!' Niall exclaimed. It was the American girl staring at him fixedly that made him add that whatever happened he would get away and very far away indeed.

It was the mother who answered him: 'Yes, of course, you're bound to feel you must find yourself sooner or later.' Now he was silent, thinking about the strangeness and impossibility of finding oneself. Where and who was he? Where should he look and what exactly should he look for?

'And what's more, I expect you'll need to get right away on your own to do it,' the woman went on.

'Yes, of course,' said the boy. 'And I'll be making for America. What about you? Have *you* found yourself?' he added rather accusingly, turning to the girl.

'Oh no, right now I live with my parents and my brothers and sisters in my own city. I've got cousins too. Most of my aunts and uncles are close by. So I'll never find myself at that rate, will I? Of course I've got to get away. Los Angeles may sound good to you, but it's certainly not my idea of heaven. I'll have to make the breakaway, and that's all there is to it.'

A few of the young foreigners outside the hostel drew near as if to support this remark. Again the girl looked up at the tall house with its delicately balanced doors and windows, its decoration of lines and scrolls and wreaths. 'That's theatre again,' she said. 'It reminds me of a play. Yes – but what? Shakespeare, maybe. Anyway, it's awfully romantic. The love at first sight thing. Would it be "Romeo and Juliet", with all those balconies and windows?'

'No, it would not,' Niall replied. 'Romantic? I don't think so. Could be a play about builders or house-cleaners, though, or even painters. Of course I don't know what's happening inside that house. I'm speaking about the outside.'

'One day, before very long, when I've made some money, I *will* come back to Edinburgh,' said the girl, still staring up, with a white disc of moonlight falling on her chin. 'I'd like to keep in touch with it, one way or another. Anyway, I'll be flying back here again, Festival or no Festival.'

Nearby, the whole group of young persons quickly turned their heads to Niall, their mouths half-open like gulls, waiting hopefully.

'In that case we'll be able to pass one another in mid-flight,' said the gallant young Scot.

Protectively, the others gathered the girl into their midst and walked quickly away. Niall listened to their steps going further and further into the distance. He thought of calling out or running after them, but did neither. He was left standing alone in the courtyard, his head turned away. It was very silent in there until a cough coming from the narrow steps behind startled him. He went closer and saw a dark figure sitting against the wall. 'Are you all right?' he asked. 'Do you want me to help you up?' The man stared up at him. 'You're asking if I'm drunk. The answer's no. I'm simply played out. I'm not a tramp either. As a matter of fact I'm a clergyman.'

For a moment Niall stared at the rim of white collar above the black suit. 'You mean you were a clergyman in a play?' he asked.

'No, real life,' said the other. 'Naturally for a few days nobody will have the faintest idea what's real and what isn't. That's the worst about Festivals, or the best if you like. People imagine it still goes on – the kings and queens, acrobats, clowns, dancers, devils and angels. It takes some time to sort it all out and get back to normal. If you think you know what normal means.'

'I don't,' said Niall. 'I've just insulted a very pretty girl, a visitor. That's not normal, is it? It's the effect of all those fireworks, of course. What I really wanted to do was to show off. Instead I sent her packing in double quick time.'

'Yes,' said the other, 'that's how it goes. The people you most want to keep near you, get chased away. It's the very devil. I know it, but I can't explain it.' He got up and brushed himself down. 'Black cloth shows everything,' he added, 'where you've been – on a beach, on a bench, on the dustheap.'

Niall now looked him up and down. 'I've always wondered,' he said, 'why religion has to be black?'

'It doesn't,' said the clergyman. 'In other countries its devotees have been in yellow, red, white and pink. With some it's simply body decoration – stripes, circles, bells, shells, beads and feathers. Don't ever think of it as smooth and black. Well, I'm off to the station now. You'd better help me up.'

'I'll do that,' said Niall, 'and we'll go together, seeing it's on my way.'

In the streets the crowd had thinned out and a few buses were getting through. They boarded one and got out at the place where a steep flight of steps led down to the trains. This spot was dangerous on windy nights. From the top of these steps people had occasionally been whirled off their feet into the street. Indeed high winds had been forecast tonight and protective screens were already up. Down below the place was beginning to empty.

'Nightmare places – stations,' remarked Niall's companion, looking round him. In the waiting hall people were slouched on seats in front of a long noticeboard, staring anxiously at the big black numbers on the white. Every few minutes these numbers changed with a click and appeared to cause more and more anxiety. Some persons jumped to their feet and peered ever closer at the board as if temporarily blinded by worry. Afterwards they might go from one official to another, making absolutely certain of their trains. They would hurry to the Information desk. What train, what time, what platform? Sometimes they wrote it on scraps of paper, continually consulting first the scrap and then their watches. Through the whole place there were hurrying figures bumping along with heavy cases or steering awkward trolleys through the tight groups at platform gates. 'Thanks for your company,' said Niall's companion, 'but don't hang around here, whatever you do.' He walked off quickly to a southbound train. But the boy stayed on for a few minutes. It was obvious the station was a complex knot of intense anxiety. It was also the place of expectation and hope. Above all, it was the point of escape. You could be totally lost and frightened like Kate's group of straying children had been, or else you could find yourself as the Americans had implied. He wasn't ready to step out yet. In five or six years, he reckoned. Nothing could hold him back. Money? He felt he had talent, nerve and wit to make enough. He would leave his beautiful city. How would he see it clearly if he stayed? Or see himself. Yet he could see himself swaggering back one day, a grown man, full of tales. 'Didn't you miss it terribly?' they would ask. Everyone wanted the straight 'yes' or 'no' to questions. Long ago he'd decided to say both 'yes' and 'no' to everything.

Once up out of the station the boy set off again. He hadn't far to go towards home. But now he felt himself able to move beyond it along endless, unseen lines which led in all directions. They were like the ancient and magical lines of Aboriginals communicating across thousands of miles in Australia. They were like the tracks of light running over the entire universe. At home it would seem dark. As usual the angles of the walls would appear to be more acute when he went in, the ceiling lower. A constricting shadow might fall upon him as he opened the door, and only a little light would follow him in from the street. But one day this door would close behind him. Before it shut he would pull all the darkness there into his own black shadow. Once liberated, it would flow easily, companionably at his heel, following him all the way on his long, lonely trek towards light.